A HELL OF A DOG

A HELL OF A DOG

A RACHEL ALEXANDER AND DASH MYSTERY

Carol Lea Benjamin

WALKER AND COMPANY

New York

ISBN 0-8027-3325-5 (hardcover)

Series design by Mauna Eichner

Printed in the United States of America

For Stephen, my

gueleebte

The Cast, Human and Canine:

Rachel Alexander and Dashiell, a pit bull
Alan Cooper and Beau, a German shorthaired pointer
Tina Darling
Boris Dashevski and Sasha, a Rottweiler
Martyn Eliot
Bucky King and Angelo, a Tibetan terrier, and Alexi
    and Tamara, borzoi
Samantha Lewis
Tracy Nevins and Jeff, a golden retriever
Beryl Potter and Cecilia, a border terrier
Cathy Powers and Sky, a border collie
Chip Pressman and Betty, a German shepherd
Audrey Little Feather Rosenberg and Magic, a pug
Rick Shelbert and Freud, a Saint Bernard
Woody Wright and Rhonda, a boxer

Acknowledgments

The author wishes to thank

Polly DeMille and Richard Siegel

Detectives Daniell O'Connell, Frank Fitzgerald, and James Abreu of the Sixth Precinct, Greenwich Village

Larry Berg, Dennis Owens, Beth Adelman, Sidney Shulman, Steve Martin Cohen, Warren Davis, Gina Spadafori, and Stuart Turner, DVM

Michael Seidman and the rest of the team at Walker, especially George Gibson, Linda Johns, Krystyna Skalski, and Chris Carey, with special thanks to everyone who played ball with Flash one afternoon last fall

Gail Hochman

And Dexter and Flash, constant companions

To know and to act are one and the same.

—Samurai maxim

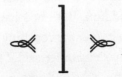

MAN PLANS, GOD LAUGHS

L ess is more. Except when it comes to money and sex. These unassailable truths may explain why I found myself checking into a hotel barely a twenty-minute cab ride from my front door.

I'd been asked to work undercover at a weeklong symposium for dog trainers, which meant I'd be paid to lecture about dog behavior, a paean to my former occupation, and paid again as I practiced my current one, private investigation.

So much for the money part.

My PI firm was an equal partnership, and my partner and I always worked together, which may explain why the elevator operator whistled and stepped back as we boarded his car.

"Hell of a dog you've got there, missus," he said, both hands dropping rapidly to cover the area directly below the brass buttons of his jacket. "Pit bull?" His back was against the wall.

I nodded.

"He okay?"

I looked down. Dashiell looked up at me and wagged his tail. "He's not complaining." I waited, but nothing happened. "Want me to drive?" I asked.

"Sorry, missus. Where to?"

I held up my key. While he read the room number, I read the name embroidered over the breast pocket of his jacket. "Home, James," I told him. But once again, nothing happened. There was another customer approaching. And another big dog.

"Rachel," the other customer said. "I didn't know *you*'d be here." Ignoring Jimmy, who by now was the color of watery mashed potatoes, Chip Pressman and his shepherd, Betty, stepped onto the small elevator. "Three, please," he said, never taking his eyes off me.

Dashiell was staring, too. Either he'd gotten a whiff of Betty, or Chip had a roast beef in his suitcase.

"I've been meaning to call you," he said, the elevator, its doors gaping open, still on the lobby floor.

"Go sit," I said, pointing to the corner farthest from Jimmy. Both dogs obeyed, squeezing into the spot I had indicated. I have no issues when it comes to dogs, but some men turn me into Silly Putty.

Jimmy closed the folding gate and turned the wheel. The old-fashioned open-cage elevator began to rise, albeit slowly.

"Can we have a drink before the dinner tonight?" Chip said, looking at his watch. "There's something I need to tell you."

Somehow, the way he said it, I didn't think it was going to be something I'd want to hear.

Out of the corner of my eye, I saw Jimmy turn slightly, perhaps to make sure he wouldn't miss any nonverbal response, a nod, a shrug, one hand demurely placed on my flushed cheek to indicate both pleasure and surprise.

"Can't," I said.

Jimmy exhaled.

"I have to straighten out some things with Sam before the symposium begins," I lied.

The elevator stopped at three.

"Well, I guess I'll see you at dinner, then?"

"I guess."

He got off. Betty followed him. Dashiell followed Betty, play-bowing as soon as he was in the hallway. He must have had ad-joining rooms on his mind. I thanked Jimmy and got off, too.

"We're on the same floor," Chip said.

I looked down at my key. "Looks that way."

We stood in front of the closed elevator door, neither of us moving, the air between us thick with pheromones and anxiety. He could have used a haircut. I could have used Valium.

"The reason I didn't call," he said, pausing and looking down for a moment, "even though I told you I would—"

"You don't have to do this."

"But I do, Rachel. The thing is, shortly after I saw you at Westminster, I—I went back to her, to Ellen. For the sake of the children."

That ought to work, I thought, the arrow he'd shot piercing my heart.

"Hey," I said, as sincerely as I could, "no problem. I hope it works out for you."

"Rachel," he said. He appeared to be gathering his thoughts. Lots of them. Too many, if you ask me.

"I have to run," I said, as if we were standing so awkwardly not in the third-floor hallway of some hotel but on the track that goes around the reservoir in Central Park.

"Well, okay, I'll see you later."

He seemed disappointed. But was that a reason for me to

hang around and listen to the touching story of how determined he was to make his marriage work, or to hear about how he tried but found he couldn't live without Ellen's cheddar cheese potato surprise? I didn't think so.

We walked down the hall. I stopped at 305. Chip and Betty continued another two feet, stopped, and turned.

"We're next door," he said, looking down at his key to make sure.

"Right," I said, nodding like one of those dogs people put on the dashboards of their cars. Then I stood there in the empty hall for a few minutes after Chip and Betty had disappeared into 307.

This wasn't exactly how I had imagined things would go when I was wrapping the black lace teddy in tissue paper and packing it carefully in one of the pockets of my suitcase.

Man plans. God laughs.

So much for the sex part.

Or so I believed at the moment.

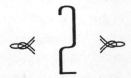

DON'T SAY A WORD, SHE SAID

I'd been reading the fashion section of the Sunday *Times*, most of which gets delivered on Saturday morning, when the phone rang. I liked being up on the important news a day ahead of people who bought their papers at the newsstand. Nails are big, the article said, especially in unreal colors.

The phone rang again. I picked up my toasted bagel and took a bite. The model's nails were considerably longer and bluer than mine. I heard Dashiell bark three times, my outgoing message. Then I heard that it wasn't my sister, so I picked up. "Alexander," I said.

"Oh, good. You're there," a deep, whiskey voice said. "Well, here's the story in a nutshell. I've arranged a weeklong symposium for dog trainers in New York City, the first of its kind, but it seems the participants all absolutely detest each other, and I'm afraid it's only going to go downhill from there. You know how these things are, I trust. So I got in touch with Frank Petrie, who

I know from way back, because I decided that what this situation needed was a guard with a gun, you know, just to keep things from getting out of hand. Perfect solution, right? Wrong. He said what I needed was you."

"Can I get your name?" I asked, pulling over a pad and a pen.

"Of course, Samantha Lewis."

Sam Lewis, I thought. I'll be damned.

"Look, Rachel, I've got a problem here—can I call you Rachel? Please call me Sam. Everyone does. The symposium starts in just two days, and I'm beginning to panic here. I'm still dealing with totally annoying last-minute changes in the program, and I've got to get this security business nailed down, too. God, I hope you're available. Maybe I ought to explain what I've done here. Do you have a minute?"

She actually stopped and waited for an answer.

"I do," I told her.

I had a lot more than that. The only thing in my calendar was an appointment to get my teeth cleaned, and that wasn't until the middle of next month.

"I've been running individual seminars for years now," she said, which was sort of like Lassie calling to tell me he was a dog, "and I decided to see if I could get these people together, if I could encourage them to stop the methodology wars and form a community so that people could share information the way they do in other professions."

That ought to work, I thought.

"But the more I thought about it, the more I thought I was asking for trouble. I wondered what on earth I could've been thinking when I dreamed this up. So I figured, okay, it's not lost yet. I'll play it safe. I'll call Frank, get a uniform. It would be well worth the expense. But Frank said no, he said I should hire you, get you to work undercover. 'You don't want your people to know why she's there,' he said, 'they won't open up. You'd be surprised what people say to each other. Sometimes you can stop some nasty business before it gets going. Stick her on a panel. Have her teach,' he said. 'Let her walk the walk, talk the talk, pal around with people, listen to what's being said. She'll fit right in. She's a dog nut.' "

"You're actually concerned?"

"I am. I was hoping I could get them to bury the hatchet. Now I need you there, to make sure they don't bury it in each other."

"Look, Sam, true, the lack of community is appalling, the attitudes less than professional, the bad-mouthing rampant, but—"

"I make a substantial amount of money doing this, Rachel. I can afford the peace of mind I'll get just knowing I have someone troubleshooting for me. Since you used to be a dog trainer, you *are* the logical choice. And Frank said you were a pretty decent operative, for a girl." She laughed. "That's when I knew it had to be you."

"His words?"

"Precisely," she said. "I guess that's why I'm still looking for Mr. Okay. There are too many Frank Petries in this world, too many annoying nerds, too many guys who like guys, too many gorgeous hunks who don't bother to tell you they're married, too—"

This time I laughed.

"Don't say a word," she said. "I know it's my own damn fault. I have terrible judgment when it comes to men. And even worse luck."

"Who doesn't?" I was thinking about my ex, not to mention a dozen or so other guys desperation and loneliness had made look an awful lot more presentable than they actually were.

"Well, that aside, right now I have a job to do. So, Rachel, would you do this much for me, would you let me buy you dinner and hear me out? Then if you decide you don't want to do this, at least I'll feel I did my best. Your choice of a restaurant. And make it expensive."

"How about the Gotham Bar and Grill?" I'd always wanted to go there when someone else would be picking up the tab. But then I had second thoughts. "I don't think you can get a reservation the same day."

"Watch me," she said. "Can you meet me there at seven?"

"No problem."

That's when I knew I'd be working for Sam Lewis. Still, I was curious to hear what she'd say to convince me, not knowing she was preaching to the choir.

I spent the rest of the day wondering which trainers would be there and trying to picture them getting along with each other, but no matter how I grouped them in my imagination, as soon as the group exceeded one, a heated argument would break out. Maybe having me there, just in case, wasn't such a bad idea after all.

Late in the afternoon, Dashiell and I took a walk along the waterfront, New Jersey twinkling across the Hudson. Perhaps it was only meant to be seen from a distance.

Back home, I decided to wear black. Dashiell wore his usual too, white with a black patch over his right eye, his Registered Service Dog tag prominently displayed on his collar. I was about to rouse him so we could leave when I realized I didn't have my keys. They weren't in my jacket pocket. Nor were they on the green marble table outside my kitchen, where I often dropped them.

"Dashiell," I said, "find the keys."

He looked up from where he was sprawled on the sofa, his eyes glazed over with sleep.

"Keys," I repeated, chopping the air with a flat, open hand, his silent signal to search an area.

Dashiell got off the couch and began dowsing for my lost keys. First he moseyed over to my jacket, which I'd tossed over the arm of the sofa. He pushed the pocket with his muzzle to release a puff of air so that he would know what was inside. Then he shoved his big nose in, just to make sure it wasn't fooling him.

He did a paws-up on the marble table. No keys, but he knows my habits, you have to give him that.

He looked around the living room, moving his head from side to side, trolling for the scent he was after. Then he headed up the stairs, his short nails clicking on the wooden steps. A moment later I heard the keys jingling as he descended the staircase. He dropped my key ring into my hand, sat, and barked. I scratched one of his top fifty favorite spots, one of the ones behind his right ear.

"So where were they?" I asked.

But I didn't wait for an answer. I know his habits, too. He's the strong, silent type, not in the least inclined to divulge hard-won professional secrets.

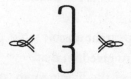

THIS IS WHERE YOU COME IN

Walking toward Twelfth Street, I was thinking about Sam, wondering if she'd be large and homely, like so many of the women I'd met in dogs. Unlike most people, animals love you anyway.

I pictured her waiting for me at the bar wearing shapeless pants and an oversize top, her ample derriere draping over the sides of the bar stool, her mousey hair pulled back in some nononsense, no-style look, her unpolished nails gnawed to the quick.

As I turned east on Twelfth Street, I wondered how I'd know her. Then it occurred to me that it wouldn't exactly be an issue. When I walked into the Gotham Bar and Grill with a pit bull, chances were good she'd know me.

"Super," she said in that husky voice, "you're early, too."

I turned around, but where was Sam?

Behind me, smiling, was a woman about my height, also late

thirties, as thin and stylish-looking as if she'd just stepped out of the pages of *Vogue*. Her straight black hair was cut short in a bouncy Dutch boy bob, her makeup flawless, her dark eyes as bright as a schipperke's.

"I always used to arrive fifteen minutes ahead of schedule when I had to meet my dad," she was saying, "and there he'd be, scowling and looking at his watch, because *he*'d gotten there half an hour early. It's warped me for life."

She raised the hand that wasn't holding a glass of wine, and a solicitous maître d' appeared to show us to our table. He glanced at Dashiell's credentials, then led the way, Sam following him, Dashiell and I following her. She was wearing a totally gorgeous black suit, probably a size four, the jacket nipped in at the waist, the skirt a good ten inches above her knees. She had the best legs I'd ever seen, unless you count this one transvestite who sometimes hangs out at the Brew Bar on Eleventh Street. If Sam Lewis was having trouble with men, I might as well get myself to a nunnery.

The maître d' took us to a table for four instead of a tiny two-person table, one of the advantages of bringing a dog along. A pewter-colored Statue of Liberty loomed majestically over our table, and high above us were gigantic light fixtures shrouded in off-white cloth, looking like upside-down parachutes suspended from the ceiling of the cavernous space.

Sam ordered a bottle of Montrachet and plunged right into work. "Here's the deal," she said. "I've been keeping a database of dog trainer wanna-bes from all over the country, you know, the ones who follow their favorites to seminars and hear the same talk, and get to see their hero, over and over again. Most of them teach an obedience class, free, for their local dog club, hate their jobs, and want to train dogs for a living. I did a huge mailing, got an excellent response, then got a great deal at the Ritz. I wanted a location that would let us use Central Park, of course, because I didn't think we could do tracking in the Roosevelt Ballroom. Am I right?"

She stopped to inspect the wine bottle the waiter had brought, watched him uncork it, sniffed the cork, sipped the wine, and nodded to him to indicate that it was acceptable.

"The program is fabulous, Rachel. And because we'll have so many of the most respected practitioners in the field, I felt we could offer a certificate of attendance at the end, the way Cornell does for its weekend workshops, and that, of course, allows us to charge more."

"But how did you convince the trainers that it would be to their benefit to work together?"

"I'm good at that," she said, rubbing her thumb and forefinger together. "Anyway, I knew that once I started getting some of them to agree to do it, the others would fall right in line. They might not want to do it, but they were more afraid of being left out. Do you want to order?" she asked, all in the same breath.

I picked up my menu and began to read, but I didn't get very far.

"It's a beautiful setup. Most of the people attending have no way at all of getting a good education in the field. They're out in podunk somewhere, and there isn't a decent trainer within a three-day drive. This way, they get all the top people, all the important topics, great demo work, hands-on practice, slide shows, videos, even the contacts they need for further study, those who want to and can afford it. And the trainers got so into this that several of them suggested we do advanced professional workshops, restricted to those who are speaking, before and after each day's program. No one, it seems, plans to sleep. I know *I* certainly don't."

She picked up her menu and began to read.

I reached for mine. Monkey see, monkey do.

"I still wasn't thrilled with the numbers, but then I was talk- ing to Bucky King about how hot dogs are now, since that Eliza- beth woman's book, and he came up with the idea of opening up the last day to the public. He's a total genius, that man, do you know him? Of course you do. You know everyone. So now we have three hundred pet owners signed up for Sunday, basic train- ing, a panel on problems, a slide show on body language, and to end the day, a little trick work. Once that had been arranged, I went after the vendors. After all, we have one hundred and sixty- two people in for the week, plus an additional three hundred the last day, and my bet is they're going to want every book and gadget on the market."

"It sounds terrific," I said, picking up my menu again. But I didn't look at it this time. I turned toward the huge windows in the rear that looked out into the lit-up garden and waited.

"Except—"

I lowered my menu.

Sam leaned closer and spoke in a whisper. "I think some of our participants, the less successful ones, actually believe they would reap the benefits if a competitor were"—she paused and tucked some hair behind one ear—"out of the way. As if that would make the work fall to them. Do you know what I mean?"

I nodded.

"From where I sit, I can guarantee you, there's plenty of money to go around. It's not some other trainer who's stopping any of them from making it. It's only themselves. But that's not the way *they* think, Rachel. The venom between some of these people is unbelievable. This is where you come in."

"They did agree to work together, didn't they?"

"Yes and no."

"Meaning?"

"I never did tell them who else would be there."

"How did you get away with *that*?"

"Each time I called someone, even the first of them, when they asked who else had agreed to attend, I said, 'Don't even ask. I don't have the time to read you the list. Just assume everyone will be there.' Then I apologized for getting to them last, mea culpa, terrible oversight, would they ever forgive me?"

"Didn't any of them pressure you?" I knew from personal experience how dogged trainers can be.

"For sure. Marty Eliot said he wouldn't commit until I told him whether or not Bucky would be there, because he knew if Bucky had agreed, there'd be lots of great PR. So I said, 'What do *you* think?' "

I didn't think Bucky would wipe his ass if the press weren't present to record it, but I took a sip of wine instead of saying so.

"Point of fact, Bucky's arranged for TV coverage for the last day, for a five-part PBS special. But I saved that tidbit, in case I needed additional artillery to convince any of them. The funny thing is, I never had to use it."

"You're shameless."

"I know. I let them jump to their own conclusions." She grinned, a lady who was used to peering down at the rest of us from the catbird seat. "It worked for *me*," she added. "This way had another advantage. I didn't have to listen to all that *stuff*, you know, mention a competitor's name and you hear, 'Why are you having *him* there? He's *so* overrated,' or 'Her? You mean she's still alive?' You know what I mean, don't you? After all, you were one of them, in a manner of speaking."

"Well—"

"Of course, *you* weren't like that. But some of them. The funny thing is, they all pretend to love and admire each other. At least, at first. They're loath to appear to be as small and petty as they actually are," she said, taking another sip of wine. "It's a riot when you know the truth. The other thing I had working for me was that they don't want *me* for an enemy. I've been booking these people for seminars all over the U.S. and Canada for years, making them a fortune. These are people not only promoting their methods, they're selling their books, pushing videos, gadgets, special collars and leashes, whatever. Some of the stuff is far out. One of them—oh, you'll see. Do they want me to stop booking them? They most certainly do not."

I smiled.

Sam pulled out her appointment calendar, which looked as if it needed the services of Weight Watchers, and kept going.

"I need your attention elsewhere, so I put you down for the opening talk on the last day, forty-five minutes. Give me a topic." When I didn't respond, she looked up. "Frank was right, Rachel. You are the right person for the job. So, a topic?"

"How about an explanation of alpha as it applies to behavior and training?"

"Super," she said, grinning at me. She uncapped her pen. "We'll call it 'Who's in Charge Here Anyway?' I have you down for two of the panels as well. No preparation required. Someone asks a question. You answer it. Piece of cake."

When most people tell you something is no work, what they are really saying is that it's worth no money, which is exactly what they're planning to pay you. I felt a surge of preparatory adrenaline.

"How does this sound?" she asked. "Five for your talk, two for each panel, and of course your customary fee for private investigation work, which is?" she said, looking up.

I told her. Her eyes registered no sign of surprise. She was clearly a woman who didn't mind paying for whatever it was she decided she wanted.

"Done. And, as an added bonus, you'll get to meet four of the seven self-designated 'dog trainers to the stars.' I had a feeling you wouldn't be able to resist my offer."

I didn't think too many people resisted Sam, at least not in business. She was probably lucky at cards, too.

She planned well, having me work my undercover job as speaker only when everyone else was also on stage, except for the last session, probably figuring if we got that far without an incident, we were home free.

"Who are the other participants, and what are their topics?" I asked. I thought I could be the first kid on the block to find out. I was wrong.

"Let's order first," she said. "I'm starving."

Over dinner, Sam didn't mention the program at all. She had the Bambi-Thumper special, starting with roast venison with wild mushroom risotto, then the saddle of rabbit, which she attacked as if she hadn't eaten in days. I started with chicken, foie gras, and black trumpet terrine and segued into the seared yellowfin tuna with rosemary. I couldn't finish either dish, but I didn't think it would go over big to put the plates down on the pristine stenciled oak floor for Dashiell to clean the way I would have were I at home.

"Do you ever call men?" Sam asked out of the blue after the plates had been cleared. "You know, if you meet an interesting guy at a party? Do you ever call the hostess and get his number, give him a call, see if he wants to go to the museum, or lie and say you have an extra ticket to the Knicks game?"

I shook my head. If I laid low, Sam would probably answer all her questions herself. At least, I hoped so. I didn't relish the thought of her actually leaving an opening in the conversation during which time I would be obliged to talk about my own pathetic history and arrested social development.

"I do," she said. "Maybe *that's* my problem. What about sex on the first date?" She lifted her wineglass but waited attentively for my answer before taking a sip.

"It depends," I said, hoping I wouldn't be asked to elaborate.

Sam sighed. "Your standards are probably higher than mine." She gestured toward me in a silent toast and drained her glass. Since I lied for a living, I never thought my standards were higher than anyone's, but I refrained from saying so.

"What about married men?" she asked, topping off my glass and refilling her own. But she didn't wait for my answer. "It depends," she said, "right? Well, for me, it usually depends on whether or not they ask."

Dashiell rolled over onto his side, using my foot as a pillow.

"I'd kill to meet Mr. Right, Rachel, but so far, all I keep doing is ending up with Mr. Tonight."

I did a lot of nodding. It was just as Frank said. You'd be surprised at what people say if you just give them a chance to talk.

I thought perhaps that Sam had had too much to drink, but when her dessert arrived, a tower of alternating layers of white, milk, and dark chocolate mousse sitting on a plate that had been swirled with raspberry sauce and dotted with fresh berries, she seemed perfectly sober.

"Taste this," she commanded. "You can still change your mind and order one."

It was so luscious, it might have dropped from heaven, but one bite was enough. Sam shrugged and dug in. Afterward, she finally started to tick off the names of some of the participants in the program, but she got so carried away with bits of gossip about each one that she didn't get very far.

When the waiter came with the bill, Sam glanced at it and handed him her credit card. While her purse was still open, she took out a check she had obviously written before I'd arrived.

"Two more things," she said, holding the check tantalizingly between two manicured fingers, the nails painted a classic arterial red. "The symposium starts on Monday morning. The speakers are arriving tomorrow, starting in the early afternoon, and there's a welcoming banquet for them tomorrow night at the hotel, at eight. Is that a problem for you?"

"Not at all."

"I might have to ask you to cover one more speaking slot." She reached across the ruins of her dessert and handed me a check for considerably more than I would have asked for. "One of the trainers who agreed to be part of the program early on, someone who, in fact, was totally thrilled and enthusiastic, hasn't confirmed."

"Meaning?"

"Meaning she didn't send in confirmation for her room, and I haven't been able to reach her." She looked at her watch, as if the answer might be written on its face. "She was supposed to deliver the opening talk, on breed character. So if need be, could you do that? I can put it later in the week if that would help."

"No problem." Sam's check was still in my hand. "Who was scheduled to do it?"

"Tina Darling. Do you know her?"

"We've met. You mean she's missing, Sam?"

"Well, I wouldn't say *that*. All I know is that she hasn't sent in her room form, nor is she returning phone calls. As the organizer, I have no choice but to assume she's not coming and to cover her talk times, don't I? It's only good business. Rachel, people are flying in from all over the country, even from England if you count Marty Eliot, but he's here lecturing more than he's there practicing, so that probably doesn't count. Still, I can't just tell them all there are holes in the program, go shopping at Bloomingdale's, can I?"

She looked at the check, still in my hand.

"Of course, I'll *pay* you for the extra—"

"That wasn't my concern. Of course I'll do it, Sam. Whatever you need is fine."

"Super. I already have someone to cover the slot on dealing with aggressive dogs. That's another topic we can't afford to omit."

"I see your point, of course. You have to have a backup, just in case." I folded the check in half and put it into my jacket pocket.

"You'll never guess who." She leaned forward, clearly pleased with herself.

I looked up. "You mean for the talk on aggression?"

Sam licked her red lips, the cat who'd just stolen the cream.

"He never does these kinds of things. Chip Pressman." She was grinning. "He's hard to get," she whispered.

Tell me about it, I thought.

"I've been after him for years. See—lose some, win some. It all works out."

I felt Dashiell's head lift up, brushing my leg. I knew if I looked down, he'd be looking back at me as if to ask what had happened to speed up my breathing.

"Still," Sam said, as much to herself as to me, "it's a pity about Tina. She's a wonderful speaker, astonishing for someone so young. She simply mesmerizes the audience."

"Maybe she'll still show. Maybe she's away, and planning to be back in time for her talk."

"Perhaps. I left her several messages, and I'm holding a room for her, just in case. But I can't take chances with the program."

"No, you can't."

"Of course, you'll stay at the Ritz, all expenses paid," she said, "including Dashiell's. Since the Four-Legged Gourmet wanted to be the only booth with food our last day, I insisted they supply food for all the participating dogs, gratis. We can't expect people to schlep their own dog food, can we? And I got another supplier to make up great sweatshirts for us. Wait until you see them."

She was some piece of work, Sam Lewis. Like many a bitch I'd trained, it seemed Sam too could and would do whatever it took to get her way—intimidate, whine, beg, plead, threaten, fool, even seduce.

I had once seen a little bitch flag a male, tossing her tail to the side, a sign she was willing to mate, in order to get the bone he had and she wanted. It worked, too. Of course, as soon as the prize was in her possession, she changed her tune, acting as if she thought he were a periodontist.

I wondered what my new employer's follow-up would be, if she too showed her canines after she'd gotten whatever it was she wanted. After all, when you captured your prey with honey, or as in this case, money, that wasn't the end of the story. But whatever that turned out to be, from what I'd seen so far, to help my audience really understand alpha, I could simply show them Sam.

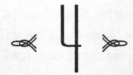

I COULD HEAR BIRDS SINGING

oom 305 was small, but the big casement window had a spectacular view east, over Central Park. I opened the windows and let in some air. The room was painted cream, with a warm gray trim around the windows and heavy gray velvet drapes in case I got tired of trees in the foreground with the Fifth Avenue skyline beyond. The gray rug was thick, and so were the walls. I couldn't hear Chip opening his suitcase and putting pictures of his wife and sons out on the small oak bureau or between the lamp and the clock radio on the nightstand near his bed. Instead, I could hear birds singing from across the street in the park and an occasional horn honking when the light changed on Central Park West. New York is a nice place to visit, but you wouldn't want to drive here.

I opened my suitcase, but I didn't unpack. I rarely wear the kind of clothes that need to be hung up. I went back to the windows and sat on the cushioned window seat looking out at the park. The trees were in leaf, and over the low stone wall that rimmed the park I could see glimpses of joggers and bicyclers, people walking their dogs, nannies out with children. The sun was shining, and from my third-floor window, the park looked clean and safe.

There was plenty of time before dinner for a long walk and a good look around the hotel when I got back. In deference to my paranoia, I hung the Do Not Disturb sign on my doorknob then, deciding to spare Jimmy, took the stairs, Dashiell running on ahead and waiting for me at each landing. We crossed the lobby quickly; this was no time to dawdle. There were trees across the street, thousands of them. Dashiell had his work cut out for him, and he was anxious to get started.

We took a path that led east into the park and then snaked its way northeast, heading deeper into the park as we headed uptown. To my left I could see the Dakota, where John Lennon had lived and died, looming high above the surrounding landscape. Looking east, beyond the roadway, I could see nothing but densely planted trees. Dashiell headed that way, doing his award-winning imitation of an untrained dog until I decided to take my chances of a hundred-dollar ticket for disobeying the city's leash law. He ran ahead, stopping whenever the road or his path would cause him to lose sight of me.

As suddenly as we had entered the copse of trees, we came to a clearing, and when Dashiell turned to ask me with his eyes if he could run on ahead, I signaled him to lie down instead. Off to the left was a group of young boys, eleven- or twelve-year-olds on the verge of voice changes, growth spurts, and the sudden appearance of hair where there used to be none. They had a couple of six-packs and a pack of cigarettes and apparently were very funny chaps; no matter who spoke, they couldn't seem to stop laughing. But what interested me was in the middle of the grassy meadow. It was Alan Cooper, a major consumer of and advocate for the products of Electronic Dog. Practicing what he preached, he was working his German shorthaired pointer with a shock collar and a remote.

Of course, in keeping with the verbal game-playing so prevalent in dog training today, Electronic Dog's literature and Cooper's book, *Instant Obedience*, never calls the equipment by such a crude, defining name. It is an "electronic" collar, and the shock with which you zap your disobedient dog is called "electronic stimulation." Most surprising of all, the brochure that accompanies the equipment suggests that the mild doses are felt as a pleasant buzz by the dog and can be used for praise; God forbid you should simply say, "Good dog." The more powerful doses correct the errant dog and make him see the wisdom of instant obedience—that is, unless he wants his fur to stick straight out from his skin for the next week or two.

I crouched next to Dashiell at the end of the tree line and watched Alan work, sending his dog out and calling him back. The first two times, the big dog was quick to obey. The third time he caught a scent in the air—a squirrel, a bird, something his genetic programming made more interesting than breathing—and he made the mistake of obeying his nature instead of his master.

I didn't need to watch Alan to know when he was making a correction. I saw it in the dog, too thin for his size, and once he'd stopped, I could see, too, that he was trembling.

I heard Alan call out.

"Beau, *come*."

The dog stood facing him, head dipped low, one front leg bent and held off the ground, as if he were pointing a bird. His docked tail pointed to the ground instead of the sky. I saw him blink twice and pass his tongue over his upper lip. Then he ran toward his master, who, holding the remote zapper, welcomed him with almost as much warmth as a rattlesnake would display.

I signaled to Dashiell to follow me, and instead of crossing the sunny meadow, we continued partway around it, staying hidden among the trees, emerging a few minutes later near a lake where Dashiell could swim.

Other people apparently had the same idea; there in the water was a large, lovely male Golden, on his way back to shore with a tennis ball in his mouth. On the shore were four humans and three more dogs—a greyhound, a Norfolk terrier, and what the ASPCA calls a Bronx coyote, a medium-size, prick-eared, pointy-faced brown dog, what third-generation mixed-breed dogs look like, in New York City and all over the world.

The greyhound, a lovely old bitch with a graying muzzle, possibly one of the many rescued retired racers that are becoming popular as pets, ran in huge circles, followed by the mixed-breed dog and the little Norfolk, who did the best he could on those short legs, barking gleefully as he ran. The Golden came out of the water, shook, and dropped the tennis ball at his mistress's feet. The dark-haired young woman reached into an open fanny pack, worn pouch to the front over her ample stomach rather than over her ample derriere as the name would suggest, and pulled out a treat, which she gave the dog. Then she picked up the wet ball and pitched it right back into the lake, the dog heading for the water before the ball landed with a splash. I wondered if she had ever considered *not* giving her water retriever a treat for doing what comes naturally.

I picked up a stick and tossed it into the lake. Dashiell marked the fall and waited. I moved my hand in the direction of the lake, and he was off, airborne over the last stretch of wet grass, his belly flop sending water high into the sky.

Dashiell and the Golden emerged together, each with his

own prize. The Golden dropped the ball and waited for a treat. Dashiell put the stick in my hand and danced his way back to the edge of the water, waiting for a toss, please God.

Like any dog that's given half a chance to be himself, it was work that thrilled the pants off Dashiell. But the pear-shaped woman with the fanny pack didn't seem to know that. She tossed the ball for her dog and came to stand near me.

"Do you want some treats for him?" she asked.

"Thanks," I said, not wanting to be deemed one of those rude New Yorkers I hear so much about, "he's fine."

"It's no problem, really. I have plenty, and Jeff doesn't mind sharing," she said as if we were in the playground talking about our three-year-olds instead of out in the park discussing our dogs. She pried open the fanny pack and showed me enough dried liver to give all of the NYPD's explosive-detection canines diarrhea for a month.

"He's happy to get the chance to—"

She pulled a card out of her pocket.

"I'm only trying to help."

Tiny beads of sweat were forming on her upper lip, and I noticed she could have used a shave, too.

I wiped my wet, dirty hand off on my leggings and took her card. It read, "The Positive Pooch. Tracy Nevins, canine behaviorist."

In my neighborhood, *positive* means you've gotten unfortunate results on your HIV test. In dog training, it means the trainer is a foodie, a practitioner of what my friend Mike Chapman refers to in his dog column as "dog training lite." Basically, the dog is viewed as a gaping maw into which you keep dropping treats. It's the method used to produce a dancing chicken, ergo an important skill to have on the odd chance you'll meet a dog with that spectacularly low an IQ.

Tracy had a 914 area code, which meant she lived out of the city. She was probably in town for the symposium, but I didn't ask. Dashiell was back, and I had *my* work cut out for me.

I pocketed the card and walked closer to the lake so that I could give Dashiell more of a swim when I tossed the stick. Later, when I turned around, I saw that we were alone.

Being a firm believer that a tired dog is a good dog, and wanting to make sure that Dashiell would be appreciative of the long down he'd have to do during dinner, I kept tossing the stick until his tongue hung down to about mid-chest level. Then, as wet as he was, because what's the point of shaking if it's not going to soak your mistress, I called to him and we headed back toward the hotel.

Coming around the lake, we heard the strangest sound. Dashiell looked at me, and I nodded, meaning he could follow it, and so we left the path and once again walked into the copse of trees that snaked around the lake.

There, side by side on a flat rock, we discovered the source of the sound, a small woman with a black pug, each with a huge white handkerchief covering her head. The pug stood as immobile as a lawn ornament, while the woman, sitting with her head tilted toward the sky, her nose poking up in the middle of the handkerchief, chanted.

Dashiell and I froze in place, just watching. I had been unable to extract the names of the speakers from Sam. Walking through the park, I was finding out what the program was on my own; a shock collar trainer, a foodie, and the self-described "dog psychic," Audrey Little Feather, here with her faithful companion, Magic. Not wanting to interrupt their meditation, and preferring my meditation in motion, I headed back the way I'd come.

Audrey Little Feather, née Audrey Louise Rosenberg, had emerged on the scene when I was still in business as a trainer. She made house calls to dog and cat owners with pet problems and spoke for their pets, explaining what was wrong and how the pet thought it should be remedied. I couldn't wait to hear her talk. But I didn't want to hear Audrey chanting now and spoil the freshness of her performance during the symposium. Nor did I want to leave the park, the air so fragrant with flowers, the trees thick with leaves, and the birds singing so loud they all but blocked out the distant sound of traffic.

There was no rush. I still had plenty of time to toss Dashiell in the tub, take a shower, and poke around the hotel before the dinner at eight. And I was sure, through my own brand of psychic revelation, that Dashiell was as reluctant to go back indoors as I was.

We parked ourselves on one of the slatted wooden benches that lined the footpath, a good place from which to watch the passing parade. Across from us, his glasses pushed up onto his forehead, his newspaper almost touching his nose, an old man in baggy plaid pants sat reading the *Times*. A few benches down was a young priest. He sat all by himself, smoking a cigarette, his legs crossed, one foot nervously moving up and down. But then Dashiell's tail was moving. I could hear it slapping against the bench. I turned in the direction he was staring and saw a large, tweedy older woman heading our way with a small border terrier bitch trotting along at her side. It was the bitch, of course, who'd caught Dashiell's fancy, and he immediately left my side to get acquainted.

Some people would be terrified to see a wet pit bull speeding their way. Not this lady. Despite the fact that Dashiell could have inhaled her little dog through one nostril, she was all smiles.

I knew that smile, didn't I?

"Oh, isn't he a handsome chap," she said.

As soon as I heard that voice, I knew who she was. Of course,

in the tapes I had, made from her British TV series on dog training, the most popular show on the air at the time, she was twenty
years younger. She'd had no jowls, no crosshatch of wrinkles on
her upper lip, and her hair had been flaming red. But even if my
eyes had been closed, there was no way I could have missed that
voice, as strong as ever, her speech dotted with her own quirky
inflections. How cagey of Sam not to mention this coup—unless,
like me, she'd been a last-minute addition.

"Mrs. Potter?"

"Oh, forgive my *rude*ness. Have we met?"

"No, but I'm a dog trainer, so of course I know who you are."

"How nice. But you must call me Beryl," she said, turning
her attention back to Dashiell. "He's a lovely boy, isn't he, dear?
How old is he, about three or four?"

"He's three," I said. "And your girl?"

"Still a pup. Only eight months old. But such a cheerful girl,
and so clever." She looked down proudly at the little dog.

Dashiell had lain down on his back, paws in the air, in the
dead cockroach position, and the little border terrier was running
in circles around him, barking all the while, stopping every now
and then to tug vigorously on his ears or tail.

"Gently, Cecilia," Beryl said. "We don't want to harm that
nice boy now, do we, pet?" We sat on a bench and let the dogs
race around behind us in the grass, enjoying their play and the
lovely weather. "I used to bring my little girl here," she said. "Oh,
we'd come every day, rain or shine, for our walk in the park."

Her eyes seemed to tear up at the memory, which must have
been as ancient as the brown leather purse she wore crosswise
over her bosom. It might have been thirty-five years or more
since she brought her little girl to the park. She was probably fifty
when she did the TV series, and that was two decades ago.

"Was it different then?" I asked.

"Was what different, dear?"

"The park. When your daughter was little. Was it safer then?"

"Yes and no," she said. "You know how it is, dear. We tend to romanticize the past, but even then, there was always the possibility of someone unsavory lurking behind a bush ready to pop out and do you in if you took the wrong path or strayed from where there were other people."

A nanny with two young charges, a boy and a girl, stopped to let the children watch the dogs play. The dogs stopped to watch a skater glide by. And two young lovers, both female, kept stopping to kiss as they headed out of the park, hand in hand.

"I guess human nature never changes."

She frowned. "Unfortunately not. But still," she said, looking down the path after the nanny, "the little ones keep us going, don't they?"

I looked at my watch, still reluctant to go.

"You and Cecilia are lucky to live so near the park," I said, thinking of how much fun Dashiell had had in the lake.

"Oh, I don't live here *now*," she said. "When I lost my husband, the baby and I went home, to England."

I looked at the little terrier, then back at her doting owner, the way Dashiell looks at something and then at me in order to let me know what he's thinking.

"But—"

"Oh, I see what you mean, dear," she said. "You're worried Cecilia will have to stay in quarantine for six months when I go home. But she's going to be an American dog from now on. She's a gift for my grandchild, you see."

"So your daughter lives here?"

She nodded.

"And we live in a little cottage in Chipping Camden, in the

Cotswolds. Well, Cecilia did. Now she'll have an American apartment, won't you, pudding?"

"Well, I expect I'll see you at dinner," I said, turning to go.

"What was that, dear?"

"You're here to teach, aren't you? At the symposium at the Ritz?" I said a little louder.

"Yes, dear. You, too?"

I nodded.

"It was nice chatting."

"It was indeed. Americans are so terribly friendly. I've always found that to be so. Especially here, in New York."

Waiting for an endless stream of serious bikers to pass, the kind who wear those skintight shorts and hunch over the handlebars, I turned back to watch Beryl heading into the park, and stood there watching as she pulled a glove from her jacket pocket and dropped it behind her. Were she someone else, I would have sent Dashiell to fetch it for her. But I didn't have to. Cecilia turned back, snagged the glove, and raced around in front of her mistress to sit and deliver. I watched Beryl bend over, take the glove, and pat her dog. I could just imagine her saying, "What a clever girl," as she did.

Outside the park, I saw the priest again, talking to a young man whose hair was dyed the color of corn. A harried-looking woman was headed our way, her fox terrier pulling so hard on the leash he was gagging. On the benches along the stone wall, a familiar-looking man sat eating a hot dog. He had another next to him on the bench, sitting on a napkin, and next to that, a giant-sized soda and a passel of greasy fries. He had just a fringe of dark hair slicked down with library paste and black as shoe polish circling a bald pate, huge eyebrows, a great, red cabbage of a nose, a heavy mustache, and a short, chunky body. I knew I'd seen him before, but I couldn't place him, like when you run into your dry cleaner at the movies.

I decided not to walk over and introduce myself in order to find out who he was and crossed the street instead; his Rottweiler was under the bench chewing on a bone so large it could only have been a human femur.

Back in my room, drying Dashiell after his bath, I realized that the man on the park bench had not been my greengrocer or druggist. In fact, I'd never actually met him. I'd only seen his face on the jackets of his books. As with Beryl, whom I'd recognized because of her distinctive voice, I had a much younger version in mind, in this case, one in which the gentleman in question had considerably less girth and tons more hair. He was Boris Dashevski, the old-fashioned yank 'em, spank 'em trainer whose books, no matter how "positive" training got, remained perennial best-sellers. It seemed that whatever dog owners did or professed to do when they were in public, they were still closet correctors at home.

When I got out of the shower, Dashiell was in the middle of the bed, fast asleep. Two wrapped packages had been left on the bureau next to a cellophane-covered basket of fruit, cheese, crackers, chocolates, and wine, all evidently delivered while I was out in the park, despite the Do Not Disturb sign on the door. There was a small white envelope there too, with my name on it. I saved it for last.

The larger package was the sweatshirt. It had a picture of a pit bull on it with the words "putting on the dog" beneath it. The smaller package, a little box wrapped in silver foil with a lavender bow, was a vial of My Sin perfume. Yeah, yeah. I really needed that.

I pulled my wet hair back with a scarf, put on a black T-shirt and jeans, hooked Dashiell's leash through one of the belt loops, and slipped a loose black jacket on so that I'd have pockets for my beeper-sized Minox camera, a mini tape recorder, my wallet, and my room key. Then, before waking Dash so that we could snoop around before dinner, I opened the envelope.

> R,
> You're off the hook for tomorrow's talk.
> S

Had I not gone to the park, I would have guessed that Tina Darling had showed after all. But I had. So I knew that all Sam's worrying had been for nothing. She'd lost an ingenue and gained a star.

⚜ 5 ⚜

HE HAD A NECK LIKE A BULLMASTIFF'S

The Truman Salon was blue with wine velvet drapes, swagged back to reveal Central Park at night—pretty as it looked, a place no sane New Yorker would venture unaccompanied after dark. The room was lit by an immense chandelier hanging over the grand oval table. The scene looked like a coed dinner at the New Skete Monastery; each dinner guest, with two exceptions, had a dog on a down-stay behind his or her chair. Martyn Eliot had no dog with him because of British quarantine laws. And Audrey Little Feather's pug was on her lap, her head covered by Audrey's napkin as if she were still meditating.

There were four empty seats. I meant to avoid the one next to Chip and sit across from him, but he caught my eye, and Dashiell caught Betty's, and that was that.

I smiled around the table, the waiter came and poured me a glass of white wine, and then the double doors opened and the vast space they exposed, room enough for a team of Clydesdales and a beer wagon, seemed filled by Sam Lewis, her arm linked around the tweed-clad arm of England's most famous dog trainer, the natty Cecilia at her side.

"I have the best surprise," Sam announced as she breezed into the salon. I heard the quiet, expensive whoosh of the tufted, leather-covered doors closing and watched the fascinating contrast before my eyes—Sam's pantherlike walk, Beryl's no-nonsense stride, and Cecilia's speedy Mr. Machine gait, her dark eyes scanning the room, looking for the most likely canine candidate to get into trouble.

Sam gestured around the table with a graceful red-tipped hand. "Rick Shelbert, Audrey Little Feather, Martyn Eliot, Tracy Nevins, Woody Wright, Rachel Kaminsky Alexander"—she stopped and grinned at me, proud of her own detective work—"Chip Pressman, Boris Dashevski, Alan Cooper, Cathy Powers"—then she turned and beamed at her surprise—"Beryl Potter."

There was a round of applause, and one at a time, everyone stood.

"Please, dear people," Beryl said without smiling. "Let's none of us make any sort of fuss now." With that, she took a chair at the near end of the oval table, then looked around for Cecilia, who was behind me, tugging on Dashiell's tail.

Sam walked to the far end of the table and pulled out her chair but remained standing. "Perhaps Audrey can address this issue when she delivers her talk on psychic communication," she said. "We seem to have lost one of our participants—two if Bucky doesn't show, but I've never known Bucky to be on time for anything. I believe that's why his mother named him Baron, to get even with him for refusing to be born until she was two weeks past the due date."

She stood there doing a Jack Benny face, eyes big and innocent, one hand on her cheek.

"You didn't know his legal name was Baron? Well, now you do. That's what happens when you're late, people, you get talked about. But we won't discuss his last name if he gets here before dessert. I think that's more than fair, don't you?"

There was nervous laughter, and one of the dogs on the other side of the table began to bark. I saw Tracy take some dried liver out of her fanny pouch and lean down to give it to her Golden.

"Well, more to the point, I've been after Beryl to come and teach here, for how long?"

"How old are you, Sam dear?"

Laughter.

"Well, nearly that long," Sam said, leaning forward and lifting her wineglass from the table. "To Beryl," she said, and once again we all stood, toasting Beryl.

"Well, as luck would have it, just when I needed her most, to discuss breed character, which she does so brilliantly, she called me to say she'd heard of our symposium, I think we were written up in the *Kennel Gazette*, among other places, and she chewed me out for not including her. Can you imagine!"

Sam bent to pick up her briefcase and pulled out the symposium programs, handing them to Woody Wright, who took one and began to pass the others around. "You'll see that Beryl is opening for the students tomorrow at ten sharp, in the Lincoln auditorium. And, as you all requested, don't blame me when coffee arrives at five-fifteen; you are meeting at six, not six-oh-one, directly across the street for tracking. Alan is laying the track tonight after dinner. Well, not immediately after dinner. At four-thirty in the morning. So when he falls asleep in his soup at lunch, folks, you'll know why."

"I can suggest something guaranteed to keep him awake," Chip said, leaning close so that no one else would hear him. I didn't respond. Everyone had started to applaud Alan for his willingness to be in Central Park in the middle of the night. Everyone, that is, except Boris.

"As for the rest of you, listen up, folks, stay out of the park after dark unless you have the National Guard along to protect you. Of course, when we go as a group—"

"Waiting a minute," Boris said.

"I know the shpeel, Boris. And I know Igor."

"Igor gone. Sasha now."

"Whatever. The point I am trying to make is that since you and Sasha are invulnerable, I was counting on you to go along with Alan tonight, staying off the track, of course, but making sure he's safe."

"He'll be as safe what he's ever been," Boris said proudly. "You not to worry."

"Good," she said, taking her seat. "I'm glad that's settled." She nodded to the waiter to begin serving.

After the smoked salmon *en croute* and the arugula salad, and halfway through the filet mignon, except for Boris, who claimed he was a "wegetarian" and couldn't eat an animal, apparently with the exception of the domesticated hot dog, the double doors once again opened, and there in all his glory was Bucky King, carrying a Tibetan terrier and flanked by two borzoi. You had to give it to the man, he knew how to make an entrance. His follow-through wasn't too shabby either.

"Sorry to be late," he said. "I just flew in from the coast. Angelo," he said, riding the TT up and down against his no doubt hairy chest, "had to tape Leno." He sighed for emphasis. It's a tough life, his expression said, and thank God *I'm* the one who gets to live it.

He had a neck like a bullmastiff's, a marine do, and an artificial-looking tan, like that stuff you schmear on from a bottle.

He still had his New York accent, but he'd eighty-sixed his New York pallor.

I waited in rapt attention for the rest of the puff puff, and had it not been for the fact that the gentleman to my left was trying to resuscitate his dead marriage, I would have pinched him hard on the thigh to make sure he didn't miss a word of Bucky's show.

Then it came, the rest of the obligatory, laudatory, self-congratulatory explanation for the presence of Alexi and Tamara. Bucky looked down as if he'd just noticed them standing regally at either side. "Oh, yes," he said, "we had to shoot a Stoli commercial, too." He rolled his eyes to let us know how difficult it was, and what a brilliant trainer he was to have pulled it off.

I looked across the table and saw Tracy blinking as if the light emanating off Bucky were too much for her unprotected eyes. Alan Cooper's mouth formed a thin, straight line, and his left eye had begun to twitch. I felt Chip lean sideways again, as if he were about to whisper something in my ear, but then Bucky noticed Beryl.

"Dame Potter," he said, bowing from the waist, a neat trick since you couldn't say he really had a waist. It looked more like the equator.

"Oh, do sit down, Bucky," she said. "Our food is getting cold. No one has the time to watch you make a spectacle of yourself." Then she turned her attention to the rest of us. "The queen, it seems, has neglected to inform me that I have been knighted," she said, "and until such time as she does, I'd appreciate it if you all called me Beryl."

I don't know if Bucky's tan changed colors. I wasn't looking. I heard him putting his dogs on a down-stay. When I did look, he was taking his place at the table, next to a flustered Tracy.

"Too heavy." It was Alan's subtle-as-a-sledgehammer-dropped-on-your-bare-toe stage whisper. I assumed he meant Bucky. Until he added insult to injury. "Not enough brisket."

My grandmother Sonya would have thought he was referring to her pot roast. But it was one of the borzoi he was bad-mouthing, a deadly sin if ever there was one. In this circle, you might get away with ranking out the owner, but never the pet.

"The brand of dog food you each requested is being delivered to your rooms as we dine," Sam said, "along with some special goodies for our hardworking demo dogs. If there's anything else you need, please, people, speak up."

Three of the dogs barked when Sam said "speak," which set the proper mood for finishing dinner. Sam had cued the dogs by accident, but there's nothing dog trainers love more than signaling each other's dogs on purpose, just for a goof. Giving a hand signal from behind another trainer's back so that a dog on a perfect sit-stay lies down or comes instead of staying put is irresistible to the lot of us, even those few of us who might consider ourselves mature adults. Of course, if there's another trainer within ten miles, you'd never correct your dog. You'd turn around smiling to show you can take a joke, then plan your revenge. Go big or stay home is the motto, especially when it comes to getting even.

I hoped that's all that would happen this week. And why not? If we could goof on one another, humiliate a fellow professional by getting his dog to appear to be breaking a command during a lecture or demo, let's say, wouldn't that be enough?

Chip, to my left, his back to me, was deeply engrossed in a conversation with Boris, to his left. And Woody, to my right, was chatting up Sam, clever man. I sawed my steak and looked across the table, thinking of all those people in all those singles bars who had to try to look as if they were having fun, sitting all alone nursing a drink, figuring that this was it for the rest of their lives. Rather than feel pitifully ignored, I decided to test my theory.

I turned slightly and clicked my tongue to get Betty's attention, and secure in the knowledge that I would not be heard above Boris's bombastic pronouncements, I gave Chip's shepherd her signal to search for drugs. Betty rose up without moving a paw, slowly, the way Dracula rose from his coffin in *Nosferatu*, and remaining still, nose in the air, she trolled for a scent. Then quietly, the stealth shepherd began to make her way around the table, air-scenting, occasionally stopping to poke at a purse or a briefcase to release the scents inside.

I took a peek at the program while I waited for Chip to notice. Audrey was speaking in the afternoon. I wondered how she'd feel following Beryl, but when I looked up, she didn't seem to be thinking about her talk at all, not the way she was locked in conversation with Marty Eliot.

There were thirteen of us around the table. I hoped it wasn't an omen. Nearly everyone, well, everyone except me, was engrossed in dinner and conversation with the person to his left or right. The real tension wouldn't start to build, I figured, until people started lecturing, at which point everyone but the speaker would think he'd just heard a tale told by an idiot. Watching Betty make her way around the table, I was hoping no one had a video or slide show. God knows what might happen in the dark.

Bucky was regaling Tracy with a great story, how he trained Meryl's dog, went on safari with Sly, or prepared the Laddie Boy Bulldog for his latest commercial. Rick Shelbert and Alan Cooper were arguing across Cathy Powers's dinner. Looking from one to the other, she seemed to be at a tennis match. Rick looked pretty angry, but he kept his voice down, and I wasn't able to catch a word. Then Betty made her find. She was standing behind Audrey, pulling the world in through her nose. Suddenly she sat, her nose pointing to Audrey's purse. She barked once.

Chip stood so quickly his chair tipped over. He started around the table and then stopped cold. As he turned, everyone else did too. Now they were all looking at me. I stabbed a piece of potato with my fork, shrugging as I lifted it to my mouth and began to devour it whole. Surely no one would expect an explanation when my mouth was full. Anyway, how was I supposed to know that Audrey used controlled substances to help her make her otherworldly connections? For all I knew, she really did have second sight, or whatever the hell it's called.

Betty was praised and returned to her place, and everyone else went back to the conversation I'd so rudely interrupted with my prank. I was still being neglected, but at least I felt I had set the proper tone for getting out one's aggressions. It wasn't until the plates were being cleared that I noticed Audrey staring hard at me across the table. I smiled at her, but she didn't smile back, her dark eyes burning in my specific direction.

It wasn't until she'd stopped working as a hairdresser and had started working with pets that she'd begun telling people she was one-third Indian—Seminole, I think. Or was it Cree? Whatever. I guess she learned a different biology than I did, but she was dark, and her hair was straight and black, and obviously she had a substance abuse problem. Who can say if that was or wasn't genetic? I heard that when she lectured, she sometimes wore Native American garb. It ought to be a hoot, I thought, infinitely easier to take than watching Cooper electrocute his dog trying to convince us how quick and easy electronic training is.

After dessert, there was brandy. The men started lighting up cigars, and the women all headed for the ladies' room. I didn't plan on trailing after them like Mary's little lamb, but thinking about how women instantly bond and chat in the john, I changed

my mind. Just as Sam lit her cigar, I reminded Dashiell he was
on a stay and followed the crowd.

Tracy and Audrey were at the big gilt-framed mirror, reap-
plying war paint. I apologized to Audrey for my little joke and
went into the cubicle, figuring out of sight, out of mind.

"I'm not sure," Audrey was saying. "I mean, I was with him
both nights in Phoenix, but I don't like his method."

In any other circumstances, you'd think she was talking
about someone's method of lovemaking. But here, they could
only be talking about training methods.

For a moment they stopped talking. I heard a compact close.
I smelled perfume.

"He's married, isn't he?" Tracy asked.

"He never said."

"But I heard—"

"What if he is? He never brings her. How great could it be?"

"Maybe she has money," Tracy said.

"That would explain it."

I heard giggling that reminded me of the bathroom in junior
high. Or what happened after lights-out in camp.

"Am I okay?" Audrey asked.

Since she was a psychic, I would have thought she would have
known.

Tracy must have nodded. I heard a purse click shut. And then
a door.

I left the cubicle and went over to the mirror, letting my hair
loose so that it would dry. That's when I noticed the shoes in the
cubicle to the left, so I waited.

I heard the flush. I could see the door opening. And there
was Beryl.

"Lively little things, aren't they?" she said, fishing around in
her pocket for something. "When the cat's away," she said, pull-

ing out a big handkerchief and blowing her nose, "the cat will play, won't he?"

But before I got the chance to comment, the door opened.

"There you two are," Sam said. "You're missing a whale of a *discussion* out there."

She was grinning, so I knew it wasn't an emergency, just the usual. She went into one of the booths. I had the feeling it wouldn't stop her from carrying on a conversation. Beryl had the same idea. A finger to her lips, she grabbed my arm and pulled me toward the door.

"Woody started it," Sam was saying. "He just couldn't—"

Beryl led me out and inched the door closed.

"There. That's better," she said. "I do love Americans," she said, "but you all talk too much."

So, of course, on the walk back to the Truman Salon, I didn't utter a word.

Bucky was gesturing at Woody with his cigar. "Give me the dog that air-scents every time. You're talking life and death here, people, not Stupid Pet Tricks. If the victim goes in circles for an hour, then the—"

"I have no argument with that, Bucky," Woody said softly, but not so softly that everyone didn't turn to listen to what he had to say. "But you can't make a blanket statement that one method is best in all situations. In the search for evidence, for example, the dog has to track. He has to make those circles. He has to go precisely where—"

"Sometimes it's not up to the trainer," Chip said, clearly annoyed. "Sometimes the dog's method is the dog's method. What you need to do is—"

"What you need is this," Alan said. He'd slipped the remote from the holster on his belt and was pointing it at Chip as if he were an errant dog in need of a correction. Or a TV whose channel needed changing. "This is what makes all the difference, gets the dog to keep his mind on his work, get to the victim as quickly as possible. I bet you that—"

"Don't bet nothing, you'll be sorry if you do," Boris said. "Because you'll not only lose your money, you'll lose expression, too."

"Face, Boris, face," Alan said, rolling his eyes. "You've been here how many years? Ten? Twenty? Isn't it time you mastered the language?"

Bucky sat back, puffing on his cigar, stroking Angelo, who was on his lap. He seemed to be enjoying himself, one of those people who thrived on conflict.

"I've found that dogs are really getting mental pictures from the victims and that they—"

"Half the time they're *dead*, Audrey," Alan shouted at her. "You think they're sending mental pictures after they've died? Or after they've been eaten by a bear? When I was living out in Montana, we had to try to locate a guy who'd gone missing eight months earlier. We were in the mountains for five days, looking for something that would let his wife sell his business and go on with her life. Finally, we found it. She had him declared dead on the basis of a belt buckle. It was all that was left. Sending pictures!"

"Ladies, gentlemen," Woody said, standing up to make sure he had our attention. "We're all here to teach and learn. Couldn't we—"

"*Learn?*" Alan sneered. "From whom? A psychic? Duh."

"From each other," Sam said, glancing quickly over at me, as if to say, See? then looking back at Alan. She was standing in the doorway and had probably heard the "discussion" from down the hall. "Wasn't that one of the appeals of doing this?"

"You'll learn from the students too," Woody said, "if you listen to their concerns and their questions."

"They won't have anything to teach us about tracking, because they won't be present," Alan said in disgust, "and tracking is what we are discussing, isn't it? I wish the rest of you could stay on the track. Cutesy-poo pet owners coming to this mistake are going to illuminate professionals on a subject they know nothing about? Get real," he said, shaking his head.

"You really are an ignoramus, aren't you?" Bucky said. "I've been trying like hell to understand why anyone in his right mind would choose a method as unnecessary and inhumane as the one you use and promote when dogs are so willing to learn and work, and now I know. You're just plain stupid."

"Maybe you'd understand better if I did a reading on Beau," Audrey said to Alan. "I can tell you already, he has a lot he wants to share with you, but he's been afraid to try."

With that, Alan turned to Cathy Powers, at his left, and repeated what Audrey had just said, using a high, squeaky voice that was meant to imitate hers, his arms up, his wrists limp.

"Maybe you'd understand better," he said, "if I did a *reading* on Beau," he began, exaggerating for emphasis.

Cathy didn't know where to look.

"I can tell you already," Alan squeaked, grimacing as he spoke, "he has a lot he wants to *share* with you." He stopped and turned toward Audrey, who was holding Magic up on her shoulder as if the pug were a baby in need of a burp. "Give me a break, Pocahontas. You may fool the naive pet owner with that mumbo jumbo, in fact I hear you do pretty well for yourself, but here? Please."

"It's not necessary to get so personal, folks," Chip said, getting up to leave.

"Good idea," Woody said, "why don't we call it a night?"

"Yeah," Alan said, "we have a whole week to become mortal enemies."

"Oh dear," Beryl said. She was still holding my arm and now began to tug me toward the doorway.

Once more I heard Alan committing a cardinal offense. This time it was Betty he was maligning, just as Chip was leaving with her. "Isn't she tall for a shepherd?" he asked no one in particular, just loud enough so that he would be sure everyone heard him.

"I've had enough. Haven't you?" Beryl asked.

Only two of the guests had paid any attention to us, so both saw us gesture and got up to follow. Once outside the dining room, they cut loose, tearing up and down the hallway, chasing each other as if there were no tomorrow.

"Let's take them out for a little air," I said. "It'll be safer if we go out together."

"I could use a little air myself," she said. "Not that there wasn't plenty in there—all of it hot, though." But then she looked at her watch. "Where does the time go?" she said. "A quick piddle for you, my sweetheart," she said, addressing the terrier and not me, "and then off to our room. I've a call to make before it gets much later. And then to bed."

It was nearly eleven, and we were due to meet for tracking at six. Still, I wondered if I ought to go back inside. Had they been arguing about food training, I'd have stayed. That could get deadly. But an argument about tracking wasn't going to go anywhere. In the morning, after Chip's demo, everyone would still believe what they believed tonight, no one's opinion altered, no harm done, except to the possibility of camaraderie, just as if they'd been arguing about religion or politics.

Beryl and I walked out of the hotel onto Central Park West. Cecilia went straight to the curb. A moment later, Beryl scooped her up and carried her back inside.

I headed north, toward the Dakota, Dashiell running on ahead, then waiting for me at the corner. At Seventy-second

Street I stopped and looked up at the turrets standing out against the moonlit sky. Then, thinking of the astonishment that must have been on John Lennon's face in the last conscious moment of his life, I turned back toward the Ritz, Dashiell close at my side.

WE SAW THE *TODAY* SHOW

When I passed the Truman Salon, I could hear their voices. As I was contemplating going back inside, Woody Wright opened the door and came out, followed by his flashy brindle boxer bitch, her tail docked but her ears natural.

"They're still going strong," he said, holding the door for me.

"Had enough?" I asked.

"Years ago." He let the door close. "I thought you left the business, Rachel. I haven't seen your ad for a long time."

"Oh, lying low," I said. "Working on referrals and trying to write a book."

"That's definitely the way to go. Do a little Oprah, get a big reputation, host your own TV show. I guess that's what Bucky's aiming for."

"How about you?"

He ran his hand through his short, curly gray hair. "I don't think so, Rachel. I'm happiest when I'm outside, working the dogs. Writing, that's too scary for me." He put a warm hand on my arm and gave it a squeeze. "See you in the morning."

I watched him walking away, Rhonda's cute little tail pointing straight up at the ceiling and then suddenly wagging furiously from side to side like a miniature metronome. She began sneezing, too. Woody must have just asked her if she wanted to go out.

I looked down at Dashiell, who was looking back at me. As soon as he had my eye, he looked at the door to the Truman Salon. I guess he needed to see if Betty was still inside.

Alan was gone. I would be too if I had to get up before five. But Boris, who also had to get up an hour and a half before the rest of us, was still there, his cigar butt smoldering in an ashtray, "wodka" in his hand instead of brandy.

I saw Betty, but no Chip. Audrey was gone. So was Tracy. And as I joined the party, Sam got up to leave. A tired-looking waiter asked me if I wanted a brandy. I nodded—when in Rome and all that—and sat back in my chair, listening to Bucky King, who was still going strong. Some people will do that as long as they have an audience, even of one.

" 'So,' Brad said, 'does he bite?' " Bucky was saying. "And I said, 'Not *you*, pally. He's a borzoi. The only thing he wants in his mouth is caviar.' "

He took a sip of brandy.

"Truth is, the dog had taken a real dislike to him, but we had to get the scene shot, didn't we?" He grinned. His dead white caps stood out against his chemical tan.

Chip walked in and took the chair next to mine. We were down to five—Chip, Bucky, Boris, Rick Shelbert, who hadn't uttered two words all evening, and myself. For a moment there was only the sound of dogs snoring. It seemed like a good idea to me.

I got up, which woke Dashiell, and we headed for the door. Before it had closed behind me, I saw Chip getting up too. I walked toward the stairs, hoping to avoid another embarrassing exchange, but then Betty was in the hall and there was no way I could get Dashiell's attention without being obvious.

"This is pretty much why I don't do these things," he said.

"But Sam seduced you this time."

"The money was irresistible," he said quietly. "You, too?"

"More or less," I said.

"That's usually not how I make my decisions. But Ellen—" He stopped and looked at me for the first time. "She's been talking about moving to California, so the extra cash will come in handy."

Why did my stomach tighten at the thought of never seeing Chip again? What difference did it make if he was in New York or California? He was cementing himself to someone else, not me. Next thing I knew, he and Ellen would be having another kid. My sister and brother-in-law were about to go on a cruise. Jack and I had redecorated, as if a little paint or a new couch would do the trick and bridge the void between us. The things people did when their relationships were deteriorating always astonished me. Anything seemed preferable to the thought of being alone.

"California. That sounds great," I said, starting to hate the sound of my own insincerity. Who was I fooling here?

"Rachel, it's—"

"Time to turn in," I said. "Dashiell needs his beauty rest." And before he could finish whatever he had started to say, I called Dashiell and headed for the stairs.

I guess Chip still had to walk Betty, because when we'd walked up the flight to three, the hallway was empty. I unlocked the door to 305, tossed my jacket onto the end of the bed, and without bothering to turn on the light, walked over to the window and pulled the drape aside.

It was raining lightly. The park across the street looked as pretty as it did in those picture postcards tourists from Iowa send home to their neighbors.

"We saw the *Today* show.

"I had my hair done at Macy's.

"Wish you were here."

The maid had turned down the bed, and Dashiell was on it, smack in the middle, licking himself noisily. I looked back out the window and saw Chip and Betty walking along the stone wall that limned the western border of the park. Betty was slightly ahead of him, looking out for danger. I watched until they turned into the park and I could no longer see them.

Every dog person has an Achilles' hock joint. Mine was a recurring flare-up of the Jiminy Cricket syndrome, the belief that despite overwhelming odds what I wish for might come true. I watched a moment longer before letting the drape fall closed.

I tossed my things onto a chair, brushed my teeth, washed my face, then gave Dashiell a nudge so that he'd move over and give me some room.

I lay in the middle of the bed, where he had been, suddenly aware of something trainers stricter than myself didn't know. If you let your dog up on the bed, you get to sleep on a wet spot without the mess and bother of actually having sex.

Despite exhaustion, I stayed awake for what seemed like ages. It wasn't until I heard the jingle of Betty's ID tags out in the hall that I was able to fall asleep.

I WATCHED CHIP CROSSING THE STREET

We were a quiet group, quite a change for dog people. You usually have to call the cops to get any one of us to stop offering gratuitous opinions. But at six in the morning, after a night of heavy drinking, heated discussions, cigar smoking, and frustrated sex drives—though in truth I could only speak for myself on the latter—no one was saying much of anything.

There were ten of us huddled together without exactly touching at the Sixty-fifth Street entrance to the park. We had walked our dogs and left them in our rooms. This was to be a demonstration, with Betty tracking and then Chip talking to us about her performance at breakfast. Chip was wearing a windbreaker and jeans, his hair rumpled as if he'd rolled out of bed two minutes before. Betty was in harness, whining and pacing, wondering why she couldn't get started. Still, there was no Alan.

"Boris," Chip finally said, "why don't you just show us where the track begins, since Alan isn't here."

"Sure. Easy for you to say."

"Didn't you and Sasha go with him?" Chip asked.

"Boris not see him since dinner when he promise to meet me quarter to five. He want to give you track one hour old. But when I show up, no one here. I wait. I wait. No Mr. Know Everything. I go to room. No answer knock. I think he stay asleep. Too much drink. Weak system. Not like Russian man, can drink wodka day and night and—"

"Boris!"

"I ask desk to call. No answer phone. I go to Columbus Street—"

"Avenue," Rick said.

"Whatever," Boris said, waving Rick away as if he were an annoying insect, "I get coffee, I come back to place he tell me to meet him, no here. Maybe he lay track. Maybe not. Who know?" Boris shrugged. "Not reliable. Russian man give his word—"

"Did anyone see him after dinner?" I asked, looking around the circle. That's when Cathy Powers showed up, running across Central Park West against the light, but not in much danger at this hour. The only traffic was a taxi, and that was several blocks away.

"Did you see Alan this morning?" Chip asked.

"Me?" Cathy asked, her face flushed from running. "What do you mean?"

"He wondered, we all wonder, if you might have seen Alan Cooper. He's not here, as you can see, dear, and it appears he may not have laid the track for Betty's demonstration," Beryl said.

Cathy looked around at each of us and shook her head. I noticed she'd taken the time to blow-dry her hair. It was light brown, long, and smooth. Too smooth, if you ask me. She was wearing a pair of to-die-for suede boots that were going to be ruined the minute she stepped into the park. Didn't they have mud in California? The rest of her outfit was equally ill-suited for tracking, skintight Calvins and a revealing white sweater that was sure to be appreciated by several, if not all, of the gentlemen present. In fact, when I looked around again, several of them were appreciating her sweater while waiting for Alan to show up and tell us where the track began.

"Why don't we assume he laid the track," Chip said. "Wait here. I'll go back to the hotel and see if Sam can get me into his room. I can cue Betty with the socks he wore last night, and we can have a much more interesting lesson than I'd originally planned. If he was out here, Betty will find the track."

There was a murmuring in the group, some of us starting to look alive, even awake, at the thought of seeing Betty start her search from outside the park without knowing where the trail began, if indeed there was one.

I watched Chip crossing the street toward the hotel, Betty at his side.

"Oh, please," Bucky said. He put the last piece of his Danish into his mouth and continued talking around it. "They planned this." He hadn't shaved. In fact, the only man who had was Martyn. "It's just like those jerks to do something like this, high drama. 'Oh, golly, there's no marker, but Betty the Wonder Dog will find the track anyway, from a pair of the track layer's dirty socks.' Does this smell like a setup, or what?"

Woody began to laugh. "Leave it to Pressman. No one loves a goof better than he does. We were doing Schutzhund, oh, ten years back, and he was supposed to be the guy hiding in the blind. We had really green dogs, beginners. So my turn comes. I have a young Dobie, a red male, barely one and a half, still not too sure of himself but coming up nicely. He begins his search, and we get to the blind where Pressman is, and he's got a paper bag over his head. Damn dog emptied his anal glands all over my pants. I never got the stink out, had to throw them away."

"He wasn't goofing," Bucky said. "He was just showing you your boy wasn't ready. Didn't have it yet."

A couple of veins hitherto not visible were sticking out on Woody's neck and forehead, but he said nothing.

"I don't think he lay track. I would have seen him," Boris said. "If not going into park, coming out from park. I wait long time." He had what looked like a fresh grease stain at the bottom of his windbreaker. Coffee, my ass. He probably had a steak for breakfast, something to stick to his big, fat ribs while he made a major production about eating only salad at lunch.

"You said you went for coffee," I said. "You said you went back to the hotel to—"

"I watch here, this spot, like he tell me, all time," Boris said.

"Hey, who's to say?" Bucky said to no one in particular, "maybe Superman isn't the only one with X-ray vision."

"Perhaps he simply got up earlier. Perhaps you misunderstood the time, Boris. Or the place. Perhaps he went another way," Martyn said, "downtown, or further uptown. The way we were drinking last night, perhaps *he* got the time or place wrong."

"He probably finished it before you got out of bed, Boris. Did anyone check the breakfast room? He's probably sitting there right now, drinking coffee, eating his pancakes," Bucky said.

There was more mumbling, no one wanting to go back and look, and then Chip was approaching again, with Betty.

"I had the desk call up. There was no answer. I guess we'll have to reschedule this. What's on for tomorrow morning?"

"Not be so off the wall. Boris lay track," he said.

Everyone turned to look at Boris, who was grinning because he'd fooled us. Or was he grinning over his mastery of American idiom? I couldn't be sure.

"When he no show, not answer door, I leave Sasha in room, come back, and lay track for you."

"Oh, I get it," Bucky said. "It was Boris and Chip doing the goof. Fine, we're ready. Surprise us." He gestured with his hand when he spoke, his fingers as plump as Ballpark Franks.

"We've already wasted half an hour," I said. "Let's get started. Boris?"

Boris led us a few feet into the park and pointed to an area between two trees.

"She'll move pretty fast once she gets the scent," Chip said. "Boris, you better go have another breakfast since you laid the track. You'll confuse her if you stay."

"No difficulty," he said, smacking himself hard on the stomach. "In case you get lost, Boris do opening speech. You still not back, Boris eat your lunch and do afternoon, psychic readings by Boris. Boris hope you find way back by dinner. Radio predict more rain."

"We're onto your scheme," Rick said. "Time to confess, Pressman. The charade is over. So the three of you cooked up this little goof, right?"

"Whatever you say, Rick. I'm ready. Anyone for coming along?"

We each took one step forward. Even if it was a scam, hell, more's the fun if it was, we surely wouldn't want to miss seeing how it would play out. Maybe Betty would lead us on a long chase through the densest part of the park, and at the end of the trail Alan would be lying on the ground, mouth open, arms and legs askew, the found victim. Or he'd be sitting on a blanket in the middle of the Sheep Meadow with Sam, and a great, huge picnic breakfast for us all, both of them laughing.

Chip addressed Betty. "Good girl," he told her, whispering urgently, "go find." She began to sniff and circle, then suddenly she was moving, nose to the ground, Chip hanging tight to the long line attached to her padded harness. Going at a moderate pace at first, she headed farther and farther into the park. Every once in a while she'd stop and search the ground, circling or moving left or right. Or she'd sneeze, clearing the way for new scents, just as the family dog riding with his head out the car window does, then she'd be off again, pulling Chip behind her.

We all followed, running to keep up, finding ourselves being led through thick low bushes, our shoes sinking into the wet earth, winding our way around trees, being careful not to trip over roots and fallen branches as we snaked around the park. Betty was going at a steady clip, across the path and onto the grass, all of us following after her.

"Couldn't just do it straight," Bucky mumbled, starting to get out of breath as we all hurried to keep up with Chip and Betty. "They had to make a big production out of it."

"Be quiet," Tracy said. "Let's just do this." Her face was damp, as if she were a plant someone had just misted, but unlike Bucky, she kept up.

Betty veered toward the copse of trees where just yesterday I had taken Dash and then seen Alan working his dog in the meadow. So it was Alan after all, going exactly the same way he had gone yesterday. No imagination.

But Betty was already off in another direction. She didn't go into the meadow, nor did she continue along the way Dashiell and I had yesterday, toward the lake. She was heading north now, and she was covering ground fast.

We crossed over the bridle path, half our band having to wait for some early-morning riders to pass and hopping around the fresh manure as they rushed to catch up. Betty was whining, moving at a full clip toward a deserted pathway thick with trees on both sides. Suddenly her cries revved up. Whatever Alan,

Boris, and Chip had cooked up, we were there. But for those of us expecting the big gag, there was only disappointment. Sure, Betty had followed the track. She held a glove in her mouth to prove it. She and Chip were doing tug-of-war with it now, her reward for a job well done. But that was it. We had been promised tracking, and tracking was what we got. It was time for breakfast at the Ritz and no doubt a continuation of last night's argument about the relative merits of tracking versus air-scenting.

I wondered why I'd thought Alan would be waiting for us with a picnic of goodies from Zabar's, or be lying faceup in the dirt, a small red circle over his heart and ketchup drooling out of his mouth. Alan Cooper, as far as I could tell, had no sense of humor whatsoever. Perhaps that was why he used a shock collar to train dogs, because he lacked the capacity to laugh at himself when a dog made him look like a fool. Hell, you can't do that, you don't belong around dogs.

So what did this all mean—that Boris was simply telling the truth? If so, where was Alan?

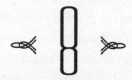

OLD-FASHIONED

"That's what Jack Godsil always told me," Bucky was saying between bites of bagels, lox, and cream cheese in the Ritz breakfast room. "Every handler ends up with the dog he deserves."

Chip tugged at my sleeve, just like the old days, to let me know he, too, knew the real source of that quote.

" 'Bucky,' he'd say . . ."

"Put a zipper on it, King," Rick Shelbert said. Then he looked startled by his own boldness.

"It's amazing how many students a trainer picks up after he's died," Woody said. He put some milk into his coffee and took a sip. "Rachel, weren't you telling me the other night that you were taught by Blanche Saunders?"

"You know, my dears," Beryl said, "none of the students coming today would have any idea what you are talking about." She picked up a knife and slid a little pot of marmalade closer to her plate of toast. We didn't only have our own pots of jam and jelly, we had individual creamers, sugar bowls, salt and pepper shakers, every amenity for people who usually ate greasy hot dogs on the fly between training jobs. "For them," Beryl continued, "history begins with the people out there teaching seminars now, some of you, some far younger and far less experienced. Nor do they study breed differences. They choose a gadget and advertise themselves as experts. I hope this week inspires one or two of them to better scholarship."

"I wouldn't count on that," Bucky said.

"At my age, I don't count on much."

"I don't think that all the changes are bad ones, Beryl," Rick said, putting down his coffee, ready for battle.

"Of course you don't," Beryl said, dismissing him.

"I think the introduction of scientific—" Rick started to say, but Beryl didn't let him finish.

"Scientific? Scientific only means you have no feeling for dogs, no insights, no respect for their intelligence and ability to learn, no—"

"My good woman—"

"I am not your good woman, nor anyone else's." Beryl pinned Rick with an alpha stare. "You are about to be very condescending toward me, and I suggest you rethink your position. Actually, rolling over, exposing your neck, and urinating would be more appropriate."

Rick opened his mouth as if to respond, but began wheezing instead, his face turning red as he struggled for breath. I could hear the air whistling its way down to his lungs while he fished around in his pants pocket and came up with his inhaler. That was when the door opened and Sam appeared in the doorway, her face as pale and dry looking as chalk.

She came over to my chair and bent over so that her lips were right next to my ear. "Something terrible has happened. I need you outside *now*," she said.

I followed her out the door and partway down the hall.

"There's been an accident," she said.

"Alan?"

She nodded, then covered her nose and mouth with her open hand.

"What happened?"

Her hand came slowly away from her face and landed lightly on my shoulder.

"He's dead," she whispered, her voice hoarse from tension.

I thought immediately about the park. It must have been a mugging.

"He must have gone to lay the track alone. There must have been two—"

She shook her head. "The police have been here since shortly after you all went out to do the tracking, checking the room and asking questions. They want to talk to Audrey, Bucky, and Beryl, because they have the rooms closest to Alan's, to see if they heard anything. I think we'll be able to go on. They seem pretty sure—"

"You mean he died in the hotel? Not in the park?"

Three men in coat and tie and a woman in a navy skirt suit, her long hair pulled back and clipped at the nape of her neck, came up the stairs at the end of the hallway.

"Detectives O'Shea, Flowers, DeAndrea, and Mullins, Rachel Alexander," Sam said.

They nodded. The woman put out her hand. "Diane Flowers," she said. "Rachel, I was wondering if you saw Mr. Cooper after he left the group last night?"

The other three detectives and Sam walked back toward the breakfast room.

"No, I didn't."

"You didn't run into him walking his dog when you took your dog out?"

I shook my head.

"Did any of the others mention seeing Mr. Cooper later in the evening, either out with his dog, or back at the hotel?"

"Not to me," I said. "What happened?"

"And you heard nothing last night?"

"I believe Mr. Cooper's room is on four," I told her. "Mine is on three. No, I didn't hear anything. And no one," I said, looking back toward the breakfast room, "mentioned hearing anything last night or this morning." I saw one of the detectives walking down the hall with Audrey at his side. "He was supposed to lay the track for us, for one of the dogs to follow, and he didn't show up."

She was writing something in her notebook. A second detective passed us, Bucky King walking next to him.

"Yes, across the hall. But I sleep with the air conditioner on," he was saying as they passed us and headed down the stairs.

"Was Mr. Cooper here by himself, Ms. Alexander, or did his wife accompany him?"

"As far as I know, all the lecturers are here without family. Except for our dogs," I added.

She looked up and smiled at me. Then she looked back down at her notes. "Did Mr. Cooper seem depressed?" she asked. "Or agitated, you know, upset, jumpy, anything that seemed out of the ordinary to you?"

"Not that I could tell."

"My dear young man." Beryl and the third detective were in the hall. "Once I take out my hearing aid, there could be a five-alarm fire at the hotel, and it would go unnoticed in my room."

Detective Flowers reached into her pocket and pulled out a card. "If you think of something you might have seen or heard."

"Detective—"

"Detective DeAndrea is going to explain what happened in a moment," Flowers said. "Come with me."

We headed back to the breakfast room, where I took my chair and looked around the room. Woody raised his eyebrows, but all I could do was shrug. I leaned toward Chip. "Did they ask you anything?" I whispered.

"Just if anyone had seen Alan last night after he left the group. What's the deal here? Did Sam say? Where's Alan?"

I didn't get the chance to answer. The door opened, and Audrey, Bucky, and Beryl came in quietly and took their seats. Sam and the three detectives were right behind them. While the others remained near the doorway, DeAndrea stepped closer to the table. He stood with his feet slightly apart, ready for anything. Muller, standing next to Sam, was putting his notebook away. When he clasped his hands behind his back, I could see the bulge of his gun under his navy jacket. Detective Muller was apparently ready, too.

"Folks," DeAndrea said, "I'm sorry to inform you that one of your colleagues, Alan Cooper, has had an accident."

Tracy stood. "What happened? Is he okay?"

"No, ma'am. He's deceased."

Detective Muller walked over and assisted Tracy back into her chair. "Can I get you some water?" he asked, even though there was a glass of water at every place setting. Tracy shook her head.

"What happened?" Woody asked.

"It appears that Mr. Cooper had moved the clock radio from his nightstand to the towel shelf over the foot of the tub so that he could listen to it in the bathroom. It seems that when he got up to get out of the tub, he slipped and grabbed for the shelf to catch himself. He took the whole shelf down with him into the tub, including the radio."

Cathy covered her mouth with both hands, Audrey was trying to shred her cloth napkin, and Rick's dead white skin seemed even paler than usual. I looked over at Sam, but she wasn't looking in my direction. Woody and Chip got up. Then Bucky rose.

"Sit down, if you would, folks. There's nothing for you to do. Ms. Lewis here has given us the information we need. The hotel staff has been very cooperative. We've been in touch with Mrs. Cooper, who'll be here this afternoon to pick up his personal effects and the dog. It's unfortunate, in the middle of your convention, but accidents happen. I'm sorry for your loss," he said, looking down for the first time. "I hope you'll be able to settle down and get on with your work."

He turned his back to us and whispered something to Sam, who nodded, and with that, the officers left. Sam started to take the empty chair that would have been Alan's, pulled it out from the table, and then hesitated, resting her hands on the back of it instead of sitting.

"Elizabeth Cooper is on her way from Connecticut. I have Beau in my room. He's pacing a lot, but Elizabeth says he always does that. We have"—she stopped and looked at her watch—"an hour and a half before my little welcome to the students and Beryl's very important talk on breed character. I thought I'd take Beau out to the park and then see if I can get him to eat something. I think each of us needs to find a way to calm down so that we can go on with our work."

The room was silent. Sam pushed the chair back in and turned to leave. But then she turned back to face us again.

"The detectives have questioned the staff and those of us whose rooms were closest to Alan's. Nothing unusual was heard or observed and they have assured me his death was—" Sam looked up for a moment, as if she were trying to stop the flow of tears. Then she picked up a napkin from the table and blotted her eyes. "Accidental," she said when she was able. There wasn't another sound in the room. "Does anyone have a question?" She held out her hand, as if she were asking for spare change.

"How did they—" Cathy asked.

"The manager called me after Boris and Chip had gone to the front desk to inquire about Alan. I've known Alan Cooper for ten years, and I know many of you don't like the method he used with dogs; however, I have always found him to be a responsible, reliable speaker. Had I not, I wouldn't have asked him to participate this week. It made no sense to me that he'd agree to do something and then just not show up, so I asked the manager if they could check his room and see if he was there, if perhaps there was some problem, if he was sick. He sent up one of the maids, and she found him. She spoke to the police, and then she was sent home. She was pretty shaken up."

Sam waited. No one else, it seemed, had anything to say.

"If that's all for now, I'm going to take care of Beau. I'll be back in my suite in forty-five minutes, should you need me."

"Walk Beau on this." Chip had a nylon slip collar in his hand. I took it and passed it to Sam.

"Do you want me to go with you?" I asked.

Sam didn't answer right away, as if she were thinking over my offer.

"You're all great," she said. "I knew you'd come through. It's tragic, what happened to Alan. But it could have happened anywhere, at any time. I just knew you'd all—" She looked away for a moment. "You're all terrific. Together we're going to do this thing. And we'll be great." Then she turned toward me. "Thank you, Rachel, but I hope you understand, I'd rather be alone just now. Thank you all for being so wonderful."

I followed her out into the hall.

"I can't believe this," she said. "What a freak thing to happen."

"What you said in there was perfect, Sam, setting the tone for cooperation. They're all going to pull together and make this happen. You'll see."

"Do you really think so?"

"I do."

"Poor Alan," she said.

"Sam, what else did the police say?"

"That from the position of his legs they're pretty sure he was getting out of the tub when the accident happened. His left heel was on the rim of the tub, and there was a lot of water on the floor. They said the water was very soapy, which is what made the tub so slippery. Of course, the final determination of cause of death rests with the medical examiner.

"They said the shelf Alan grabbed to try and stop himself from falling was never meant to hold anything except a few extra towels. It could never have held the weight of a person." She shook her head. "It pulled right out of the tile."

"Sam, are the police finished with the room?"

"Yes, but they don't want the hotel to release it yet, not for twenty-four hours. They said I could go in and pack his things, though, that that would be okay."

"Let me do that for you. You've got enough to do taking care of Beau. And yourself. Anyway, you have to be available to the others, in case there are some second thoughts later, anxieties to be dealt with, questions."

"Thanks, Rachel. I certainly want to have everything ready for Elizabeth. I don't want her to have to be in that room at all." She reached into her pocket and took out two keys, checking the room numbers, and then handed one of them to me.

"I'll pack and leave the bag at the front desk, okay?"

"Why don't you just bring it to my suite after you've cleaned up and changed?" she said. "I'm in 501. Of course, you already know that, don't you? Thanks for this, Rachel. It'll help a lot. The hotel offered to have it done, but I said no. I think we owe it to Alan not to have a stranger—"

"Not to worry. I'll see you later, okay?"

I stopped on three for Dashiell, then took the stairs up one more flight. Standing in the empty hallway outside 408, I took a deep breath, preparing myself as if Alan's body would still be in there, one foot sticking up out of the tub, his face locked in a grimace of pain and fear. But the room was empty, the curtains open, the sun streaming in onto the rumpled bed, the electronic collar and remote lying on top of the dresser.

I put Dashiell on a down just inside the door so that I could look first. I could see that the nightstand was still pulled away from the wall. I guessed that Alan intended to return the radio to its place after his bath. There was a pair of pants over the back of a chair near the window, a pair of shoes near the bed, the socks he'd worn tossed over them. The bedcovers were in a great pile on one side of the bed, and the pillows were one on top of the other. I bent and looked under the bed, and found Alan's shirt there. Perhaps he'd tossed it on the bed and it slipped off when he'd gotten up, then got kicked beneath the bed by accident. I pulled it out and did the best I could to fold it, pushing the covers over to make room for Alan's suitcase so that I could pack up his things, as promised. I thought I'd do that first and save the bathroom for last.

But when I pushed the covers over, I saw something that made me stop. Had I only been looking at Alan as someone whose training method I disliked intensely, that all changed when I saw the tennis ball pushed under the edge of the bedclothes, placed there by a hopeful dog who wanted one more toss. Many dog trainers have two sides to them, the one they show in public and one they keep private. But in most cases, the public side is the gentle one, and the rougher training techniques are used when no one else is watching. Here was a case where the public side was one many considered harmful to dogs. But, alone with Beau, Alan had played ball with him.

Come to think of it, there'd been a ball just inside the door. I was so used to seeing dog toys on the floor, it hadn't really registered. When I turned to look for it, it was between Dashiell's paws. I picked it up and held it in my hand. Did he let the dog sleep up on the bed, too? I wondered, putting the ball in my pocket and running my hands on top of the spread to see if I picked up dog hair.

I couldn't find any fur on the spread, nor could I find any pajamas tossed anywhere. They were probably in the bathroom, I thought, wincing. He probably hung them on the back of the door before he got into the tub. Or if he didn't wear any, no wonder he wouldn't let the dog in the bed, I thought. You can get some nasty scratches sleeping naked with a dog. I flipped up the end of the covers, finding Alan's polka-dot boxer shorts there. So, no pajamas. He just kicked off the last article of clothing after he was already under the covers.

I put Alan's things in his bag, including his shorts, looking through his seminar notes and placing them in one of the pockets, using the plastic bag the hotel provided for his shoes, as if it mattered now, even folding the slacks as smoothly and neatly as I could, as if he were going to wear them again. Then I walked over to the bathroom, opened the door, and looked in.

The tub was empty and looked as if it had been cleaned, so despite what my mother called my overactive imagination, I figured it would be safe to start breathing again after only a few seconds. Unfortunately, I was wrong. The stench of feces was too strong to be masked by air freshener, especially since there was no window in the small bathroom. I picked up a clean washcloth, wet it, and held it over my nose and mouth.

I looked at the outlet next. It was as old-fashioned as everything else in the hotel. Had there been an outlet with a ground fault interrupter, the way there is in the bathrooms of more modern hotels, Alan Cooper would still be alive.

The bath mat was gone. It must have gotten soaked when Alan fell back into the tub. The wet towels and the broken shelf had been removed, but the radio had not. It had been placed on the floor next to the foot of the tub, and there it sat, the loose cord behind it. It was useless as evidence. You wouldn't be able to get fingerprints from an object that had soaked in hot, soapy water. From what Sam had said, the detectives would only expect to find Alan's prints on it anyway. There had been black powder on top of the nightstand. Tomorrow or the next day they'd confirm that Alan was the one who'd moved it out so that he could have music while he soaked in the tub.

There was a terry robe the hotel supplied tossed over the closed toilet, something to put on when you got out of the tub. And Alan's toothbrush and shaving things were out on the sink.

The trash basket had only a couple of used tissues in it. I picked up Alan's things and went back into the bedroom. I packed the rest of his gear, putting his bathroom supplies neatly into his dopp kit, checking the closet again to make sure I hadn't left a pair of shoes on the floor or a shirt on the shelf. I slipped the collar and remote in last. Then I sat on the window seat and looked out at the park.

It was after nine already. I still had to get Dashiell out for a short walk and shower and change before Beryl's talk. I stood near the window looking around one last time, then zipped up the suitcase, released Dash from his stay, and was about to leave when I realized I hadn't checked the wastebasket near the bed. So while Dashiell filled his nose with Beau's smells, I walked back to the bed where Alan Cooper had spent the last night of his life and found another bunch of wadded-up tissues in the trash. Guy must have had one hell of a cold, I thought. Or maybe he was allergic. It was the season for it.

"Maybe that's why he was soaking in the tub, to help with chest congestion, what do you think?" I asked Dash, being one of those New Yorkers who uses my dog as an excuse to talk to myself.

But Dashiell wasn't listening. He'd found a third tennis ball, this one under the covers on the other side of the bed, and since I'd spoken to him, he figured maybe I wasn't busy any longer; maybe, in fact, I'd be as interested as he was in a little game of fetch. He trotted over and tossed the ball at my feet, backed up, barked, and wagged his tail.

One ball on the floor and two shoved under the covers didn't mean a game. It meant Beau was hoping for a game and was being ignored.

So instead of responding to Dashiell's invitation, I busied myself pulling the top sheet and blankets all the way off the bed.

Bright sunlight was streaming in through the window, lighting up every corner of the room. With the covers off, I quickly discovered why Beau had had no response to his pleas for a game of fetch. His master, it seemed, had been otherwise occupied. As far as I could tell, right up until the end, Alan Cooper, God bless him, had made wet spots the old-fashioned way.

Now all I needed to find out was who wore skimpy leopard bikini underwear. Because whoever it was, she'd left a pair in Alan Cooper's bed.

WOULD YOU MIND? SHE ASKED

I took the empty place in the last row next to Woody for Beryl's talk, then looked around to see where the other female trainers were, wondering if it had been one of them who had so generously entertained Alan on the last night of his life. I'd overheard Audrey in the bathroom saying she'd been with someone in Phoenix who was in New York now, someone with whom she was contemplating breaking the laws of God and man again.

Could she have meant Alan? It was hard to believe. He'd been so cruel to her at dinner. Still, you never know. Her whole schtick was fixing bad relationships, wasn't it? Perhaps she saw him as an irresistible challenge. Or maybe his nastiness had turned her on. I'd have to find out if Alan had ever shocked dogs and humane trainers in Arizona, and one way or another, if it was he who had charmed the pants off Audrey last night.

On the other hand, many of the students had arrived last

night, and their names had been gleaned from lists of people attending previous seminars, including Alan's. For years I had heard stories about certain male trainers who crisscrossed the country teaching seminars, hopping from bed to bed instead of hotel to hotel as they moved from city to city. One of them had even bragged to me about how much money he'd saved, revealing the name of the lady who'd so kindly put him up, and making sure I knew he hadn't slept on a foldout couch or in a guest room. A real gentleman.

"It is character, dear people," Beryl was saying, "that makes or breaks a relationship, character that becomes the red thread of a life, no matter if we are discussing a canine or a human, and therefore understanding character should be a prerequisite for choosing a dog and for educating a dog as well."

"Rotten piece of luck about Cooper," Woody said, his voice serious.

"Along with the issues of size, strength, activity level, and trainability," Beryl was saying.

"What did I miss?" Chip said, taking the seat next to mine.

Woody leaned across me. "I was saying to Rachel here that it was a rotten piece of luck, Alan's accident."

"Not so rotten for dogs," Chip said. He was watching the stage, Beryl at the mike, the screen down for her slide show.

I'd been wondering exactly how long respect for the dead would stave off comments about Alan's training method. He'd been dead only five or six hours, and apparently the moratorium had already run out.

"So it is the work function of the dog which must be examined," Beryl was saying, "for therein lies the blueprint for understanding the animal, the way he thinks, moves, gets on with others."

"Still, I found the news shocking, didn't you?" Woody said.

"It certainly has everyone talking," Chip said.

"What have you heard?" I asked, watching Beryl imitating a golden retriever waiting to be sent for a duck. And then doing exactly the same expression again, saying it was the same dog, now waiting for its owner to chuck a ball.

"Rumor has it that Beau stood up and pulled down the shelf with the radio on it," Chip said.

"Poetic justice," Woody said.

"Most dogs, like the Golden, will happily swap some game for the function for which they were created and bred, as long as that game contains the elements that were genetically strengthened over the years in order to make the dog a more efficient and dedicated worker."

"That the ASPCA hired the mob to—"

"Will someone in the back please turn down the lights?" Beryl said. A young man across the aisle jumped up, and in a moment we were sitting in the dark.

"And the usual stuff. 'How did Alan Cooper find the dog-training seminar? Electrifying.' You know, that sort of thing. I mean, if they did it when the *Challenger* went down, why not now?"

The first slide was on the screen, a border terrier digging for a rodent. "This very tenacity—" Beryl began. Then Chip leaned across me to speak to Woody again.

"Where's Sam? Did she say if they're doing an autopsy?"

"She's probably still with Elizabeth. It's too soon for any results," I said.

"So that if you are training a proper terrier, it should—" Beryl said as the next slide clicked into place.

"It's not an easy way to go," Woody said. "Better to die in your sleep."

"I wonder if he had time—"

I turned to look at Chip. Woody leaned across me.

"I'm just saying, they said he fell. They didn't say if he was knocked out before the radio hit the water. So I wonder if there would have been time—"

"To try to get out after the radio fell in?" Woody said. "Trust me. That's not an option."

When I was kid, my sister Lillian used to take me to horror movies, and I would put my hands over my eyes when the scary parts came on so that I wouldn't get nightmares. But then, I couldn't help it, I'd spread my fingers apart and look anyway.

"Time to what?" I couldn't resist asking.

"To rethink his training method," Chip said, watching Beryl on the stage, the podium light throwing weird shadows onto her face.

Woody and I groaned.

"I hope the students don't find out," he said.

"Do you think they'll miss him?" I asked. "He's on the program. And some of them must have come just to see *him*."

"I can't imagine why," Chip said.

"Because he promised them the magic pill," I said, "a way they could get what they were after without actually working for it. Isn't that why the lottery works?"

Chip leaned across me to say something to Woody.

"Shhh, Beryl's speaking. I want to hear her." I punched him in the arm for emphasis, the way I used to in the old days, before he spoiled our friendship by getting divorced and reconciled.

"Do you know what Sam is going to do about his time slot?" Woody asked.

Beryl was showing a slide of a Rottweiler herding sheep.

"She'll probably ask one of us to fill it," I said. "You wouldn't have a problem with that, would you?" I asked him.

"Not as long as I don't have to electronically stimulate any dogs."

"Maybe she'll add another panel," I said. "Wasn't Alan speaking about problem correction? We could do a problem panel, take questions from the students. There's one on Saturday, for pet owners. But we could do this one for professionals, you know, talk about client problems as well as dog problems."

"Sure," Woody said, "why not a panel, the three of us and some foodies. Why stop at one death?"

"Sam will come up with something. She just needs to spend some time with Elizabeth first."

"I hope she dumped that damn shock collar," Chip said.

"I packed Alan's stuff," I said.

Woody and Chip turned to look at me in the light of the next slide. It was a gazehound, and Beryl was saying something about the difference between dogs that work closely with man, genetically predisposed to taking direction, and dogs that hunt in packs, working off their instincts rather than instruction and therefore less cooperative as training subjects.

"I gave Sam a hand, that's all. I packed Alan's stuff so she wouldn't have to do it. She was nice enough to get Beau out, try to calm him down. And she's the one dealing with Elizabeth. It was the least I could do."

"And?" Woody asked. "What about the collar?"

"I packed it."

"Oh, Jesus," he said.

"What would you have done?" I said loud enough to get shushed by the mountain of a woman two rows in front of us. "Throw it out with the trash the maid was collecting in the hall? Don't you figure there are more of them back at the kennel, should Elizabeth want to continue electrocuting her dog once she sheds her widow's weeds? Anyway, married couples hardly ever train alike, even in professional families."

"Tell me about it," Chip said, and when I turned to look at

him, his brow was furrowed, and he seemed for the moment to be far away.

"I mean, sometimes you can't even get a husband and wife to use the same vocabulary with the dog. Anyway, Elizabeth will have other things on her mind," I said, looking back at the screen, "at least for a while."

"So that in testing the intelligence of a dog not genetically attuned to working with a human handler," Beryl was saying, "what are you actually testing? If the dog is not prone to being cooperative with humans in a work situation, in a partnership, as it were, then why would he care about the artificial tests devised by some scientist with no knowledge of breed differences?"

That's when I zeroed in on the back of Audrey's head, the little black pug looking over her shoulder, her bug eyes watching everyone watch the slide show. Even if neither of them had been in Phoenix, suppose Alan had changed his mind and accepted Audrey's generous offer of a psychic reading on Beau, perhaps noticing the blue-black shine of her hair or the wonderful roundness of her tight little derriere. So then I sat there trying to figure out if that wonderful little derriere was the size that would fit into the leopard bikinis I had stuffed into my pocket before leaving Alan's room. From there it was a hop, skip, and a jump to wonder how that little tramp—how *anyone*, no matter how desperate— could go to bed with a shock collar trainer.

I was dying to ask at least one of my companions that very question, but instead I merely slid lower into my seat and tried to concentrate on Beryl's talk, suddenly seeing her younger, saying these same things, on the tapes I had at home.

"That the Lab is harder and cooler than the Golden, that the—" Beryl was saying.

"They're not going to get this," Chip whispered. "It's too subtle."

"Maybe it will start them noticing things they never saw before. That's really all you can hope for."

"Some of us won't get it either," I said.

"Tell me about it," Chip said.

But I didn't have to. Beryl was saying it for me.

"And so of course any method that ignores breed character, that treats all dogs as if they were the same, is foolhardy at best. Sadly, to ignore character differences is also to miss out on—"

"Who's on after lunch?" Woody asked.

"Audrey," Chip said.

I sank lower in my seat and concentrated on the stage as Beryl wrapped up.

"And that in addition to breed character, we as trainers must pay attention to individual differences, how bright a particular dog is, how quickly he responds, to the limitations and determinations of body type, to humor and how each dog expresses his own version of it, to the level of dominance in each individual, to stubbornness and tenacity above and beyond what is to be expected for a certain breed and whether we are dealing with an issue of character or a training problem. So you can see, dear friends, that the underlying factor is always the character of the particular dog you are training, how to understand and best approach it for a successful dog-and-human relationship."

Then everyone was clapping, and Beryl was waving away the applause.

"Is there a question period?" Woody asked. "God, I hope not. I'm starving."

I pulled the program out of my jacket pocket, nearly dislodging the leopard bikinis along with it. "Weird. Sam put it at the end of the day, both speakers together."

"She does that to keep it lively. Where's the lunch?" Woody asked.

"The Nixon Room," I said.

"You're joking."

"Right."

But before I got the chance to tell him where the lunch was, the fat lady who had shushed us was at the end of the aisle, and we weren't going anywhere without her permission.

"You're speakers?" she asked.

"Guilty as charged," Woody said. "Rachel Alexander, Chip Pressman, and I'm Woody Wright."

"Oh," she said, disappointed. That's when I noticed the point-and-shoot camera in her hand.

"Bucky's in the front, on the left side," I told her, hoping once she'd left I could get out of the aisle and on with my life.

She looked over toward the front of the room, toward the crowd around Bucky, but she didn't stir. "But you're all on the program," she said. "May I?" She held up the camera, and as we were about to lean together and say "cheese," she held it out toward me. "Would you mind?" she asked.

I took her picture with Woody and then with Chip. I was about to hand the camera to Chip so that I could pose with her, too, but she was thanking them, and then she was off, leaning first to one side and then the other as she duck-walked down to the front to have her picture taken with the king of dog trainers.

"Lunch is in the Carter Café," I told Woody. "I think we're eating in the garden. You coming, Pressman?"

"I'm going to take Betty out for a walk," he said. "Want to join me?" He was staring at me the way Dashiell does when he has some desperate need he's trying to communicate. But the only need I was interested in just then was my own.

I needed answers. I needed to know who fell panting into Alan Cooper's arms last night. And then what? Did she steal away before dawn, unable to find her panties in the dark and too considerate to put on the light?

Or was she still there in the morning when Alan had slipped into the hot, soapy tub? And if so, considering the circumstances, what business was that of mine?

"Rachel?" he said.

"I can't. I have something really important I have to do," I told him, because at least I was sure about the answer to my last question. Even if I weren't dying of curiosity, Sam's check had made it my business.

I STUCK MY HAND INTO MY POCKET

I ran up the stairs to my room. I needed some time to be alone and think. At twelve-thirty I took Dashiell for a walk around the neighborhood, dropped off the film I had shot on Sunday at the closest drugstore, and returned at one to hear Audrey's talk. A worried-looking Sam, standing outside the door, called me over.

"Audrey refuses to speak this afternoon. She says the vibes are too negative, because of Alan's accident."

"Won't anyone else switch with her?"

"Yes, but I'm worried about all these last-minute changes. People expect to hear what's on the program."

"Who's speaking in Audrey's place?"

"Rick said he would. He's very sweet. But he's such a boring speaker. I was hoping to slip him in later in the week."

"It's after lunch, Sam, half the audience will fall asleep anyway. More than half if he's really dull."

"Audrey would have kept them up. Even if you don't buy a word she says, she's so entertaining. And she gets everyone to participate."

"You mean the whole audience will be sitting there with handkerchiefs over their heads, chanting?"

"Exactly. Try sleeping with *that* going on. But it's not only that. She tells these sad, charming, funny stories about what the animals tell her is wrong with their lives. None of it is their own fault. It's all human error. People lap it up. It gives them somewhere to put their free-floating guilt. Anyway, now Rick has the afternoon, which means he and Beryl will be together for the question period. You know how *she* is, she's so overbearing, she won't let him say a word."

"I wouldn't worry about it, Sam. It'll be good for Rick to tangle with Godzilla."

I smiled wickedly at the thought. So did Sam.

"Maybe you're right," she said. "At least *that* part will be lively. I know I'm fretting too much. It's just that talking to Elizabeth was so draining."

"I can imagine. Any news about Alan?"

"Detective Flowers came back when Elizabeth was here, in case she had any questions. And she did. She wanted to know everything. Flowers was totally straight with her. She said that unfortunately Alan had been conscious during the mishap. That's what she called it, the mishap. She said the fall hadn't knocked him out. It only knocked the radio in." She made a face. "She also said his hand was on the faucet, that he might have been trying to right himself and get back up, but that that was what made the current go through his heart. Otherwise he might have survived the shock."

"So it was definitely an accident?" I asked her.

"What else?" she said, lowering her voice and looking at me seriously. "Rachel, you don't think—"

"No, no, it's just that he wasn't alone last night."

"Who was?" she said. "And whatever difference could that make? Rachel, the man's dead. And everyone screws around at these things. It's expected, you know, it's one of the perks. People like to get away from the routines of their life. What harm does it do, a little flirting, a little fling at a seminar? It doesn't hurt anyone."

"The way eating bacon out when you keep a kosher home doesn't count?" I said, a little edge in my voice perhaps. "Is that the theory? That God only watches when you're at your legal home address?"

What on earth was *I* so angry about? I wondered. No one was breaking down my door insisting I break any commandments with them. I was free to be just as moral—and lonely—as I pleased.

"People are unhappy, Rachel."

Tell me about it, I thought, seeing again the look in Chip's eyes when I turned down his invitation for a walk in the park. He'd looked as sad as a shelter dog.

"They need a little treat once in a while," she said, "a little pick-me-up. It doesn't destroy their life at home. No one takes it seriously."

But some do, I thought. Some take it very seriously. Hadn't my own brother-in-law, burdened by guilt from his little pick-me-ups, confessed much too much to his unsuspecting wife, neatly transferring the anvil of pain from his shoulders to hers?

I stuck my hand into my pocket and for a moment wondered if one other person had taken things seriously, the person whose underwear was now in my hand.

"Sam, did you ever book Alan in Phoenix?"

"Phoenix? Yes, last fall, October. What makes you ask?"

"Oh, no special reason. It's just that I overheard Audrey talking about someone she'd been with in Phoenix that she might be with again here. That's all."

"Rachel, it was an accident. That's what the police said. Please keep in mind that any other conclusion could ruin me. Anyway, most of them have been in Phoenix. What you heard, it didn't mean anything. And if you do find out who was there with Alan, then what?"

"I only wanted to return these," I said, holding my pocket open so that Sam could see what was inside.

"*There* they are," she said, slipping her hand into my pocket and gathering the bikinis into her fist.

My mouth opened, but nothing came out. Anyway, don't the Chinese say, One pair of underwear is worth more than ten thousand words? What was there to add?

"Where'd you find them?" she asked, opening her purse and dropping them in. "Never mind. I don't want to know. Anyway, thanks, Rachel. I knew you'd earn your wages."

I tried to imagine Sam and Alan, but it was as unthinkable and distasteful as trying to imagine one's parents having sex, which everyone knew only happened very early in their marriage, and only as many times as there were offspring.

"I'm grateful it was you who found them and not the police," she whispered. "Can you imagine how much fun *that* interrogation would have been?"

She turned and held the door open for me. "Come along," she said. "Rick is about to begin. It's nap time." And with that she led the way, then continued on up to the stage to introduce him after I dropped off near the back and slid into an empty seat two rows behind Martyn Eliot and Cathy Powers, signaling Dashiell to lie down in front of me.

"There's been a slight change in the program," Sam was saying. "This afternoon, we are lucky to have Rick Shelbert, dog behaviorist to the stars and author of *Positively Perfect*, talking about some of his most fascinating cases. Dr. Shelbert, as you know, has a Ph.D. in psychology and has been working with dog owners for twelve years. Let's give him a warm welcome."

Dashiell lifted his head during the applause and put it back down as Rick approached the microphone, hoping perhaps to be first to fall asleep, but he didn't come close. Rick's Saint Bernard, Freud, who had been asleep near the chair in which Rick had been sitting during Sam's introduction, never woke up when his master moved. From where I sat, I couldn't be *positive*, but chances were good he was snoring and drooling too.

As Rick began, I noticed that not everyone was listening. Martyn seemed to be more engrossed in his conversation with Cathy than he was in what was happening on the stage.

In fact, I seemed to being having trouble concentrating on Rick myself. I thought the acoustics might be better if I moved up a row. But I thought that might be too obvious, so instead I leaned forward, resting my arms on the empty seat in front of me, then leaning my chin on the back of one hand.

"Her father left the family when she was just a kid, you see," Martyn was saying. He was so wrapped up in Cathy he hadn't noticed me practically breathing down his neck. "It really messed her up badly."

Cathy nodded as he spoke. She was pretty wrapped up herself.

"There's no way I could leave her at this time," he said. "It would seem a repetition of her past, as if I were doing to her what her father had done, as if it were happening all over again."

"How sad."

I thought I detected a touch of sarcasm in Cathy's voice, but Martyn didn't seem to notice.

Rick was talking about a collie he'd worked with. The dog

was afraid of men, so Rick had had the owner play a tape of men speaking and offer the dog bits of liver while it played.

"Next," he said, "we took him out, and whenever a man came into view, we'd offer treats to the dog. Eventually we were able to get some men to offer the liver directly to the dog, so that he would begin to perceive male strangers as bearers of pleasant things—"

"She's in therapy," Martyn was saying. "Perhaps in time—" He didn't bother to finish the sentence, leaving it to Cathy's imagination.

I leaned back and tried to concentrate on the stage.

Rick was talking about aggression now, first a problem with a shih tzu who hid under the bed and bit the bare feet of the boyfriend when he tried to get out of bed. Rick's suggestion was that the couple eschew sex for several weeks, during which the boyfriend was supposed to feed bits of dried liver to the dog whenever he came over. Sounded to me like a program most people would stick with.

"I don't know what's right anymore," Martyn was saying.

Next was the case of the Doberman who tore the house to shreds whenever the owner went to work. Rick began to drone on about separation anxiety, saying he suggested the owner take a few weeks off from work and go through the motions of leaving without leaving, going to the coat closet and then returning to the couch with a treat for the dog, getting his coat out and then hanging it back up, offering a treat afterward, putting his coat on and then taking it off, giving the dog some more liver as he did. I felt my eyes starting to close, the way Freud's had the minute he got up on the stage. I thought if I fell asleep, chances were I'd drool, too. But I didn't fall asleep. I kept thinking of how sick this dog must have gotten eating all that desiccated liver.

"Sometimes I wonder if I'll ever have any happiness in my

life," Martyn was saying, his eyes appropriately downcast now.

Rick's guy was still going to the closet and sitting down, still giving treats but getting nowhere, certainly not out the door. I wondered why Rick didn't suggest a little obedience training and a shitload of exercise. How could anyone expect a young, strong, large animal to sit and do nothing all day long when he had only been out to relieve himself of the end product of digestion and not the purpose of it, to produce the energy with which to work and play? But he never did.

Rick had apparently finished with the Doberman. Now he was talking about a four-year-old pug who slept on the bed and growled at his owner whenever she rolled over during the night. I was waiting to hear him suggest the owner sleep with liver in her hands when I heard Cathy instead.

"How tragic," Cathy said. For a moment I was confused. I thought she must be talking about Rick's consultation advice. But she wasn't looking at the stage. It was apparently Martyn's plight she found so tragic.

Tragic? Maybe we were listening to different conversations. All I heard was a guy trying to get laid.

It was working, too. You could have fried eggs on the look that passed between them.

Cathy leaned close and whispered something I couldn't hear.

"Do you think so?" Martyn said, apparently astonished by whatever he'd heard.

Where were the Oscars when they were so richly deserved?

"I do," she said.

I leaned back. Sitting that close to them, I was in danger of getting diabetes.

"We all so hate to punish our doggies," Rick was saying.

Talk about diabetes.

"So what might you do about the dog who loves the sound

of his own voice too much when he's put out in the yard? Well, to be honest, you can help these behaviors disappear without giving a single correction. We behaviorists call this process extinction. When we simply ignore the behavior, its frequency diminishes, and eventually the unwanted behavior disappears altogether." He smiled out at us. "And this way the dog will not think of you as a punisher."

I heard applause. Dashiell lifted his head, but Freud did not. Then Beryl was on the stage, and hands were up all over the room. Beryl pointed to the owner of one of them.

"Why the great divide in dog training?" a young man in a green T-shirt asked. He must have been one of those rude New Yorkers you hear so much about, going right to the heart of the matter with no polite small talk to cushion the thrust of his question. "Why don't the trainers who use food get along with—"

Rick leaned toward one of the mikes, but he was too slow.

"Because, dear man, some of us find it devastating to have the public taught that dogs are nothing but furry little garbage disposals rather than sentient, thinking beings."

Half the audience laughed. The other half started grumbling.

"And much as I detest having to disagree with my esteemed colleague, it is imperative that I point out to you professionals that barking is self-reinforcing, even at those times when it hasn't just chased the postal person away. You cannot extinguish it by not reinforcing it, because the act itself gives the dog immense pleasure. You, my dear friends, are beside the point. The same, of course, is true with chewing problems. You can extinguish some bad habits by doing nothing. But why not do something? Why not take an active role in your dog's education? 'No' is not a four-letter word, people. It's merely one of the ways you can communicate annoyance, displeasure, or impending danger to your companion animal."

Rick leaned toward his mike again, but clearly Beryl had no intention of relinquishing the floor.

"Moreover, you cannot discuss these issues logically, though heaven knows, that's what people think they are doing. Instead, they are working off unconscious emotional needs set in childhood, using the dog to rewrite history, so that the owner with the cold parent becomes the indulgent good parent to his pet—"

Cathy got up. I slid down in my seat and tried to look as if I were completely absorbed in the Q & A session.

"So that they are both the parent and the child in this scenario, indulging and being indulged, the way we may be all the characters in our dreams." She turned to Rick, finally giving him a chance to respond. But it was too late. He looked shell-shocked. Beryl had just given him a powerful demonstration of the effectiveness of negative reinforcement as well as the principle of alpha.

Beryl shrugged and pointed to a young woman whose hand had been waving frantically in the air all the while Beryl had been speaking.

"Is there any breed that's truly hypoallergenic?" she asked.

As Rick began to respond, Martyn gathered up his things and quietly headed for the door. He looked lost in thought and didn't seem to notice me.

"I've been reading about drive training," a man in the middle of the group was saying. There was something pinched and tight about him. Looking at the back of his head, I imagined his lips would be pursed. Perhaps it was the perfect little voice that put me off, the way he enunciated every syllable so carefully. As he continued, I realized he was speaking too slowly, even for a midwesterner.

"Could each of you explain how a dog's drives can be used when obedience-training a client's pet dog?" he said, reminding me that Ida once said that talking very slowly can be a passive-aggressive act, a way to hold someone's attention without earning that right. The result, she'd said, made the listener intensely irritated. It worked for me. I felt like slapping him.

"How using the dog's desire to fetch," he droned on, "could be a pathway to training, for example, or—"

"Clever trainers have always motivated dogs by capitalizing on what the animal finds exciting, dear," Beryl interrupted. "Do you have a dog with you?"

He was slim and narrow-shouldered, even smaller looking when he stood than he'd appeared seated. A handsome, lively flat-coat trotted along as he walked toward the stage.

"Show us his recall, dear."

The precise little man, every hair glued in place, his tie just so, left his handsome boy on a sit-stay and crossed the stage. He turned, took a few hundred breaths, passed a few birthdays, and applied for social security. Then, snapping his fingers, he said, "Watch me, Dicky. Dicky, come."

Dicky walked slowly toward his owner and sat, as precise and dutiful as his master, clearly as bored as we were.

"Now let me try," Beryl said, reaching into the pocket of her navy blazer and pulling out a tennis ball. Instead of placing Dicky on a stay or commanding his attention, Beryl bounced the ball, scooping it out of the air with a smooth, practiced move, the way the dog might have were he close enough.

When Dicky turned in her direction, it was as if he were the Christmas tree in Rockefeller Center, and someone had just thrown the switch.

"Dicky, dear," she said in an animated voice, "come to Beryl," and with no further encouragement, Dicky flew across the stage and sat in front of a complete stranger, gazing into her eyes as if she were the Messiah, for indeed, to Dicky, that's exactly who she had just become.

"Good lad."

She tossed the ball to Dicky, who rose and caught it to a round of applause.

"There, dear, does that answer your question?"

The little man nodded and left the stage, Dicky still holding the ball in his mouth.

"Just a little thought about who the dog is, and you can enliven his response and keep his mind on the work at hand."

Rick, standing still on the stage, began to look as if he were smoldering. Were I closer, I might be able to see his aura, red as the rage he was trying to control as Beryl eclipsed him with her quick, confident answers.

I remembered reading a story that the psychic Edgar Cayce told. A friend of his had once been waiting for an elevator, and when it arrived and the door opened, no one aboard had an aura. She let the elevator go and took the stairs instead. When she'd reached the lobby, she found that one of the cables had snapped, and the elevator had fallen, killing everyone inside.

I'd always wondered why she hadn't warned them. Was it part of her belief, and Cayce's, that the man who is destined to drown will drown in a glass of water? Did they think there was nothing one could or should do, that the people on the elevator were all fated to die, like strangers who share the same terrible lot in airline crashes or train wrecks?

Just because you see what's coming doesn't mean you can interfere, does it?

I thought about Alan Cooper then, and the way he'd died. Could anyone have prevented that accident, or was it *bashert?* What a burden it must be to see the future if, no matter how well-meaning you are, you can't do a damn thing about what you see.

HOME OF THE BRAVES

The mood at dinner was almost manic, people shouting across the table at each other instead of chatting sedately with the person to their left or right. They gesticulated, too, as if everyone were on uppers, celebrating some great victory we'd all worked so hard to achieve rather than grieving over the loss of a young friend who had died that very morning.

For one thing, no one had considered Alan a friend—with one possible exception, I thought, glancing over at Sam. Perhaps our evening was merely a wake instead of a funeral. Surely we were drinking as if it were. Or maybe it was just the escape from reality we all needed. No one was anxious to retire and be alone with his or her own thoughts. It seemed the consensus of unspoken opinion was that we should do whatever was necessary to delay that eventuality for as long as possible. After all, what had happened to Alan Cooper could just as easily have happened to any of us.

Months back there had been a little piece in the *Times* reporting the recall of some eight thousand hair dryers because they posed the risk of electrocution if dropped in water when they were plugged in, even if they were turned off at the time. I remembered the piece because until that time, I'd always thought an appliance had to be on, its juice flowing, to pose any risk.

Juices were certainly flowing when the dessert was served. There were so many of us talking at once, so much loud laughter, that I don't even remember for sure who did the first trick. As I recall, pickled as I was on vodka, drunk (in every sense of the word) the way Boris suggested, ice cold, neat, and not sipped but swallowed a shot at a time, it was Tracy. She put a piece of peach pie, just a mouthful, on Jeff's nose, held up a finger for him to wait, and then told him Okay. We all watched while he flipped the morsel high in the air and then caught it in his mouth. When we applauded, most of the dogs began to bark. With that, Audrey led a group howl, dogs and trainers, all of us tilting our heads up toward the ornate molding that circled the chandelier and making mournful sounds. I remember thinking of Alan then, the sadness making my chest feel heavy.

I think I made the first toast. It's hard to be sure. There were so many. But I remember thinking even as I held my glass aloft, saying, "To Alan," that I'd already had too much to drink. And I think I put my shot glass down without drinking. At least that time.

Bucky's toast was next. He asked us each to make a silent prayer, but the mood had been set, and it was far too late in the game for us to be serious twice in a row. "To Alan," he'd said, but Boris couldn't let well enough alone.

"To Alan," he'd seconded, holding his glass high, dipping his head for drama, then, looking back up so as not to miss our reactions, he added, "electrocutioner to the stars."

That gave Bucky the silence he'd been after. After a moment, to break the somber mood, he put Angelo up on the table and signaled him to stand on his hind legs and dance in a circle. Then Bucky stood and tapped his chest, and Angelo touched his front paws down, then launched himself forward, landing in Bucky's arms. We all applauded, and those who could whistled, which got Sky up. He ran to the opposite side of the table, took the perfect balance point, crouched, and waited, as if we were sheep he needed to move as soon as his mistress gave him leave to do so. We all turned to look at Cathy to see what she'd do next; obviously, even if any of us were ovine enough to let the small dog move us toward her in other circumstances, there wasn't one of us sober enough to have gotten up just then without tipping over.

Cathy whistled twice, tilting her head to her left, which sent Sky moving to his right. Going from person to person, sticking his long, thin nose where it didn't belong, Sky began to pick our pockets. Each time he found a set of keys, he'd snag them, continue around the table to Cathy, toss them onto her lap, and then go back to his search. When he came to me, I could feel his cold nose through the lining of my jacket pocket. Next I felt his teeth as he grasped the key tag and slipped the key out.

Cathy, flushing slightly as she did so easily, despite her California tan, just watched him work, offering neither encouragement nor redirection. In the end, he'd picked six pockets, and Cathy scooped up six hotel keys from her lap and tossed them onto the table. The applause was wild, and those of us who could manage it gave her a standing ovation.

"Untie," Audrey said, putting Magic down onto the rug.

The black pug started with Martyn, who sat at Audrey's left, because we were sitting in exactly the same places we'd sat the night before, except that there were twelve of us now instead of thirteen. When we heard growling, and when Martyn began to laugh, we all ducked our heads under the table to have a look-see. There was Magic holding the end of one lace and shaking her head from side to side, backing up as she did, keeping up her ferocious sound. When she'd untied one shoe, she proceeded to the next and then around the table, until everyone not wearing slip-ons had their laces dangling loose. We all stayed with our heads under the table, too enthralled to miss a shoe.

Woody picked up a little basket of chocolate mints that the waiter had placed on the table after clearing the dessert plates. For a moment the basket disappeared, then Rhonda came around serving the mints, the handle of the basket tucked into her big undershot jaw, the basket swinging below her pugnacious-looking chin.

We took mints by the handfuls, junking up on sugar and chocolate as the perfect accompaniment to the booze. As Rhonda worked her way around the table, we got louder and louder.

When someone's cell phone rang, it set us off anew. I sent Dash to fetch it, and he slipped it off Woody's belt and brought it to me. I held it up as if to answer the call, pretended to listen, and then said, "Only a smile. What are *you* wearing?" When it rang again, I passed it to Woody.

Rick surprised us all by asking Freud how old Sam was, and after he'd barked about ten times and showed no signs of stopping, the saliva flying out of both sides of his mouth, Sam jumped up and grabbed his big, drooly mouth to stop the count. Whoever would have guessed that Rick Shelbert had a sense of humor? You never know.

Woody had walked away from the table and turned his back to us. I could see him nodding as he talked into the phone. I could see the tension in his neck and shoulders. When he took his seat again, he was frowning.

Then Boris got up and walked away from the table with

Sasha. "Sasha now sink Star-Spangled Banner," he said so seriously that for the moment there wasn't a sound in the room. He hummed, as if to give Sasha the right key, then he turned back to face us again. "Boris teach this to Sasha because he is happy to be American dog trainer." He bowed his head and turned back to face the big Rottie, lifting his arms as if he were about to conduct the Boston Pops. No one was breathing. He turned again, the dog waiting patiently for his cue. "Boris loves this land, land of the free, home of the braves."

Boris waited, then turned to us yet again. I felt my stomach lurch, as if I were the one doing all that turning.

"You must be much more drunk than you look," he said. It took us a moment to realize he was right; honest to God, until then, we were waiting for Boris's Rottweiler to sing "The Star-Spangled Banner."

Everyone began to look around the table sheepishly. "We do have to work tomorrow," Bucky said. "I think I'll be the first." He reached into the pile of keys and picked out his. "Good night, folks."

Cathy picked up the remaining five keys.

"404," she said. Rick began to stand, stumbled, and sat back down hard. We all laughed, relieved that it was he and not us. Cathy whistled and Sky picked up his head, but she tossed Rick's room key to Freud. And when he caught it, everyone clapped.

"305."

I raised one hand, and she tossed the key. It landed with a thunk on my dessert plate to thunderous applause. Once again, we were on a roll.

Cathy palmed the next key and dropped it on her lap. But Sky hadn't picked her pocket, had he?

"405," she said.

"Oh, that's me, dear. Have your clever dog bring it over. Beryl's too potted to catch it."

But Cathy merely handed the key across the empty space where Alan Cooper would have been sitting. "That leaves key number 306." She held up the last key, the brass tag with the number of the room hanging down. Sky, Cecilia, and Dashiell all stood. Sky barked. Dashiell did a paws-up and turned to look at me. Cecilia landed on the table and walked between, but never on, the dirty dishes. But she stopped before getting to the dangling key. There was a lovely piece of brie on one of the dessert plates, and it made her forget why she'd jumped up onto the table in the first place.

"Naughty girl," Beryl said, lifting her off the table. Boris stood and reached for his key. Then one by one, we gathered ourselves up, took our dogs out front for a quick one, and headed off to what we dreaded, the silence of our own rooms and time to think, although with the amount of vodka consumed in the last few hours, only those of us with cast-iron stomachs would be awake for long.

I walked down the front steps of the hotel with Dashiell and turned south, walking downtown toward the tip of the park, glad I had stopped drinking halfway into the evening. There were times I was happy that Dashiell was a pit bull and not a Chihuahua, and this was certainly one of them. The streets were empty; even the traffic was sparse. I walked Dashiell down to Central Park South, hoping the sight of all those hotels and restaurants would cheer me up, but everything was closed up tight until morning.

We headed back to the Ritz, Dashiell close to my side. As we approached the hotel, I looked up at the stone facade, almost medieval looking, the way the building loomed over the street, most of the large windows draped and dark. None of the others were out. They had probably just gone across the street and walked their dogs along the wall that separated the park from the avenue.

I took the stairs, noticing the way the carpet was worn on the side nearest the wooden banister rather than in the middle or on the side of the wall. I could hear the whine of the elevator when I got up to three, but it continued on up to a higher floor.

My room was dark. I kept it that way. There were only a few hours left until morning. I spent one of them sitting at the window, staring out at the park and up at the dark sky above, thinking about life and death and the stuff that happens in between, afraid to give myself over to the possibility of dreaming until staying awake any longer was completely out of the question, at which point I was grateful for the second time that evening that I harbored a pit bull rather than a Chihuahua. Pressed against Dashiell's back, I finally fell into a fitful sleep.

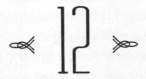

I HOPE YOU'RE WRITING YOUR PARENTS

Since we'd heard about Alan's death, no one had mentioned an early-morning program for Tuesday. It was a miracle we were all up for breakfast and to attend Cathy's talk on basic training for puppies at ten. Twice I saw little pill vials being passed left, then right. Excedrin, I figured, or Advil. Even Boris was quiet, for Boris. But he had ordered more food than anyone else, perhaps just his way of showing off his powerful constitution. It remained to be seen if the food would actually be eaten.

Cathy poked at a small bowl of fruit, rearranging it rather than eating it. I was wondering where she'd get the energy for her talk.

Audrey had ordered a soft-boiled egg, but she was feeding it to Magic and hadn't even touched her coffee.

Chip had finished two cups of coffee already and was signaling the waiter to bring a third.

Martyn was eating a sweet roll. The sight of the gooey icing made me look away.

Beryl was finishing off a plate of bacon and eggs. Her half grapefruit, looking like a toothless mouth now, had been pushed off to the side, and there was an empty cereal bowl near her plate as well.

Rick Shelbert had an appetite too. His food arrived just as I sat down, a big bowl of cereal with bananas, apples, berries, and whole almonds on top. He began picking off the fruit and eating it even before adding milk and sugar.

But Boris was clearly the champion. He seemed to already have consumed a Russian man–sized portion of pancakes, and was starting on a plate of runny fried eggs with home fries, mopping up the first leaking yolk with a hunk of buttered white bread. I watched for a moment to see if Sasha was chewing, but he was fast asleep behind Boris's chair, which meant not only did Boris have an appetite, but he'd had the energy to take his dog out for a long hike before breakfast.

"American police," he said, shaking his head, "I don't understand how people think in this country. Boris gets ticket in park. Spoils whole day."

Pieces of pancake and bread were stuck in his mustache. At least, that's what I hope was stuck there.

"Dogs aren't allowed off leash in Central Park, Boris," Bucky was quick to tell him. "You're American dog trainer," he said, looking around at the rest of us for appreciation of his wit, "you ought to know that, pally."

"Sasha was on leash, wise guy."

"Then why the ticket?" Sam asked, an unbitten piece of toast in her hand.

"For answering call of nature."

"Didn't you pick up?" Audrey asked.

"Ticket not for Sasha's call. Boris had call."

No one spoke, but Boris had our attention.

"What you supposed to do? Boris have coffee. Boris walk dog. Boris have to go. Cop gives hundred-dollar ticket. Sasha doesn't get ticket for doing same thing. Why Sasha's pee okay, and Boris's pee no good?"

We all started laughing, but Rick began to laugh so hard he couldn't stop. For a moment, I watched him enjoying himself. But then I noticed tears coming out of his eyes and running down his cheeks, and a moment later he was drained of color and gasping for air. I expected to see him reach for his inhaler, but he didn't. Still wheezing, a look of panic on his face, he slid off his chair, knocking it sideways as he fell, the spoon he was holding still in his hand.

Chip jumped up and began lifting him.

"Get his inhaler out of his pocket," I said, standing and almost knocking over my chair.

"He's choking," Chip said. He sat Rick up and put his arms around his chest, trying the Heimlich maneuver, but nothing popped out of his mouth. Still, it must have helped, because that awful wheezing noise had stopped. There wasn't a sound in the room. I figured whatever he'd been choking on had come loose.

Chip, still sitting on the floor with Rick leaning on his chest, looked relieved. I heard him take a deep breath, but then a look of horror came over his face. Rick's eyes were open, but his chest wasn't moving.

"We're losing him," Chip shouted.

Rick wasn't just pale now, he was ashen, and his lips were turning blue. Woody stood, pulled out his cell phone, and punched in three numbers. Martyn was up now, too. He and Chip were laying Rick flat on the floor. As a veterinarian, even though his specialty was behavior, Martyn was the closest thing we had to what Rick so desperately needed. He wiped the spittle and food off Rick's mouth with his napkin, then opened it and swept inside with his pointer, wiping whatever was there onto his own pants leg, cradling Rick's head with the other hand as he did so.

Chip pulled off his jacket, rolled it up, and placed it under Rick's neck so that his head would tilt back. I saw Martyn reach for Rick's nose, then lean forward to blow air into his mouth, and for a moment all I could see was the back of Martyn's head, his neck glistening with sweat.

I ran for the front desk. Even if Woody had dialed 911, the front desk might get faster results calling the closest hospital or the local precinct. But no one was behind the desk. I rang the bell that sat on the counter and waited, banging on it again when no one seemed to be responding. But then the heavy oak door to the left of the counter opened, and the clerk appeared, a man in his seventies who moved as if he had all the time in the world. I didn't. And neither did Rick. I wanted to leap over the counter and pull the clerk toward me to make sure he understood what I was going to say.

"There's been an accident in the breakfast room. I want you to call the nearest hospital."

"Another accident?" he asked, incredulous.

"Someone choked on food. Please make the call, now."

"Nine one one's the fastest," he said, picking up the phone and searching the number pad for the nine. I heard him repeating what I'd told him and giving the address of the hotel. "They said they're on the way," he said, placing the phone down carefully. "Do you want to wait out front for them?"

"No," I said. "Just send them to the breakfast room as soon as they get here. Tell them to run."

But when I got back to the breakfast room, I saw there was no longer a reason for the emergency medical team to hurry.

Chip, holding his rolled-up jacket in one hand, caught my eye and shook his head.

Rick was lying where he'd been placed, just behind the chair he'd been sitting on, the remains of his breakfast still on the table, the cereal spoon still in his hand.

"He's gone," Martyn said. "I couldn't save him."

I looked for Sam, but she was no longer in the room. When I walked out, she was coming toward me, down the hall.

"I don't understand," she said. "Why is this happening? Two of my speakers are dead in two days. This is a nightmare." She opened her purse and took out a pillbox.

"What's that?"

"Generic aspirin. Why?"

"Never mind," I said, noting that the two pills she shook into her hand were tamperproof caplets. "I just wanted to be sure—"

Sam stopped, her hand holding the pills cupped beneath her mouth. Then she dumped them back into the pillbox, turned on her heel, and walked toward the lobby. I followed behind her and caught up.

"I don't want you even *near* the EMS or the police, Rachel. If this is something more than another ghastly accident, they'll tell us. I'm sure they'll autopsy, especially considering how quickly my speakers are dropping dead. But for God's sake, don't you put any ideas into their heads." She looked at her watch. "It's thirty-five minutes to show time," she said. "I hope Cathy can pull herself together."

"What are you going to say when the ambulance arrives?"

"That it's their fault Dr. Shelbert is dead. It's twelve minutes since they were called."

"More like fifteen," I said. "I think Woody called them on his cell phone."

"Rachel, help me out here."

"I'll talk to Cathy, make sure she's up to her talk."

"Tell her she's got to be."

The ambulance had arrived. I could hear the techs in the lobby, joking around and taking their time. Sam headed in that direction. I hurried back to the breakfast room.

Cathy was sitting at her place with her head between her knees. The persons who sat on either side of her for meals were both dead. Tracy stood behind her, holding a napkin against Cathy's neck. I watched as she took it away, dipped it into a water glass, and then put it back on Cathy's neck, her other hand holding Cathy's forehead.

I called Beryl over to the doorway. "Would you help me out?" She nodded without asking what it was I wanted.

"See if you can get everyone out of here, but keep them together. See if the café is open, and take them in there. Sam asked me to get Cathy out of here and help her to pull herself together. She's on in thirty minutes."

"Right you are, dear. The show must go on, and it's not doing anyone any good to sit here staring at poor Dr. Shelbert lying there dead."

As I walked over to Cathy, I heard Beryl clearing her throat to get everyone's attention.

"You're speaking this morning." I took the napkin from Tracy and dropped it onto the table. "In thirty minutes, to be precise. You need to get out of here, get a little air, and get your thoughts together."

"I don't think I can—"

"Look, Cathy, there are people out there who know nothing about what just happened. They've come from a great distance to hear you, to hear all of us. As tragic as this is, it would be a disaster to cancel the symposium and send them home. In fact, we can't do that. The hotel has been paid for the week. Speakers and students alike have nonrefundable tickets. And we all owe Sam. If for no other reason, we have to come through for her. Now, can you do this?"

"But Rick—"

"Not doing your talk won't help Rick one bit, now will it?"

"No. I see what you're saying, but—"

"Let's go up to your room for a few minutes, okay?"

Cathy nodded.

"Let me see your key." She reached into the small purse she wore hooked onto her belt and took it out.

"Fourth floor. Good. Let's walk," I suggested, thinking it would be good for her to move. "I've heard such good things about your puppy seminars, Cathy. I've always wanted to see you in action. How many pups are being brought in for your demonstrations?"

"A dozen. Half are coming from a shelter, and the other half from breeders." Her color improved as we climbed the stairs and talked about her work. She was still holding the key. I took it from her when we reached her room, unlocked the door, and stepped aside so that she could go in first. Sky was lying on the neatly made bed, a scented tennis ball between his white paws. I could smell the mint the moment I'd opened the door.

"Martyn looked so upset when he realized Rick was gone."

"It must be just terrible, to work on someone like that and fail. I'm sure watching your talk will help him take his mind off this tragedy. It'll be the best medicine for all of us, to stay involved in what we're here for, isn't that so?"

I could see towels on the bathroom floor and dog hair all over the gray rug, but the bed was neatly made. Cathy hadn't slept here last night. She'd just come back in the morning to shower. Without thinking, I glanced over at the clock radio, happy to see it safely on the nightstand where it belonged. "Do you want to change?" I asked her.

"No, I'm okay." She had stopped in the middle of the room, near the foot of the bed. She didn't seem to know what to do.

"You look great," I told her. "Do you have notes for the talk, or slides?"

"No. I don't need notes, Rachel. I've been doing this talk on puppy basics for six years. Sam's booked me all over the country and in Canada, but even before I met her, the local kennel clubs were inviting me to speak at their meetings. The breeders like to invite the pet-owning public to this talk because they want their pups to start out right. They care about them, but it also means fewer headaches for them, if people know what to do."

As she spoke, her voice got stronger and deeper; her confidence returned. I glanced back at the clock radio. We had ten minutes left.

"Do you use Sky in your seminar?" I asked. He cocked his pretty head at the sound of his name, got up, picked up the tennis ball, and with a flick of his muzzle, tossed it right to my hand. I snatched it from the air and threw it back to him.

"He'd only drive everyone crazy," Cathy said, cocking her head toward her dog. "If I didn't throw the ball for him, he'd go looking for some sucker who would." She smiled at Sky's latest sucker.

"Does he need a walk? Or food?"

"I had him out earlier, playing Frisbee. He's fine."

"Shall we go, then?" The tennis ball came back, like a bad penny. "The room is probably full already. And you might want to take a look at the puppies before you work with them."

I tossed the ball to Sky, closed the door, and slipped the key into my pocket. Cathy, too preoccupied to notice, wouldn't have cause to discover it was missing until after her talk, which, alas, I was planning to miss.

I did sit in the back of the room long enough to watch Cathy begin. She was every bit as terrific as I'd heard, demonstrating beginning training with the puppies that had been brought in for a morning's work. She used no collars or leashes, just her voice and high energy, mesmerizing each pup in turn so that it saw nothing but her. In no time seven of the pups, one at a time, none over twelve weeks of age, were following Cathy back and forth across the stage.

The audience, trainers and wanna-be trainers from all over the country, were mesmerized too, hoping that they would be able to work as gracefully and effectively with their clients' pups when they got home, considerably richer in knowledge than when they'd left.

I stayed longer than I'd planned, watching Cathy teach sit and down, still without a leash and, even more surprisingly for a Californian, without food rewards. She lured a little blue-flecked Australian cattle dog, nine weeks old that very day, to follow her and then sit when she stopped. Her hands, moving like birds, were as exciting to the pup as toys or treats. His eyes stayed on Cathy, no matter where she moved. Two Dalmatians, the oldest of the pups, worked side by side, following, sitting, then lying down. One lay down slowly, his eyes on Cathy's eyes. The other threw himself to the ground as if he were pouncing on a coveted toy. And both stayed as she backed away, then went tearing into her arms when she called them.

When I saw Sam come into the auditorium with Freud, I slipped out the back door. If Sam was here, it meant the police had left. I headed for the front desk to begin my work.

The slow old man was behind the counter this time, his maroon blazer with the hotel emblem at least two sizes too big for him. He sat on a tall stool, his bony forearms lost in their sleeves, resting on the counter. Despite all the recent excitement, he looked dead bored. I thought I might be able to change that.

"Hello, again."

"Good morning, miss," he said, no sign of recognition in his eyes though I'd just talked to him an hour or so earlier about a medical emergency. "What can I do for you?"

"I wanted to write a few letters," I told him, "but there's no stationery in my room."

"You've come to the right place." He slid off the stool and pulled his jacket down over his thin body. "You just wait right here," he said. He started toward the office door, then turned and came back to the counter. "Unless you'd like it sent up."

"Oh, no, I can wait." I shot him a Kaminsky family grin.

As soon as the door closed, I ducked under the shelf at the right side of the counter and began to look for Rick's box. I didn't know if he'd been carted off to the morgue with his key still in his pocket, but there were usually two, so that husbands and wives could go out and do their own thing and illicit lovers could arrive and leave separately, fooling only themselves, never the staff. I reached in and took the spare key from the back of the box for room 404, but didn't get to crouch back under the shelf in time. The skinny old coot was standing in the open doorway to the office, a surprised look on his wrinkled, dry face.

"I was coming to knock, to save you a trip," I said. "I need a pen, too. I was sure I'd packed one, but you know how it is; you're always wondering, What will the weather be? Do I need a raincoat? Are these shoes dressy enough? You always leave *something* home. This time it was my pen," I said, shrugging and trying to look honest and harmless.

He walked over to the shelf, unlatched it, and held it up for me. "Insurance regulations," he whispered. "Guests aren't allowed back here. It's not that I'd mind a little company. This isn't exactly Grand Central Station. But rules are rules. I'll get you something to write with." He walked slowly back to the office, adding, "I hope you're writing your parents."

I was still behind the counter even though I could get to the other side without bending. I needed other keys—well, one more. What I really needed was a passkey. But the only keys I saw were the ones in the guests' mailboxes, and the old man had left the office door ajar so I couldn't go pulling open drawers behind the counter. Besides, the office, where he was, was more than likely where the passkeys would be kept.

I walked around to the appropriate side of the wooden counter and waited. He came back with a pen and laid it on top of the pile of stationery and envelopes he'd brought out the first time.

"You need anything else, just ask. And when I go off, you can ask my son. Works the second shift."

I remembered a woman on in the late afternoon, a tough old bird, looked like a retired cop. Or like some of the women who hang out at Henrietta Hudson's in my neighborhood, the ones who pick up the tab and sometimes, when tempers flare, the bar stools.

"Name's Jimmy. Anything you need, even from the outside, he's your man. Don't request nothing from Mabel. She's like to take your head off just for inquiring."

So he meant to keep the tips in the family. I picked up the stationery and the pen.

"I met him when I checked in. He seemed to have a little problem with some of the dogs. I've been taking the stairs."

"No need to do that. He's got to take you. That's his job. Though, to tell the truth, he nearly wet hisself the day you all checked in."

I headed for the stairs, the old man's chuckling following me all the way up to two. I stopped on three for Dashiell before heading for Rick's room. There's something so creepy being in someone else's private space. Even when it's a hotel room and all you get to see is what brand of toothpaste they use, it still feels as invasive as checking their bank balance, seeing if they're a grasshopper or an ant, or hiding behind the curtain and watching someone else have sex. Just as thrilling, too. Perhaps it was how I'd replaced the rush of working with aggressive dogs. That aside, it was how I earned my living, and I needed my partner to share the load.

❦ 13 ❧

SO YOU'RE PERFECT? MY MOTHER USED TO SAY

There was no crime scene tape sealing Rick Shelbert's room, a courtesy to the hotel, I suspected, since it might well have caused a mass exodus. I unlocked the door and stepped inside before Dashiell. Then I called him to follow me, put him on a down-stay, and let the door go. It locked, as they all did, automatically.

Had I expected anything extraordinary, I would have been disappointed. Rick Shelbert was apparently pretty much of a neatnik, even away from home. The only glitch in the system was Freud. Saint Bernards are not neat dogs, and while Freud himself wasn't present, traces of him were everywhere. Looking around the room, I could make a case for those hotels and motels that charge guests with dogs security deposits. Of course, the big dog wasn't a chewer. Nor was he unhousebroken. But when loose-flewed dogs shake their heads, saliva flies. It sticks to the walls like chunks of plaster, stains most fabrics, and when it dries it resembles the foam the ocean leaves behind at low tide, a web of schmutzy-looking bubbles.

The bed had been slept in, but Rick had pulled the covers and spread up before he'd gone downstairs for what would turn out to be his last meal. There were no clothes draped over the chair, the window seat, or the bureau. When I opened the dresser drawers, all Rick's things seemed to be there, neatly folded, ready to use. So no one had packed his things yet either.

His calendar and address book were in the top drawer of the bureau. I opened the address book to the front, and there, of course, he had filled in all the required information, including whom to call in case of an emergency. It was a Mrs. Rick Shelbert, a lady who apparently had not only not kept her maiden name but lost her first name as well.

I opened the appointment calendar next, a current of excitement shooting down my arms as I did. But the week of the symposium was blank. I looked back at the weeks before, and they were filled with appointments: eleven-thirty, "Rog," beagle mix, destructive chewing; one-thirty, "Chester," Dalmatian, dog aggression; and so on. There was a check near each appointment to indicate they were kept. And at the bottom it said either cash or check to indicate the method of payment.

I walked into the bathroom, wondering what it was I'd expected to find. The towels were all neatly folded on the racks, none lying on the floor as they were in my bathroom. I touched a couple of them that were still damp. God, I could have used this man for four hours once a week at home.

I looked at Rick's shaving things, his comb, his toothpaste. He used Sensodyne for sensitive teeth, and he had two extra inhalers with him, one in his dopp kit, the other that I'd seen sitting on the nightstand, along with a small bottle of Tylenol and a glass of water, ready for any contingency. I pulled back the shower curtain and looked at the tub. He had even rinsed the loose hair out before dressing and going downstairs, perhaps so the maid wouldn't consider him messy. Such a precise person, I thought—why hadn't he chewed his food more carefully? But suddenly I felt a chill down my back, as if I'd just gotten out of the shower and forgotten the air conditioner was on. In a milieu of envy and venomous competition, two of my former colleagues were dead, both dying accidentally. The shock collar trainer had been electrocuted. The foodie had choked on a piece of food.

Right.

I put my hand in my pocket and felt for Detective Flowers's card. But if I called her now, what could I say? That the hair on my arms was standing up? That I thought there was something fishy going on at the Ritz Hotel? What if I were wrong? What would a phone call like that do to Sam?

Walking back into the room, I released Dashiell and told him, "Find it." While he checked the place out with his nose, because you never know, I poked inside Rick's suitcase, which was empty, and then turned to look at the almost perfect bed. I looked under the pillows first, to see if Rick had folded his pajamas and put them there. He had. Then I pulled down the spread, to see if Freud had drooled on the dark gray blanket, and that was why Rick had put the bed back together. And then, as long as I was at it, I pulled down the top sheet and blanket and found not what I had discovered in Alan's bed, the detritus of a last night of ecstasy. In this case, I found a sheet so clean the maid might have pulled it tight and left it on instead of changing it.

I sat at the window, looking out at the park, waiting for Dashiell to finish his snooping. That's when I heard the sound, his rabies tag hitting against the wastebasket at the far side of Rick's bed, once, twice, three times. Something in there interested my dog, more than likely an empty can of Pedigree

Choice Cuts that he was trying to swab out with his tongue.

"Leave it," I told him, getting up almost as slowly as Jimmy's old man and walking over to where he was. I hadn't eaten, and it was catching up with me. Maybe there'd be something for me in the trash as well. And indeed there was.

Under the morning's paper and a wad of tissues, I found what Dashiell had been sniffing. I took a plastic Baggie out of my pocket and slipped it over my hand, the way I do when I have to pick up after Dashiell outside. Then I carried the wastebasket over to the window seat, where there was the most light. Reaching in, I picked up what my dog had discovered—two used condoms, one of them broken.

I walked back into Rick's bathroom and rechecked those towels. Three of them were pretty damp, as if they had been used after a shower—or two. One was dry, but the middle of it felt as if it had been starched. According to the Young Detective's Handbook, that meant it had probably been spread out under someone's cute little *tochis* in order to keep the sheets clean.

I wondered who his companion had been; someone, I hoped, who used birth control pills; someone, it seemed, who didn't find Rick's fastidiousness as big a turnoff as I did.

"So you're perfect?" my mother used to say. "Life is about compromise," she'd say if she were here.

My grandmother Sonya, made practical by a childhood of poverty, would have had a comment, too. *Nifter, shmifter, a leben macht er?* she might have added. What difference does it make as long as he makes a living?

No matter the cost, my family only wanted me to be married, to have someone to take care of me, as if I were not a woman but an invalid. I wondered if Mrs. Shelbert's family had felt the same way.

Then I stood in Rick Shelbert's bathroom, thinking about

Freud. Not the man, the dog. What an odd thing it was for such a tidy person to have chosen a slobbering heavy shedder for a pet. It hadn't been an accident, a dog he'd purchased on impulse at the pet shop in the mall. He worked with dogs for a living. He had to know what it would be like to live with a Saint Bernard. Was his choice simply a testimony to how bonded we humans are to the canine species, that what we would never consider allowing in another person's behavior, we patiently accept from our dogs, and have been doing so, according to the latest study, for approximately 135,000 years? Even if dogs were slow learners and not the clever opportunists I thought them to be, that was sufficient time to practice not only helping in the hunt, warming the sleeping area, and protecting the cave, but manipulative skills as well. Speaking of which, I heard Dashiell summoning me from the bedroom.

I went quickly to see if he had made another find. He had. There he was, my hero, sitting in the closet, barking at a twenty-pound sack of kibble.

IT WAS HIS HEART

Leaving Rick's room, I went on to frisk Cathy's, then caught the very end of her talk. After two and a half hours, the puppies she was working with could have earned their livings doing TV commercials. In fact, one of the things I'd learned was that Sky was the Huffy T-shirt border collie. Cathy had five of the shirts with her, though I hadn't seen her wearing any so far. On them Sky was airborne catching a Frisbee; sailing over a fence; staring down a huddled mass of sheep; carrying a tennis ball in his mouth; and on the last one, doing agility weave poles. He certainly was a clever border collie.

I also discovered, through perspicacious detective work, that Sky had a dozen tennis balls, all mint scented—and those were just the ones that had been packed for the trip—that he shed as profusely as a Samoyed in spring, or fall, come to think of it; that he ate organic dog food; and that his mistress wore underpants made from undyed, bleach-free organic cotton, not a pair of skimpy silk bikinis in sight, leopard or otherwise. "You're going to believe what you're told?" Frank used to say. "Find another way to earn a living."

Two people from a New Jersey shelter and six breeders were retrieving their now-well-mannered puppies up on the stage, and Cathy was standing at the edge of the apron answering questions. I walked up onstage, petted a few of the puppies, and handed Cathy her room key. She slipped it into her jacket pocket as she kept answering questions and handing out her business card, too absorbed in her adoring fans to take any notice.

As I walked off the stage and back to where I'd left Dashiell on a down-stay, I noticed Chip and Woody talking to trainers in the rear of the auditorium. Beryl was on her way out the door with Cecilia when I got there.

"It's off to the park, dear. Do you and your boy want to join me?"

"No lunch?"

She patted her stomach. "Too many lunches, I'm afraid. I made an awful pig of myself at breakfast as well. At my age, the metabolism doesn't do what it used to. It hardly seems to do anything at all.

"Throughout my twenties," she said as we walked through the lobby, "I could drink a milk shake if I was thirsty and not gain an ounce. Now"—she rolled her eyes—"well, you can see what happens now. I'll probably gain a pound skipping lunch and walking Cecilia in the park."

We crossed at the corner and walked uptown along the outside of the park until we reached an entrance. Then we turned east and headed for a grassy area where we could keep watch for the park patrol and let our dogs play off leash.

"My Carl liked big dogs," she said. "Bullmastiffs. I prefer the little ones, border terriers. I like their energy, the way they fling themselves into life with such enthusiasm over the least little thing."

We stood and watched Cecilia run, with Dashiell following behind her.

"Although I did quite fancy Charles."

"Charles?"

"The bullmastiff, dear."

"Oh."

"Then, so very suddenly, Carl was gone, and by the time I sold his practice, Charles was gone too."

"How did it happen?"

"Bloat," she said.

"I meant Carl."

"Oh, I see, yes, of course you did, dear. It was his heart."

"So it was quick?"

"A complete surprise. And afterward, I took our little one and went home. But you already know that part, don't you, love?"

I nodded. "Was that when you became a dog trainer?"

"Oh, no, Rachel. I've always been a dog trainer. My mother used to say that my teething ring was a feed pan. My father was a veterinarian too, and my mother bred Irish terriers, wild things they were, so full of the devil. I adored them.

"As far back as I can recall, I was teaching the dogs, manners and commands, tricks, tracking, anything I could. I had one, Hubert, who I taught to ride a three-wheeler, clever thing. The dogs were my companions, my dearest friends. And when you learn on terriers, well, dear, you can train anything, anything at all, so while I was still quite young, eleven or twelve, neighbors began to ask me to straighten out their pets for them and paying me to do so. It was, I think, a perfect childhood."

"Time for leashes." I pointed out the green truck of the park rangers, visible as it passed on the other side of the trees that grew at the edge of the grassy hill where the dogs were playing. We called them to us, hooked on the leashes, and headed for the path.

"Hello, there." The voice was breathless. Someone had been running. "I see I'm not the only one skipping lunch," she said, the little pug puffing along behind her. "It's too much food, isn't it?"

"Yes, dear. I was just saying that very thing to Rachel. Walking is a lot better for the waistline. Besides, no doubt Samantha has another feast set for this evening."

Dashiell stopped to sniff Magic's rear and genitals, and then stood motionless, not even his tail moving, as she sniffed his, the traditional doggy handshake. When we turned onto an isolated dirt path, we let the dogs off leash again.

"I can't believe what's been happening here," Audrey said. She picked up her hank of thick, dark hair and twisted it around in her hands nervously. "These accidents."

But before Beryl or I could respond, we saw Tracy up ahead with Jeff.

"It seems we left Samantha and Cathy with all those good-looking men," Beryl said.

"What's left of them," Audrey said. "I don't know if I can—"

"Of course you can, Audrey. If you don't speak, the rest of us will have to carry an even bigger load."

Jeff spotted the dogs and came running, his tail wagging. Tracy turned and waved, heading our way.

"She's perfectly right, dear," Beryl said. "Grace under pressure is the mark of a true professional. 'Chin up, dear girl.' That's what my mother used to tell me. 'Soldier on,' she'd say, 'no one wants to hear you snivel, so just get over it.' She'd say that no matter what it was. And I believe she was correct. It's the best thing for you, to plunge ahead, do what's expected of you; it's absolutely therapeutic."

Audrey took a big breath. "I know you're right. I'll tell Sam I'll speak tomorrow afternoon."

"Brilliant. You're exactly what we need, too. Meditation. Good for the soul."

"Are you talking about Audrey's talk?" Tracy asked. "Oh, please say you're doing it. You're one of the reasons I came."

"We'd best head back, dears. It's getting to be that time."

"Who's speaking this afternoon?" Tracy asked. "I forgot to look."

"Boris Dashevski," Beryl told her, and we all groaned.

"Audrey, would you do the walking chant on the way back? It'll make us all feel so good," Tracy said. "Is that okay with you guys?" she asked me and Beryl.

"Certainly," Beryl said.

"I'd love it," I told them, hoping no one I knew was in the park. For a hard-boiled New Yorker, being seen chanting in Central Park would be almost as bad as being spotted waiting on line for the elevator to the top of the Empire State Building or catching a breeze on the ferry that went to Liberty Island.

Audrey Little Feather stopped, closed her eyes, and moved her arms in circles, the way old ladies do at the beach, splashing handfuls of water on their sunburned bosoms, chanting about what a blessing the coolness is with each splash.

After a moment Audrey's eyes opened, and her arms were still. Magic was sitting right in front of her, looking adoringly at her face. I thought about the way Dashiell always comes close when I practice t'ai chi, wanting to bathe in the sea of moving energy.

"Ah la," Audrey sang, her voice as clear and poignant as the call of a bird looking for a mate. "Ah la."

And so we walked back toward Central Park West, "ah la," the dogs running ahead, lagging behind, chasing each other in circles around us. Audrey reached out her hands for ours. I took one, Tracy the other, and then Tracy reached for Beryl's hand. We couldn't fit four abreast on the narrow walk. Instead we moved in a wavy line, holding each other's hands and chanting as we worked our way back to the Ritz.

Something funny happened in the park. I began to feel a pleasant buzz, the mantra sweeping through me and leaving a feeling of serenity in its wake. I no longer felt silly about chanting in the park, no longer cared if someone I knew spotted me. I was starting to like these women too, even when that meant getting past a training method I didn't think much of. There was a generosity here, and camaraderie.

The fighting that had been going on since we got here was mostly among the men. Males were, after all, the major perpetrators of violent crimes. They were more prone to aggressive outbursts, less likely than women to talk things out. Or work things out. They were more competitive, too.

That was also the way it was in most other species of animals, certainly among any of the Canidae. For wolves, survival is based on competition. When there isn't enough food to go around, the fact that the stronger, smarter, and therefore higher-ranked animals eat first ensures the survival of the species.

Were we more like animals than we wanted to admit, sleeping in a heap with our dogs for the physical comfort of another warm body, putting up with nearly unbearable unhappiness rather than choosing to live alone, the way my sister was doing, the way Chip seemed to be doing? In the wild, a lone wolf would not survive, unless he was somehow able to get himself accepted by another pack. More often than not, he'd find no takers. Wasn't that true for us, too, especially as we grew older?

I'd been thinking these "accidents" might be the work of a black widow spider, one who wore leopard underwear, underwear I didn't believe belonged to my clever employer. But maybe she was right about one thing, that the mating practices of the species had nothing at all to do with the deaths.

So what was happening here? Were the "accidents" the results of one of the men killing off the competition in order to safeguard his own survival? Wasn't it exactly that fear that had inspired Sam to hire me? Perhaps one of the seemingly civilized wolves she'd brought together found himself unable to stop at scent-marking and posturing in order to assure himself that the territory was his, that he was top dog after all.

BORIS TELLS IT LIKE IT IS

What could you have been thinking, pally, telling all those people that taking the dog away from the owner and correcting the hell out of it is the only way to begin a consultation?" Bucky was pointing a fat finger at Boris. "You're one of the reasons why this profession has a bad name," he shouted.

"Boris is only one here who is honest." He drained his third glass of merlot, stabbed his tofu steak with his fork, and then let go. The fork he'd been holding in his bandaged hand fell over sideways, taking the tofu with it and making a jarring sound as it hit the edge of the plate. "You like to put on kind face for owners, train with treats, handkerchiefs, toys. Boris tells it like it is."

"You mean like it *was*," Bucky said. "Yank 'em, spank 'em. Jesus. Hasn't anything that's happened in the last fifty years touched you?"

"Boris can't respond to stupid questions."

"And will you stop referring to yourself in the third person. Who are you supposed to be, the king?"

"You should talk. What is Bucky's motto?" he asked, looking from face to face around the table. "The King of Dog Trainers." Boris began to nod. "The King," he repeated.

"It's my *name*," Bucky said between his teeth. "It's a play on my name. I have every right—"

"Your name, Baron?" Boris said, again looking around for approval.

"Who? Who?" Bucky turned to look at Sam, who was deep into her cold poached salmon, the choice for those of us who preferred something in between a slab of bleeding meat and a dead white square of soy product with a side of roughage.

We all waited as Sam put down her fork, patted her lips with the napkin, and looked up at Bucky. "You sound like a damn owl," she said. "Now will both of you please contain yourselves. It's perfectly fine that there are a variety of methods from which both professionals and the pet-owning public can choose. Just leave it alone. Everyone here is earning a living. Doesn't that tell you something? Doesn't that show you that the public—"

"The public is naive," Bucky said. "They hire Boris not understanding that—"

"Gentlemen," Sam said, tapping her spoon on her water glass the way the guests at weddings do when they want the bride and groom to kiss. "Please."

"Bucky's right," Tracy said, looking down into her lap as she spoke. "Telling people who are trying to learn how to be better dog trainers that you have to take a dog apart and put him back together, why, that's so barbaric I—"

"Did anyone get up and walk out?" Woody asked. But he didn't wait for an answer. "You don't give the students enough credit. Shouldn't they hear it all, every possible way of working with dogs, and be given the chance to make up their own minds? After all, there are lots of ways to train, variations on a theme. In certain situations you need to be firmer. Don't you think people ought to know this?"

"Firmer?" Bucky shouted, his face red and sweating. "His methods are downright cruel. They're antiquated. Weren't you there? Didn't you see what he did to that chow?"

"Weren't *you* there? Didn't you see what that chow did to Boris? He was only defending himself against further injury. Look, Bucky, those people who agree with you will ignore what Boris has to tell them. Or they'll find, in all he said, a couple of points they can add to their own spin on training. No one's going to sit out there and swallow anyone else's method whole. If they did, they'd choke on it."

For the next few minutes, no one spoke. We all poked at our food, moving things around but not actually picking anything up and eating it.

"I apologize. I didn't mean to—" Woody sighed. "It's been a rough week," he said, as much to himself as to any of us.

"We need to do something positive together," Cathy said. "Something fun. We can't just sit around brooding and fighting. Perhaps we can agree to disagree about our training methods. Just leave that alone, as Sam suggested. Let's get the dogs out to the park this evening. It's a beautiful night. There's a moon, so it won't be completely dark. And if we're together, we'll be safe. What do you say? We can set up some easy agility games. We can use whatever we can find in the park, branches, low walls, ourselves instead of weave poles. We can have the dogs jump over each other. We can—"

"Super," Sam said. "This is the way I hoped it would be. Boris? Bucky? Everyone?"

There was grumbling, but there was nodding, too. There

were two sides here for each of us—the fierce belief that whatever each of us did was the only effective, humane way to train, and the insatiable hunger for talking about dogs and working them with a group of people who knew what they were all about and who loved them as excessively as we ourselves did.

"In fact," Sam said, "let me see if we can have coffee and dessert afterward instead of now. Maybe they can leave us something in the tea room. Wouldn't that be lovely?"

For a while, we ate quietly, no one shouting across the table or pointing at someone else with their knife or fork. Sam had gotten up to talk to the waiter. When she came back, she merely put her napkin back over her short skirt and continued eating her dinner. When everyone was finished, she called over the waiter who had been standing attentively in the doorway in case anyone needed more water or wine.

"Kevin will have everything we'll want when we return set up in the tea room. You're a darling," she told him.

The smile she gave him was so glowing, for an instant I wondered if Kevin was going to be Mr. Tonight.

"Why don't we meet right out front in twenty minutes. Bucky, will you bring the whole family?" she asked. "That way Martyn and I can join in, too." Bucky nodded. "Excellent. Twenty minutes, then, people. Don't keep the rest of us waiting."

I waited with Sam until everyone else had left. "Do you think this will turn things around?" I asked her.

"It better." She dropped her napkin onto her plate and stood. "I'm running out of speakers."

≪ 16 ≫

HOW ABOUT HIDE-AND-SEEK? CHIP SAID

Lying on the damp grass, looking up at the stars, I heard Tracy's voice loud and strong, sending Jeff. A moment later I could hear him thundering across the grass toward me, the sound coming closer and closer, and then there was only the sound of my own breathing as he sailed over the three prone bodies lined up side by side on the ground, landing clear of us on the other side. With Woody pressed against me to my right and Audrey to my left, for the moment I felt completely happy, the way you do when you're a child and now is the only thing there is.

"Shall we try four?" Tracy shouted out in the darkness of the Sheep Meadow.

"It depends who's on the end," Woody said, and we began to laugh so hard I thought we'd never be able to stop.

"I'll do it," I said, and before I could get up and go around him, he'd rolled me over his body and dumped me on his other side. Audrey scrunched over, and Cathy lay down next to her on the damp grass.

Tracy called Jeff back to her. I thought he'd go back over us, making me first and Cathy last, but he went around us instead. I could hear him thudding along on the grass, and then Tracy sent him again. Something danced in my stomach as I heard Jeff coming our way. He sailed over us, but low enough this time to make me wonder if trying five would be a sane idea, knowing in my heart we would, and that once again I'd be on the end because I found the fear intoxicating.

I was only half right. Suddenly Chip was lying next to me, so close that if we'd stayed that way for weeks, the grass couldn't have grown up between us. Playing in the dark, not one of us seemed to have a serious thought in his head, as if two of our colleagues had not just died.

Sometime between Central Park West and getting to the Sheep Meadow, a miraculous transformation had begun to take place. Instead of pointing at one another with accusations and recriminations, instead of hostility and rage, there was cooperation, there was camaraderie, there was even joy. Under the moon and stars we cavorted with each other and our dogs as if there had never been any conflict, as if nothing at all were wrong, as if we were children and best friends at that. I, for one, intended to enjoy it as long as I could, all night if it lasted.

"Ready for five?" Tracy called out.

"Oh, no," Cathy said. "At least send Magic instead of Jeff." And once again, we were giggling like kids.

"No five," Boris said.

We all groaned.

"Six. Boris on end."

And with that, Chip Pressman did something I would have

thought was impossible. As if to make room for Boris, he moved closer.

"There's a whole park out here," I whispered, looking not at him but up at the stars.

"I know."

I could see the Big Dipper.

"I thought we should all get as close as possible so that Jeff can make the jump without landing on Boris." He scrunched closer still.

"Jeff not to land on Boris," I heard from the other side of Chip. And then I heard Tracy, and Jeff was coming our way. I closed my eyes this time, waiting. It seemed to take longer this way, nearly forever. Perhaps Tracy had backed up to give the dog a better chance of making the jump. And then I felt him and heard him land, heard the others clapping for him and shouting his name. I sat up. Boris was already standing, taking a bow. Jeff was back with Tracy, ready to go again.

"Let's make it seven. I'll take the end." It was Beryl, coming to lie down next to Boris.

"Let's try something else, give another of the dogs a chance." That was Cathy, the voice of reason. She had changed to one of the Huffy T-shirts, the one with Sky doing weave poles on it.

"How about human weave poles, then?" Beryl asked. "I'll send the doggies through, just tell me which ones know how to do it."

Some of the dogs were on down-stays, others were on their own in the meadow, chasing each other or sniffing all the wonderful new odors. I whistled for Dashiell, and Sky came too. Beryl called Cecilia. Betty came on her own, curious to see what all the fuss was about. Bucky had been sitting with Tamara, who he'd said would only work for him. Sam was next to him, with Angelo on her lap, and Martyn had Alexi at his side and was stroking the big dog's neck. Far off at the edge of the meadow, Sasha was pacing. Boris said Sasha was American dog, keeping the world safe for democracy. But the truth was, he was keeping Sasha away from the other males. The Rottie people say Rotties will never start a fight, but they'll never back down from one either. I say, show me a dog who'll never back down, and I'll show you a dog who will start a fight, any chance he gets. Looking around, I wondered which of us was like that. In the middle of our work, who had taken things so irretrievably far? And why? Then Tracy grabbed my hand and pulled me into the line with the others.

All the dogs except Sasha were lined up for Beryl to send. The rest of us held hands, standing as far apart as we could this time, leaving room for the dogs to weave in and out as they ran down the line as quickly as they could.

Cecilia did the human weave poles like the puppy she was, jumping up for kisses on whichever people she fancied she could manipulate into responding to her cuteness, stopping to pull up some grass, barking when she got to the end, so pleased with her own performance she couldn't keep quiet about it. Alexi and Tamara walked through, as if they were strolling down Fifth Avenue in the Easter parade. Bucky, who held my other hand, squeezed it as his dogs passed around us. Betty was precise, centering herself on each turn and not touching any of us. Dashiell was the opposite, smacking into as many legs as possible on his way. Sky streaked through the poles like a bolt of lightning, never touching any of us, and when he reached the end, turning and running back through, ending with a smart, neat sit in front of Beryl, as if to say, How was that for weave poles, amateurs?

"That's it," Audrey called out, dropping the hands she was holding and breaking the line. "No one can compete with Sky. Time for something new."

"How about hide-and-seek?" Chip said.

I thought he'd be shouted down, that Boris would suggest we find a wall for the dogs to scale or that we do a relay race, each of us running with our own dog. I saw that Cathy had a bag of Frisbees and that Woody had brought a couple of gloves for scent discrimination, even though we said we'd use what we found in the park. But suddenly they were all shouting like five-year-olds, hide-and-seek, hide-and-seek. And then before I knew what was happening, Chip had grabbed my hand and we were running toward the line of trees, Betty and Dashiell at our sides.

"We'll give you fifteen minutes," Beryl shouted, "then we're coming to get you."

All I could hear was my breathing as we ran in the dark, through the trees and to a narrow dirt path on the other side.

"This way," he said, pulling on my hand, holding it so tightly I couldn't get it free. He was running in an arc, heading east first, then north, then west. At one point, he stopped so that we could leash the dogs, and I realized we were at the stone wall that lined the park.

"Here, let me give you a leg up," he said, bending and linking his hands so that I could step on them. Ignoring his offer, I turned my back to the wall, hoisted myself so that I was sitting on it, and then swiveled around and jumped off, calling Dashiell to jump the wall and follow me.

"Where are we going? They'll never find us if we leave the park."

"Exactly," he said, grinning.

I stopped walking. Dashiell stopped, too.

"I'm going back."

"Don't," he said. "I never had the chance—"

At first he just stared at me. He didn't look like a five-year-old any longer. He looked significantly older. Maybe deep into adolescence.

He started coming closer, too close, if you ask me. When I saw his lips heading for mine, I ducked, leaving him with a mouthful of hair.

"Rachel," he said. "I never—"

"Yeah, yeah, I know. You never knew it could be like this. Well, the truth is, it can't. It can't be like anything between us."

"You don't understand," he said.

"But I do. I understand perfectly. Everyone is feeling frisky this week, and you feel left out. If I play my cards right, we could be part of it all, you know, the adultery that no one takes very seriously, that doesn't spoil anyone's home life. Because as you might well imagine"—I may have been shouting by then, but hey, this was New York, who the hell would even notice?—"I've been lying awake at night wishing I could have a meaningless roll in the hay with some other lady's husband and then order up some *traif* from room service because there's nothing quite like pork rinds after sex. It's a well-known fact."

I took a deep breath and continued. "I would appreciate it immensely if we could refrain from any sort of personal conversations for the rest of this week while we're stuck in each other's presence. We're here to work, and I find this sort of—"

"I hear you, Rachel. It was foolish of me to think—" Suddenly we could hear the dogs barking, coming our way. "This way." He reached for my hand again, then thought better of it and gave me the hand signal for come. "Hurry."

We headed across the street and back to the hotel, going straight to the tea room, where we began gobbling dessert, trying to make it look as if we'd been there for ages, just waiting for them to show up.

My mouth was full of cheesecake when the glass doors

opened and the others burst in. I lifted my teacup and took a slp. "What kept you all?" I said, as casual as a polyester pants suit.

"Guess you're not trying for tracking degrees with any of those mutts," Chip added.

Bucky could hardly catch his breath. "Good one, pally," he said to Chip. "You really had us going this time." He threw himself into the chair next to mine. I heard it groan.

Martyn sat across from Bucky, still holding Alexi's leash. Tracy was at the dessert table, and Beryl was pouring tea. Everyone looked happy, flushed with color, not nearly as tired as we all should have been.

"How did you ever get involved in this insanity?" Chip asked Sam.

"Don't get me started," she said, waving away the question. "Who's up for the morning?" Audrey asked.

"Good lord, it *is* morning," Martyn said. "It's me. I'd better be off to bed."

I looked around for Cathy and didn't see her.

"Have a cup first." Beryl handed him tea, but before he got the chance to take a sip, Boris walked in with a better idea, three bottles of vodka. He held the door with his ample backside, and Cathy came in behind him with a huge bowl of water for the dogs.

Boris filled eleven cups with vodka and handed one to each of us. "To American camaraderie," he said, and we all cheered and emptied our cups, holding them out immediately for refills. Martyn waved away a second and handed Alexi's leash to Bucky. Beryl got in the next toast before he got out the door.

"To England."

So of course Martyn walked back in and refilled his cup.

"To the queen," he said.

And then Boris was opening the second bottle. This time Martyn made it out the door before the toast.

"To better days ahead," Bucky said, holding up his cup. "And to Rick," he added softly.

"To Rick," we all repeated.

"He was in men's clothing," Bucky said.

"Who was?" Chip asked.

"Rick. Before his degree. He'd dropped out of college and bummed around out west for a year or so. Then he got this job on Madison Avenue, selling men's clothing. But it bored him. He said he could barely stand it. He'd wake up in the morning and not want to get out of bed. So he took a loan out, finished his degree, and went right on to graduate school. He started out working with homeless children, and he brought his dog with him to get the kids to open up and talk. Then one thing led to another, I guess."

"Poor man," Audrey said. "Alan was a teacher. High school history. He went to visit his brother, someplace in the South, one of the Carolinas maybe, or Tennessee, and they went hunting. He thought the electronic collars that the hunters all were using working off-leash dogs at great distances could also solve the problems of pet owners whose dogs wouldn't come. That's all most people want, he used to say, is for their dogs to come off leash. They don't care about the other stuff." She was stroking Magic, who was sitting, as usual, on her lap.

There was a silence.

"To Alan," she said.

Boris poured a swallow or two into Chip's cup, then Woody's. But when he refilled his own, it runneth over, and when he lifted it to drink, some of it even runneth down his double chin.

"Cake," Beryl said. I looked over at her now. She seemed drunk out of her mind. I wondered if I looked that way, too. "We need sweets," she said, attempting to get up and fetch the platter of cakes and pastries, then falling back into her chair. "Oh, my." She straightened up and fussed with her blouse. "Someone bring on the goodies." She spoke slowly, so as to get the words past her lips in good order. "The old lady's too drunk to do it herself. You know, my dears, if the queen could see me now, perhaps she would knight me." She pronounced the *k*, then fell apart laughing, as if she'd just uttered the funniest thing she'd ever heard. "Oh, dear, am I making a complete ass of myself?"

"Only partial," Woody assured her, getting up to get the platter of sweets and offering it to Beryl first.

"Sugar," she said, stopping to take a bite of a small Napoleon and getting powdered sugar and pastry crumbs all over herself as she did, "now what was I saying?"

"That sugar cures a hangover," Audrey said. "But only if accompanied by chanting."

If we'd ever be ready for Audrey, the time was now. We lifted our empty cups. "To Audrey," we all said.

"Come on, handkerchiefs over your faces. You can use napkins," she said, motioning to Cathy, who could reach them from where she sat. Cathy passed us each a large paper napkin, so we finally relinquished our vodka cups, putting them on the floor if we couldn't reach a table, unfolded our napkins, and covered our faces with them. I decided to cheat, pretending to have trouble opening up my napkin. Or did I really have trouble getting the layers apart? I watched everyone, faces covered, napkins rising up and down with their respiration.

"Just chant along with me. Ah la, ah la. At first," Audrey said, her voice low and soothing, "ah la, good, keep it up, at first you'll feel the grief in your chests, the loss of our young colleagues, ah la, ah la, and then the grief will rise and you will feel a lightness, an energy, as you turn your focus to the future and let go of the past, ah la, ah la."

The chanting became one sound, all the voices together, the syllables running together. I chanted too but without covering my face. Instead, I was watching Chip Pressman, one arm hanging off the side of his chair, his hand resting on Betty's head, which was raised as she watched us all behaving so peculiarly, trying to figure out if her master was in danger.

As I watched his handkerchief rising and falling over his mouth, thoughts of being alone with him nearly swept me away. But the overwhelming urge I felt had nothing to do with breaking the laws of man, God, and possibly even the Ritz Hotel. I was thinking about something far more dangerous, breaking one of the rules of private investigation, that body of wisdom my former mentor Frank Petrie had so carefully yelled into my face back when I was in his employ.

When I'd first called Frank and gotten him to agree to an interview even though he'd said he had no openings, especially no openings for no beginners, he'd given me a time to meet with him and directions to his office.

"The elevator only goes to twenny," he'd told me. "Get out there and take the stairs to your left down the hall to twenny-one. Don't mind that the sign says Authorized Personnel Only. I'm authorizing you."

The sign on the office door said Petrie Brothers. When I opened it, there was no receptionist. There was only Frank, sitting behind a big desk with so many phones on it, you'd think he was a bookie.

"You the kid who called?" He looked me over from head to toe and back again. "Sit down. Sit down."

I nodded, taking the plastic folding chair on my side of the desk, wondering what the hell I'd had in mind when I made the call.

"I was hoping you'd consider me as an investigator trainee,"

I said, making it up as I went along, like everything else in my life.

"Nah," he said. "Now that I see you're a girl, I don't think so."

"Now that you see I'm a girl?" I shouted, surprising myself as well as Frank. "You mean you didn't know I was a *woman* when you spoke to me on the phone? You mean the name Rachel didn't tip you off that I'd be a female? You mean I had to waste my time waiting for two hours and then coming up here to see you for you to figure out I was a fucking female and that you didn't hire women to work in your *farkuckt* agency?" By the end, I was standing, my hands on his desk, leaning forward and looming over him. "Listen, mister, there's no job here I couldn't—"

"Okay, you're hired. When can you begin? I have a case that needs an undercover operative, at a hospital in Staten Island, night shift. Ya think you can handle it?"

I sat down, stunned at my own behavior and at Frank's response.

He was grinning. "Just wanted to see if you had a little spunk, kid. You're going to need it on this one. But let me tell you right off. You're going to get in there, just like that, you're going to want to blab. You're going to want to tell just one person what you're *really* doing there. Especially you broads, you know how you are, yadda, yadda, yadda with every stranger you meet. Don't do it, I'm telling you. Because no matter what you think, you might be blabbing to exactly the wrong person, the person you're looking to finger. You know what, use everyone else's desire to blab. That's how you do this." He nodded. Then he whispered. "Mouth shut, except when asking questions. And don't only listen with your ears. Listen with your gut." He slapped his abs for emphasis.

I opened my mouth, but he didn't leave me time to say a thing.

"No. Don't say nothing. I know what you're going to say even before it comes out. You're a college graduate. Told me so on the telephone. Graduated with honors. See, I remember every word you said. You got a pen? Of course you do. Then write this down. It's rule number twelve, but maybe it oughta be number one."

I picked up a piece of paper and a pen from his desk.

"You're going to want to blab. Don't do it," he said. Then he sat back, hands behind his head, and waited while I wrote.

"There's another one, sounds similar. But it's different, believe me. It's number eight. Don't *give* information. *Get* information. See what I mean? Similar, but different. That one has to do with blabbing too, running off at the mouth instead of listening to see what you can find out. This one has to do with blowing your cover. Which, no matter what, you never do. Lie, that's okay. But never—"

"Blow my cover."

He'd nodded. I'd nodded back. But now, with years of experience and three cups of vodka under my belt, I was starting to think that maybe it was the exception that proved the rule. I was starting to think that I needed to talk things out about what was happening during this symposium, and I had the feeling that the last person who would listen to my theory with a sympathetic ear was the one person I should be talking to, Samantha Lewis. I was thinking, in fact, that it might be time to trust an old friend with the truth.

That's when I knew it was time to get moving. Frank Petrie was as pigheaded as they come, but in all the years I'd been in his employ, he had never been wrong in the advice he gave me about the work.

As Dashiell and I slipped out the door, it wasn't the chanting of my colleagues I was listening to. All I could hear, as clearly as if Frank were standing in front of me, was the cacophonous Brooklynese I had come to know and love, repeating the same phrase over and over again, as if it were a mantra: Don't do it.

DOES ANYONE NEED AN ASPIRIN?

I t was seven-thirty when the clock radio woke me, the Beethoven sonata sounding as loud as the rap music blaring from some people's cars as they drive around my neighborhood on Saturday nights trying to appear cool. I had slept a little over four hours.

Martyn, bent over his notes at the far end of the breakfast table, his blond hair falling over his brow, looked more like an adolescent than an adult. I thought I'd sit quietly at the other end of the table so as not to disturb him, but when he heard me, he looked up and closed his notebook.

"Come and join me, Rachel." He pushed what was left of his breakfast off to the side. "It's rather lonely down at this end. I was just writing my children. They love getting letters when I'm in the States. I don't think it's the letters per se they like; it's your quirky American stamps. It's so refreshing, the variety here. Not a queen in the lot."

"Oh, I wouldn't bet on that," I said, taking a hard roll from the basket on the table and giving half to Dashiell. There was an envelope next to Martyn's notebook, the address and two Bugs Bunny stamps already on it. "He came out, what, about a month ago."

"I hadn't heard. The tabloids were too full of the latest pit bull fiasco. They have one in jail again. From the photo, I'd say he was a white boxer. The last one was a Great Dane mix, confiscated from a locked car because he wasn't wearing a muzzle. Our breed-specific laws have created some bizarre behavior, but it's in the humans, of course."

"There was a push to do that here, too, to ban pit bulls first. Then of course the list would grow. Who knows where it would stop?"

The waiter came with a small pot of tea for me and took my order for breakfast.

"What are you covering today?"

"Temperament testing. In fact, I wonder if you'd consider letting me test Dashiell."

"My vicious pit bull? Sure, if you're brave enough. Are you testing the other participants' dogs?"

"Yes, except for Sasha." He sighed heavily.

"How come?"

He looked down at his letter, then back up at me. I expected that was all the answer he was going to give me.

He was small, shorter than I was and skinny as capellini. Did he feel uncomfortable around large dogs? Then why had he asked to test Dashiell?

"I think we'll probably not test Cecilia either. She's a lovely little thing, isn't she? But too young for this test. I don't think she's one year old yet, and I don't want to put this kind of pressure on a pup. How are you enjoying the talks, Rachel? Have you been attending all of them?"

"Some," I said. "Actually, parts of most."

"I must confess, I did duck out in the middle of Rick's talk." He leaned so close I could count his fillings. For just a second, I had the antic thought he was going to tell me why. "Now, of course, I'll not have another chance to hear his theories, and I do think he had an awful lot to offer. But I wanted to get over to the gift shop at the zoo and send a little something off to Graeme and Sheila early in the week so that they'd have it by the time Daddy got home. With a new brother or sister on the way, they need some positive reinforcement of their parents' affection, don't you think?"

Yeah, yeah, the zoo, a little something for Graeme and Sheila. And here I'd been thinking he'd spent tea time coming up with a little something for Cathy Powers.

He lifted his attaché case from the floor next to his chair to the table, snapped it open, and took out two hand puppets, a butterscotch-colored lion with a big mane and a pointy-faced red fox. Slipping a hand in each, he held them up. "Brilliant, aren't they? I must get over to the post office today, after the talk, and Express Mail them to London, even though that means missing Tracy's little presentation. Ah, well. Family first." He reached for his cup of cold coffee, took a sip, and made a face. "This was not the best time for me to be away, Rachel. I'd just gone home after several months of lecturing here, but Samantha's done so much for me, I couldn't very well say no to her, could I?"

The door opened, and Beryl and Tracy walked in, Cecilia and Jeff at their sides, tongues lolling.

"Is this a rehearsal for this morning's talk or just something to get Rachel to eat her breakfast?" Beryl asked, taking her place at the table just as the waiter came with my bowl of fresh fruit. "I'll have the same," she said. "And some yogurt as well."

"Me, too," Tracy added.

"Then two soft-boiled eggs, sausage, ham and toast, with a pot of tea, and let it steep, young man. I can't drink that watery brew you Americans call tea, not one more morning."

I looked to see if Tracy was going to me-too the rest of the breakfast, but she was busy feeding Jeff a buttered roll. The waiter waited, but when Tracy looked up, she merely shook her head. Maybe she was one of those secret eaters, eating delicately when with other people and snacking on tons of junk food when she was alone.

Martyn managed to get the puppets back into his attaché case before Sam walked in.

"I see some of us survived the night," she announced.

My heart flipped over, but when she took the seat next to Beryl's, she was smiling.

"Does anyone need an aspirin?" she asked, opening her purse and looking around. "Or Visine?" She took out a giant-sized bottle of aspirin, shook two into her palm, and put the bottle in the middle of the table.

"Are you using any shelter dogs for the testing this morning?" Tracy asked Martyn.

"No, not any. I'd rather not pull a dog out of such a stressful situation for a test such as this one. I'd rather see a version of the test Cathy uses for puppies used on the shelter dogs, basically just seeing how biddable they are, assessing activity level, and finding out if they're gentle enough. This test judges soundness for work. I don't think that's often an issue in shelter adoptions."

"But it might encourage—"

"We're supposed to be training professionals here." He spoke as if he were teaching a five-year-old. For a moment I thought he was going to put the puppets back on his hands to help explain things. "It's not going to be a very productive week if we have to censor ourselves and see if we're being politically correct every minute."

"Some of the service dog programs do use shelter dogs." She picked up another roll and buttered it, this time for herself.

"Then why don't *you* use one or two for your little talk, love? Operant conditioning phaseout timing, isn't it?"

Tracy's mouth opened and closed as if she were biting the air. The door opened, and Betty charged in ahead of Angelo, proving a point that was already a given. I could hear Chip and Bucky from out in the hall where they remained, too busy arguing to come in for breakfast.

"There is validity in that part of the test," Chip was saying. "You have to know how a dog will react under pressure."

"Gentlemen," Martyn said, sliding his chair back and standing. He motioned them in with a wave of his arm. "It seems my talk has inspired argument even before I deliver it. I'm flattered."

"Don't be," Chip said. "This one's going to fight you every step of the way. Thinks we ought to mollycoddle the dogs instead of testing them."

"Indeed? It should be a stimulating morning." He picked up his unfinished letter to his children, slipped it into his pocket, picked up the notebook and attaché case, and headed for the doors.

Sam knocked another aspirin into her hand. "What happened to all the good feeling we generated last night?" She shook her head and took the pill.

"Gone with the dawn," Beryl said. She looked at her watch. "Oh, dear, no time to eat all that lovely food. Just barely time for a phone call before Martyn's speech." She made a sandwich of ham and toast to take with her and, with Cecilia following at her heels, left the breakfast room.

Chip sat next to Sam. Bucky took the chair next to mine.

"I used to think he knew what he was talking about," he said, staring at Chip and shaking his head. "Not anymore." He lifted a hand for the waiter and pointed to the empty cup in front of him. "Do you have those nice blueberry pancakes this morning?" he asked.

"What exactly were you arguing about?"

"The umbrella test. I think it's excessive. I prefer being all positive with the dogs. You can find out everything you need to know without scaring the hell out of them. Chip thinks it separates the men from the boys, that it's necessary, but really, Rachel, this kind of thing doesn't give the public a very good—"

"I'd like to reserve judgment until I hear what Martyn has to say. Why did we all come here, if we're going to be so closed to each other's ideas?"

Feeling the need to separate one of the women from the boys, I tapped my leg for Dashiell. I wanted to take a quick walk before Martyn's talk.

I hadn't waited for Bucky to answer my question because I already knew the answer. Whatever reasons any of us had for coming here, having our opinions about dogs changed was not one that made anyone's list. Besides, as far as I could tell, the reason you choose to do something in the first place can change, especially when circumstances conspire to make you mad enough to kill.

HOW ABOUT YOU? SHE ASKED

Whatever you have heard about pit bulls, please forget that
now."

Martyn as a speaker was a cranked-up version of the man
I had talked to at breakfast. His voice was stronger, strong enough
for us all to hear him out-of-doors and without a mike, his
inflections were more dramatic, his posture straighter, his command of the audience complete. No wonder he had chosen to
spend most of his time lecturing about behavior all over the
United States rather than spaying and inoculating pets back
home in merry old England. As an added bonus, when he was
here, no one was going to ask him to tidy up or take out the trash.
Or expect him to sleep with the same woman every night.

Dashiell stood at my side, content to wait and see. He too
stood in a commanding way, his legs apart, his eyes benignly
scanning the audience spread out before him in the grass of the
Sheep Meadow, quietly ready for whatever might come his way.

"First of all, we are going to test the dog's reaction toward strangers, beginning with a neutral stranger who will approach Rachel, shake her hand, and ignore Dashiell. Next a friendly stranger will approach in an animated way and pet the dog. I have asked this audience for experienced assistance, and two of you volunteered"—he turned to look at two men who stood quietly to one side—"both of whom are strangers to this dog, and so can help us in the performance of this test. You have both worked on this test before?" The young bearded man nodded; the older man, who was stocky and balding, lifted one hand as a reply. "Excellent, gentlemen," Martyn said. He walked over to them, and they conferred quietly for a moment, Martyn occasionally pointing toward me and Dashiell.

I could see Cathy Powers sitting halfway back in the group, Sky lying down alongside her, a tennis ball in his mouth. There was room next to her, and I hoped it would stay that way, because it was where I planned to be after Dashiell's test.

"Let's begin," Martyn said. With that, the older man came over to where I stood with Dashiell, calmly reached out and shook my hand, exchanged a few pleasantries, and left. Dashiell sat at my side doing nothing more than absorbing the smell and sound of the benign stranger.

After a moment, the second man approached. He was smiling, and he waved at me. When he got close enough, he bent and began to pet Dashiell. Dashiell remained sitting, but his tail swished back and forth on the cool grass.

I could see Sam way in the back of the group, flanked by Woody and Chip. Betty was behind them, her tail sticking out at Chip's side. Rhonda had backed up and was sitting on Woody's thigh, as if he were a chair.

Audrey, Tracy, and Beryl were together, close to the testing area but off to my right. Jeff was sitting in front of Tracy, watching the test. Cecilia, on Beryl's lap, was trying to bite on his ears. I couldn't see Magic. She must have been asleep on Audrey's lap, perhaps with a napkin over her head. Now that I'd tried meditating Audrey's way, I couldn't blame Magic for being so cooperative.

Martyn was getting ready to test Dash's reaction to noise. As a city dog, he'd slept through sirens, car alarms, and the Gay Pride parade. There was nothing Martyn could do that would startle Dashiell.

He flew through the ten subtests, acing every one, reacting where he should have, to the hidden decoy threatening him with a riding crop, and as calm as Balto, the statue of the great sled dog in Central Park, when the younger of the two assistants snapped open the spring-loaded umbrella and lowered it onto the path we'd been asked to traverse. I looked out into the audience for Bucky, who was shaking his head, but Dashiell had not been traumatized by the sudden appearance of a large object in his path. He had gone, as he should have, to investigate and, finding the umbrella to be harmless and inedible, went about his business as if it were no longer there.

"This test is meant to show the level of soundness of a dog's temperament," Martyn said as I walked toward Cathy and Sky, "and I believe that once that information is yours, you can predict how well a given dog will work. The test does not, of course, assess genetically based skills in the way that a herding test or water test might—"

"Is he going to test Sky?" I asked, sitting cross-legged next to Cathy, Dashiell stretching out next to the border collie, sniffing his nose, and then rolling over onto his side and falling asleep.

She nodded. "I was hoping he'd do some less well-trained dogs. These dogs have proven their temperament through work. So the results are a given, aren't they?"

I nodded. "Makes a smoother show this way," I whispered. Woody and Rhonda passed us on the way up to the front. "And smooth this man is." I let that sit in the air between us.

I was looking at Martyn, but out of the corner of my eye I could see that Cathy had turned to look at me.

"Guess who made a pass?" I said, rolling my eyes in case she was still looking. "One minute he's talking about the presents he bought for his kids," I said, stopping as if I'd gotten very interested in Rhonda's reaction to the neutral stranger, listening instead for a change in Cathy's breathing pattern, "and the next thing I know, he's telling me how unhappy he is at home, that it's the main reason he travels so much. Men!"

Rhonda was walking across a plastic sheet.

"It's that seminar mentality."

No way was I going to get the answers I needed from Martyn. Deception was the man's middle name. Cathy was my only chance, and even though baiting her felt cruel, I continued. "They all have it. At least that's what Sam says."

"What do you mean?"

"You know, when they're staying in a hotel, without their wives, they feel they can do whatever they want."

I turned to face her. She was looking at the boxer investigating the open umbrella, no emotion showing on her face. Unless you counted the muscles jumping in her cheeks or that little back-and-forth movement at the corner of her right eyelid.

"How about you?" she asked suddenly, an edge in her voice. "Do you ever feel that way when you're away lecturing?" Her mouth smiled at me, but the rest of her face didn't concur.

"He's cute," I said. "You have to give him that. And he's smart. He's one hell of an attractive man."

I waited.

"But he's not *that* cute."

There was an exercise pen laid out flat on the grass to simulate a grating. Woody was walking on the side of it, and Rhonda was walking across it, as if she walked on a surface like that every day of her life, no problem.

"Even if he were single," I said, "why would I want to get involved with a guy who lived in England? Think of the phone bills."

She flicked back her long hair and looked toward where Martyn stood, explaining the test results.

"What would be the point? It's not like he's going to leave his wife."

"He might," she said. "Some men do. The divorce rate—"

"Oh, please. Not this one. There's another kid on the way."

"She's pregnant, his wife?"

"That's what he said."

"But—"

I waited to see if Cathy would say anything else, but she didn't. When Martyn called her to come forward with Sky, she got up without saying another word and walked up front, to where he stood waiting for her, a big smile on his face.

Yeah, yeah, the zoo, I thought. Wherever and whenever Martyn had bought those puppets, I was now sure it hadn't been Monday afternoon. Sam was right. Day and night, the joint was jumping.

I moved over to where Sam was sitting on the grass, sitting where Woody had been before he got back to claim his spot.

"Boris must be having one of his temper tantrums," she said as soon as I was seated beside her.

I looked around. I didn't remember seeing him in the audience. He hadn't been at breakfast either. "What's up?"

"Martyn told him he didn't want to test Sasha, and Boris stormed out of the breakfast room. He probably went back to his room to try to sleep off his hangover."

"Maybe," I said, but I didn't believe it. If someone had made Boris angry, he wouldn't go to sleep. He'd make damn sure they suffered in return. He'd be here, heckling, sitting as close to the front as he could, right under Martyn's nose. He'd probably have his dog growling too, figuring Martyn was afraid of Rotties, and why not capitalize on the edge he had and terrorize him all the more?

"I'll have the desk ring his room when we go back to the hotel."

True, the man drank a lot of vodka the night before, I thought, but wasn't he, in his own words, Russian man with constitution of iron, not weak American?

"You know what," I said to Sam, "I'll go back and have the desk call up now, see if we can rouse him."

Sam didn't seem concerned. "Let him sleep, Rachel. He'll be as grouchy as a Russian bear if you wake him. At least let Martyn finish in peace." She waved me to stay where I was, and I did. But I couldn't help wondering if Boris was really in his room, or if like Alan Cooper, when he didn't show up when he should have, he too had fallen victim to an accident.

YOU DIDN'T DO A VERY GOOD JOB

Martyn was still taking questions when I headed back to the hotel. I too was going to miss Tracy's talk on phasing out food rewards, but from what I'd seen in the park, I wouldn't be missing much.

The old guy was on, Jimmy's father. I asked him to ring 306. After shuffling around as if he'd forgotten where the switchboard was, he did.

He held the phone a few inches away from his ear and shook his head. "No one's picking up."

"Keep trying. He might be sleeping."

"It's twelve-fifteen."

I flicked my hand at him to ring again, waiting until he shook his head a second time.

"Probably out in the park with that big dog of his—bigger than yours, that one. My son's having a hard week." He chuckled, having himself a whale of a good time at his son's expense.

"Did you see him go out?"

"Can't keep track of all of you. Not with mail to sort, check-ins, check-outs."

He shook his head again. No wonder his neck was so skinny.

Dashiell and I headed up the stairs. Boris's room was across the hall from mine. Maybe a knock would wake him where the phone hadn't. Maybe he was sitting in there letting us stew, not answering on purpose. At least I'd find out if Sasha was in the room. No way I could stand outside of Boris's room with Dashiell and not get a rise from the Rottie.

Dashiell headed for our door but then followed me over to Boris's door. When there was no sound from inside, I knew before knocking that Sasha wasn't home. So did Dashiell. He went over to sniff at the sill of Betty's door.

I knocked twice, just to be sure. But if Sasha wasn't there, Boris wouldn't be there. Boris could go out without his dog, but it didn't work the other way around.

I thought about checking out the park, but who was I kidding? It was enormous. Boris and his dog could be anywhere. I wouldn't know where to begin.

I headed downstairs for the café, hoping that someone else had seen Boris, and felt a little foolish when I got to the bottom of the staircase. I could hear him from the far end of the hallway.

"It's *your* temperament that should be tested," he was shouting, "afraid to test Boris's dog. You make students think something wrong with Sasha, all dogs tested but him. What did he ever do to you? And what are you doing in dog business if you can't handle well-bred Rottweiler?"

I heard no response.

When I opened the door to the café, everyone but Sam was at the table, all of them staring at Boris, whose face was as red as it had been the night before.

"Maybe that's way things are in England, whole country maybe a little—" Instead of spelling his insult out verbally, he raised his eyebrows and rocked his hand from side to side. "Afraid of rabies coming in through Channel tunnel, have six-month quarantine, dogs can die of broken heart before you let them on your island, afraid of pit bull, ban them, shoot them, castrate them, muzzle them, now afraid of Rottweiler, what next?"

His face was redder now than when I'd come in and taken my place at the table.

"Where've you been?" Chip asked. "You missed the first ten minutes of this?"

"Powdering my nose."

"You didn't do a very good job. It's still shiny."

"High-gloss powder," I told him in Russian accent. "Deflects harmful UV rays. Keeps Rachel's skin young."

"Keep your day job," he said.

"Has Martyn said anything back?"

"Never got the chance. Besides, I think Boris has a point. He's got a well-behaved dog with a sound temperament. There was no reason for excluding him from the testing. It could give the students the wrong idea. On the other hand, someone with less of a temper, and less of an ego, would have let it go, or spoken privately to Martyn."

"I wonder why Martyn doesn't just apologize. Wouldn't that be the gentlemanly thing to do?"

"Perhaps he's not a gentleman," Chip said, as if he knew that to be the case. And didn't I suspect the very same thing?

"Enough." Sam stood in the doorway like the principal come to discipline a class that had gotten away from its teacher. "Next time you want to play the fool, Boris, kindly let the rest of us know precisely where you'll be performing so that we can fail to show up. And next time you pull a disappearing act, you can book your own future seminars. I was just upstairs banging on your door and was this short"—she held her thumb and pointer a half inch apart—"of calling in the police. After what's happened this week, I'd prefer knowing where everyone is. And I'd prefer it if none of you would listen to music in the bathroom, and when you eat your meals, I hope you'll cut your food into small pieces."

She turned and left the café, leaving the door open instead of slamming it, but the effect was the same.

"Sam's got a point," I said, barely over my own pointless worry. "There's been enough excitement this week. We need to make a real effort to get along for the next few days, and then we can agree to never lay eyes on each other again."

"But—"

"No buts, Boris. First, Martyn, do you have something you'd like to say to Boris?"

"Indeed. I apologize, Boris. You are absolutely correct that I should have tested Sasha. He's a fine dog, well trained and with excellent Rottie temperament. I hope you will forgive me. You see, I was once bitten very badly by—"

"Thank you," I said. "Boris, can we get by this now?"

"Why test pit bull and not Rottweiler?"

"Boris?"

"Boris accepts apology."

"Good. Thank you both. A few more days, people, and that's it."

Tracy was at the buffet table, a plate in one hand, a glass of lemonade in the other. No one was arguing about her talk. It was as if it had never happened.

Audrey was speaking in the afternoon. Aside from the meditation, she would talk about her psychic experiences with animals, what they had told her, and how they had revealed in their own words surprising solutions to the common problems so many dog

owners face. She said she would do some readings with our animals too. I couldn't wait. They say smiling, like sex, is good for
the immune system, and Lord knows I hadn't done enough of
either lately.

After lunch, we walked as a group into the auditorium.
Audrey started with a basic chant, and so for five minutes Dashiell
and I sat in the middle of a sea of noise, the energy rising with
people's voices. Some of the dogs joined in, too, howling along
as their owners chanted.

When it was over, Audrey lowered her head, her hands together as if in prayer, and remained that way for what seemed
like an eternity.

"I know that some of you find what I have to say foolish, and
that some will not be able to implement these skills and ideas in
order to have a better understanding of the animals you train.
But I hope all of you will try to be open, to listen with your hearts
as well as your ears, and to try the techniques instead of just
writing them off.

"What I would like to do today instead of telling you old
stories I've heard over the years from the many wonderful animals I've met is to work with some of the dogs that are here and
see if they will tell me new stories, stories of their lives with you
and how they could be made better. Boris," she said, "would you
bring Sasha up front?"

Audrey was sitting cross-legged on the edge of the stage,
wearing the same T-shirt and jeans she'd had on in the park this
morning. I was a little disappointed that she hadn't worn her
Native-American garb, but excited that she had chosen Sasha to
be a first subject. I looked around for Martyn, to see his reaction—surely this was a slap in his face, that little Audrey could
work with a dog he had declined to use—but I couldn't see his
expression. He was leaning forward, and he seemed to be writing.

Boris and Sasha were on the stage now, Boris beaming, the Rottie standing at his side.

"I'd like Sasha to be free to say whatever it is that's on his mind, Boris, so could I ask you to leave him with me and take your seat?"

Nearly everyone there leaned forward, and there wasn't a sound in the room. Some of us, at least, must have been waiting for the volcano to blow, but Boris left the stage without a word. He was so pleased his dog had been selected, Audrey could do no wrong. If she'd asked him to leave the country, he probably would have pulled out a cell phone and called the airlines right from the stage.

"Sasha, come on over here and tell me what's been on your mind." Audrey patted the stage right next to where she sat, and the big dog, his head rolling from side to side, walked slowly over to where she was and sat. Then he rolled onto one hip so that he was leaning against her. Everyone began to clap.

Audrey stroked Sasha's neck, just sitting at his side. And listening. Or so we were meant to believe.

"He says he'd really like to go to Burger King, and have one *his* way."

We all laughed. I could hear Boris from where I sat, laughing louder and longer than any of us. Then I saw him smirking at someone off to the left. He was apparently trying to catch Martyn's eye, but Martyn didn't see him. He was still paying attention to whatever was on his lap.

"He says he doesn't like to be disciplined."

Audrey was smiling, patting Sasha on the top of his broad head. There was a loud moaning sound from the humans, as if to say, Get on with it, tell us something we don't know. And as if Audrey heard those very words, she did.

"He said his leg still hurts when it's damp out," she said. "But not when he runs. It used to. But not now. And he'd like you to rub it the way you used to. He says it's much better, but it still aches when the weather is wet."

It was quiet again. Very quiet. Boris stood. "Leg was broken when he was nine months old. Sasha jump for fly in office, come down on slippery floor and skid. Break bone." He sat again, and waited. We all did.

I had once let Lili drag me to a numerologist all her friends had been raving about. It's ridiculous, I'd told her, I have better things to do with my time and money than listening to some charlatan telling me the sort of junk everyone wants to hear, call it a "reading" and charge an arm and a leg for making up stuff to fool me with. My treat, she'd said, and when I'd told her that the money wasn't the issue, she'd said, Please, Rachel, do this for me, I'd never have the nerve to go without you. And so I'd gone with her, laughing all the way, until the guy had gotten specific enough, and scary enough, to get my attention. The way Audrey had just gotten all of ours.

"What else would you like Boris to know?" she asked, her cheek against Sasha's. We waited a long time, just watching them. With nothing else to do, I wondered if Boris had told her about the broken leg, and if he'd forgotten that he had. Or if there were stitches there, an old scar she'd felt when the dog sat next to her. I thought I could feel his legs later on, see if that was the case.

"You're safe here," she told the Rottie. Then we all waited for him to answer her question, the way we'd all waited for him to sing the national anthem.

"He won't say anything else," Audrey finally said. "He's—" But she didn't finish her sentence. She was looking out into the audience, at Boris. "I think that's it for now," she said, but when the dog lay down at her side and began to tremble, Audrey continued. "He's afraid of making you angry," she said, her hand on the dog's back, her eyes on Boris. "He's afraid of you," she added, as tenderly as she could. "Of your anger."

"What anger?" Boris shouted, his arms raised, palms up. He looked around the room for confirmation of his judgment, but didn't receive any. "This is biggest baloney I ever hear."

"Perhaps next time," Audrey said.

"People come here for knowledge, not ridiculous storytelling, dog says he's afraid, wants hamburger, ach." He charged up to the stage to get his dog.

I expected him to storm out of the room, but he didn't. Audrey waited until he was seated again. "It's just that he wants to please you so badly," she said. "He would never want to make you angry at him by complaining."

Boris grunted, appeased by what she'd added.

Audrey asked Tracy to bring Jeff up, but she declined, saying that Jeff had always told her absolutely everything he required for total happiness. She was clinging on so tight, I had to wonder exactly which beans she was afraid Jeff would spill.

Boris was sitting quietly now, stroking Sasha's neck. How easily he'd gone into a rage, I thought. And then I had a psychic revelation of my own. For just a moment, there was a picture in my head, the way you remember a snippet of a dream before it blows away as quickly as it came. I saw a hand, maybe Boris's hand, leaning down on that small shelf in the hotel bathrooms, the one they leave the extra towels on, the one that Alan Cooper had put the radio on so that he could listen to music while he soaked in the tub.

Bucky had brought Alexi to the stage and had gone back to his seat.

"I can't understand a word he's saying," Audrey said. "Does anyone here speak Russian?"

But before Boris got the chance to volunteer, her hands were up, stopping the laughter and letting us know we should remain in our places. "This is the time for me to explain how psychic communication with animals works. Or more accurately, how it doesn't work. It doesn't work in words, so language differences never become language barriers. The communication is done in pictures, things the dog imagines and sends to you and things you imagine and the dog picks up. I'll ask you to close your eyes now—no, not you, Alexi, you can keep your eyes open."

There was laughter again. I looked around and saw everyone smiling, eyes closed. Audrey had won them over. Even Boris had his eyes closed.

I closed my eyes and waited for Audrey's voice to tell me what to do, but before she said a word, another picture came, an awful picture, Rick Shelbert turning pale as he struggled for air.

I opened my eyes and thought about what Chip had said when I'd told him I'd been late because I'd stopped to powder my nose.

You didn't do a very good job.

He was right. I hadn't.

I had been hired to prevent the loss of life, and yet two people were dead. I thought about the elevator falling, the people not being warned. Maybe once things were set in motion, there was no way to stop them. Maybe all I could do, like the police, was make sure that whoever was doing this would be found out, that we could have the small but important satisfaction of knowing who and why. But that wasn't enough. There had to be an end to this.

"Is there an image in your mind now?"

Her voice seemed to be coming from very far away.

"If you have a companion animal with you, change the image so that you are picturing something pleasant that includes your pet, taking him for a walk in the park, feeding him a favorite treat, or playing a game he likes. One image. And hold that image. Now see if your pet starts to react in any way, but don't open your eyes yet. Wait until you're sure he's got it."

Dashiell wasn't impressed. He was lying on his side, snoring lightly. But sitting there and watching Audrey bonding with Alexi, I was formulating a mental image that got me excited, a way that, starting tonight, I could do my job better, a way, I hoped, to interfere with fate and prevent the next senseless killing.

I'VE BEEN HEARING RUMORS ABOUT YOU

"Ante up, people," Woody said, breaking the seal on the deck and shuffling. "Ante. From the Latin, meaning 'before.' Come on, Boris. You know the American saying, A fool and his money are soon parted. Let's go here."

I tossed my chip and heard the satisfying sound of plastic against plastic as each of my cohorts did the same, the chips landing on each other and then sliding off onto the green felt cover of the round table I'd asked Jimmy to have brought to my room after dinner.

I'd gone out for the supplies myself, not wanting to leave the selection of junk food to an amateur. Boris had volunteered to supply the cigars. He'd brought vodka too, not knowing that I'd had the same idea. We had enough booze to fill a kiddie pool.

I waited until all my cards were in front of me before picking them up.

The other women had declined my proposition, each making her own lame excuse for not spending the night in a cloud of smoke. I didn't care. It was the men I was after. If they were all together playing poker, I hoped they'd all be alive in the morning. Because even without the sort of hard evidence that was needed to change anyone's opinion about what had happened to two of our male speakers, the knot in my stomach was telling me these cleverly orchestrated episodes were not accidents.

I sat next to Chip. Boris was across from me, which is exactly where I wanted him, in full view, and Woody sat at my right, Bucky sat at Chip's left, and Martyn, who had been the only voice of dissent in the group but gave in and came anyway, was sitting between Woody and Boris.

I took a look at my cards. "In," I said. I tossed in a five-dollar chip, the last of the big spenders.

"Call," Chip said.

"Call." Bucky picked up a chip with two fat fingers and tossed it into the pot.

"Boris calls."

There were two more pings as Martyn and Woody pitched a chip each toward the pot, nobody going out on a limb just yet.

"How many?" Woody asked.

"I'll play these."

"Two," Chip said. He peeled off a couple of cards and tossed them to Woody. Woody sent two back, only the three golden retriever puppies showing. I'm nothing if not appropriate.

"One," Bucky said, trying to look inscrutable.

Boris held his cards from above, his fingers coming down over the top like ivy growing over a stone wall. "Three."

"Three?"

"You heard Boris," he said, looking irritated now.

"One," Martyn said. "No, make that two."

"I'm taking one," Woody said. Then he turned to look at me and waited.

Well, let him, I thought. I wasn't here to play cards.

"Weird week, isn't it?" I said, easing in slowly.

Rhonda had gotten up on the bed. She was snoring even louder than Dashiell does.

"In or out?" Woody asked.

"A full house beats a flush, right?" I asked.

Woody slapped his cards down on the table and picked up a cigar.

"It's just that it's been a while," I said, having too much fun now to stop. "I only wanted to be sure."

They were all staring.

"Never mind," I told them, dropping two chips into the pot without bothering to look at my cards again. Hell, with my love life, who had to check my cards in the first place? Anyway, my ploy worked. I had their attention. "So here's what I was thinking—"

"Broads," Bucky said, holding the cards close to his chest. "Let one sit in on a poker game, and what do you have? A quilting bee. Yadda, yadda, yadda, all night long." He dropped his free hand to his lap and was moving it rhythmically. I hoped he was petting Angelo, but there was always that other possibility.

"Hasn't it occurred to anyone but me that two fatal accidents mean this isn't a coincidence?"

"It is unusual," Martyn said, "losing two of our major players like this. But the police said—"

"No, listen," I said, "think about dog training, you know, when a client calls you up with a string of coincidences, a shopping list of all the dog's bad behavior, and they don't see any connection between, say, the growling and the urinating on the arm of the sofa. But it's always connected. It's never a case of—"

I stopped and looked around the table. Bucky was rearranging his cards. Boris was staring across the table. Chip had turned sideways to get a better view of me. Woody was doing the same, except from the other side. And Martyn, who a moment ago had seemed interested and concerned, now looked as if he had gone on an out-of-body trip, imagining himself, perhaps, in a better place, or with a less irritating group of people. I picked up my vodka and tossed it down in one gulp. "Coincidence," I said.

"It is a bit of a stretch," Woody said, looking not at me now but at the others.

"Call," Chip said, tossing in two chips.

"Heavy," I said. "What do you have, Pressman, a pair of threes?"

Bucky laid down his cards and pitched three chips into the pot. "See you and raise you," he said. "Female hysteria is what it is. Always imagining more than there is."

"Maybe Bucky imagines more than there is in his hand," Boris said. "I look at you. I raise you," he said, picking up four chips and tossing them in.

"Fold," Martyn said, laying down his hand and taking one of the fat cigars Boris had put on the table. He slipped off the band, cut off the tip of the cigar, and reached across the table for matches.

I didn't care where this went now. I wanted them to know someone was looking at this differently than the police, that it wasn't just going down as smoothly as ice-cold vodka. I thought maybe it needed one more touch to get the message across.

"Think what you want, Bucky," I said, "but who says you won't be the next one to have an *accident?*"

"Maybe Bucky causes accidents," Boris said, and even though I'd felt like smacking him in the past, just then I could have kissed the man.

"Oh, perfect, Boris. Good American thinking. So what's the scenario, pally? Let me see if I can figure it out. I broke into Alan's room, unplugged his radio, carried it into his bathroom, placed it on the shelf over the tub, plugged it in, and then pulled the shelf out of the wall. How am I doing so far?" But it was a rhetorical question, my favorite kind. He held up a hand. There was more to come. "So what was Alan doing while I allegedly did all this, soaping his genitals?"

He looked around for support and found none.

"Great. This is great. So what did I do next? Will someone please tell me how I made Rick choke?"

When no one answered him, or came to his defense, he shot Boris a look and then picked up his cards again, rechecking them to see if his hand had improved in the interim.

Boris looked at me and winked. Then he picked up his shot glass and downed the contents, taking the sweating bottle out of the ice bucket and refilling his glass and mine before putting it back. Fortunately, my mother wasn't here to tsk-tsk about the drinking or tell my cohorts I'd always had an overactive imagination.

Woody picked up four chips and dropped them in the pot.

I threw in five more chips, raising it again, and waited.

"Are you going to call, or aren't you?" I asked when nothing happened.

"I fold," Chip said.

Bucky slapped his cards onto the table and folded.

"Rachel has big hand," Boris said. "Boris folds, too."

I turned and looked at Woody.

"Fold," he said.

"Cool," I said, gathering in the chips and adding them to the pile in front of me.

"Starter's luck," Boris said.

I picked up the cards and began shuffling, fanning them out left and then right to the melodious sound of chips hitting each other.

Suddenly Bucky gave me a concerned look, his face as wrinkled as a shar-pei's. "I meant to tell you, Rachel," he said, picking up the cards as I dealt and slipping one between two others, "I've been hearing rumors about you for the past few years, since you dropped out of sight."

He looked up at me now, to make sure he had my attention.

"They say you quit the business because you took a bite, and it scared you off."

"Really? I heard the same story about you," I told him, picking up my cards, giving them a look-see, then looking up at Bucky, grinning.

"What are you talking about?"

"Yeah, it's what everyone is saying, that you do all those commercials instead of working with clients because you lost your—"

"What a bunch of crap," he said.

I looked down at my queens and grinned some more. I've always felt the concept of a poker face was a guy thing. I prefer the grin to the deadpan gaze, Julia Roberts rather than Robert Mitchum, rest his soul. It's better for the immune system.

"Who? Who said that?" Bucky shouted.

"Who do you think?" I asked him. There'd been too many years of Bucky's game, inventing some hideously damaging insult, then passing it on in front of other people as if he were your best friend shouldering an important but difficult message.

Beware the messenger.

Bucky looked back at his hand, quiet for the moment.

"Of course," I added, "I tell anybody who bad-mouths you, whatever they are saying just isn't so. I tell them that you're a wonderful trainer, absolutely fearless, one of the best in the business, past, present, and future. And that you have huge balls."

Even before Bucky looked up, surprised, Chip had kicked me in the foot.

"Isn't that what you told them about me?"

"Especially the part about the balls," Chip muttered.

"Of course, I—"

"So, that's settled." I flashed him the Kaminsky grin, a watt or two brighter than Julia's. "Let's play cards. In or out, suckers?"

Chip picked up a five-dollar chip and tossed it into the pot.

"Fold." Bucky picked up his vodka, swallowed it, and slammed his glass down on the table. At the loud sound, Dashiell stood and barked, his tail straight out behind him. Then Betty stood, too. She gave him the eye. Dashiell's shoulders seemed to lift as his tail dropped. He went around to the far side of the bed and lay down with a sigh. There's nothing like the efficiency of an alpha bitch. I hoped I had just proven that, along with Betty.

I looked at Boris. "In or out?" I asked him. "Let's go, people. Are we playing cards here or quilting?"

I heard the ping of three chips, but I wasn't looking. I had just thought of another irritating coincidence. Maybe it was nothing, but at this point, I wanted to check out everything. I knocked back a second vodka, feeling it burn all the way down, and reached for a handful of potato chips. I had to do something to keep my strength up for all the running around I'd have to do the next day. In addition to everything else, I was on a panel in the afternoon.

I looked up in time to see Bucky trying to see my cards in the mirror on the wall behind me.

"Close to the vest, gentlemen," I said as I got up and walked over to the bathroom. I came back with a bath sheet and draped it over the mirror. "My error. We should be sitting shivah. Haven't two of our colleagues just passed on?"

When I sat down again and looked around the table, Bucky no longer had a poker face. He was scowling as he studied his cards. What was he going to do next, the slime, send Angelo to steal chips from the rest of us? Just how far would he go, I wondered, to make himself feel he was winning?

It was going to be a long night, but that was precisely the point. I'd promised myself I'd do whatever I could to keep the game going until morning.

THIS IS SO SUDDEN, HE SAID

W e need more ice," Boris said. "Wodka not cold enough."
I looked out the open window and saw the first glimmers of
pink in the sky.

"Ice, Rachel, ice."

"Okay, okay," I said, wanting everyone to be happy so they'd
stay at my party, "I'll go down the hall to the ice machine."

When I picked up the ice bucket, Dashiell got up and went
to the door. I checked my pocket for the key. None of these guys
looked sober enough by now to get up and unlock the door for
me when I came back.

"Don't any of you touch my chips. I counted them."

"Ice," Boris said, clearly a man in need.

"Ice, ice, I'm going."

I didn't bother with my shoes. The hall carpeting was thick
and soft, and the maids vacuumed it every day. They were always
there, cleaning the hallways, early in the morning when I was

going out with Dashiell. Anyway, at that point, I wasn't sure where my shoes were.

When I got to the end of the corridor, there was a candy machine and an ice machine. But the ice machine wasn't working. Someone had taped a sign on it saying there was one on four. So I took the stairs, found the working ice machine, and scooped up a bucket full of ice so that Boris could chill the rest of the vodka properly. Next thing they'd be sending out to an all-night deli for more snack food.

I headed back to my room, swinging the ice bucket at my side as if I were Jill coming down the hill, and when I got to my door, Dashiell immediately welded his nose to the doorstop, hoping for a preview of Betty. I fished the key out of my pocket, blew the lint off it, and attempted to slip it into the lock. But it didn't seem to fit. I figure I must have had more to drink than I thought I did, because it wasn't until after my third try that I looked at the number on the door and saw that I was at 405. I heard a dog sniffing and sneezing near the saddle from the other side of the door, and though I clearly was not as sharp as I could have been, I knew it was a little dog, not a German shepherd.

I turned to go back to the stairs I'd come up, though I could just as well have used the stairs near the elevator. Just as I rounded the corner where the hallway dog-legged in another direction, I heard a door open behind me. But when I walked back to see who it was and to reassure whomever it was that it was only me, I found all the doors closed.

Downstairs, I headed back toward my room, padding quietly around the turn and then straight along the empty hall. My key still in my hand, I checked first to make sure it was the right room, then slipped it into my lock and opened the door.

Boris was out for the count. Stretched across the foot of my bed, snoring, he resembled a hibernating bear. Bucky had moved to the one upholstered chair, where he was asleep with Angelo curled on his lap. Chip had apparently stood up from where he'd been sitting on the window seat and was walking toward me. I heard the toilet flush, and Woody came out, barely looked at me, and lay down on the bed perpendicular to Boris, his head on one of the pillows, curled like spoons with Rhonda.

"Where's Martyn?" I whispered. "Are we playing cards or what?"

"It's nearly dawn, Rachel. Martyn's the only one here with any sense. He left shortly after you did. He said he was still jet-lagged and had to get some sleep. I'm going to do the same thing."

I felt a flutter of panic over Martyn, but if everyone else was here asleep, he'd be perfectly safe. I looked at my bed. Then at the chair. Then I looked at Chip. What if that weren't so? What if by separating, the men weren't safe? Wasn't the whole point of this to keep them together?

I grabbed Chip's shirt. "You can't leave me here like this." Joan Crawford, minus the shoulder pads.

He looked at me as if I were talking some foreign language he hadn't gotten around to learning. I thought I better try again.

"I thought maybe I could sleep in your room," I whispered, even though I probably wouldn't have been able to wake the others had I begun demolishing the room with a jackhammer. "It's a little crowded in here."

I watched him trying to figure out what it was I really wanted. Finally, he thought he had.

"Okay, Rachel, sure. Betty and I will stay here, and you can—"

"No. I wouldn't ask you to do that. It's bad enough we spent all these hours breathing smoke. Neither of us should—"

"You weren't merely breathing it, Kaminsky. As I recall, you were smoking."

"Don't get technical." It was a favorite line of my mother's when she'd been backed into a corner of her own making.

"So what is it you want, Rachel?"

Smooth, I thought. It's a good thing this guy was back with his Mrs., because God knows how he'd function as a single man. Maybe, unlike the rest of this motley crew, he was out of practice. One way or another, I had to get through to him, because if I couldn't protect them all, he was the one I couldn't afford to lose. It didn't matter that I was saving him for another woman, as long as I was saving him. I decided to do whatever it would take to not let Chip out of my sight. And then I knew exactly what it was I had to do. But I couldn't do it where we were.

"Come on," I said. I took his hand and pulled him with me toward the door. Out in the hall, the dogs began to run back and forth, Dash chasing Betty, then Betty chasing Dashiell. I held out my hand for Chip's key.

Inside his room, I put my hands on his shoulders. "Sit down." I backed him up to the bed and pushed him onto it.

"This is so sudden," he said. He pulled me onto him and was reaching for my face. Even before I became a detective, I knew where a move like that was going.

I shoved his hand away. "I need you to listen to me, very carefully. You can't do that with me lying on top of you. And I won't be able to speak if you're kissing me. I have to speak to you right now. And you have to listen."

"Did anyone ever tell you that you're beautiful when you're angry?" he said. "Come on." He rolled me off him, and we both sat up.

The dogs were nowhere in sight. Apparently they had gone into the bathroom to see if there was any food left in Betty's dish. A moment later Dashiell emerged from the bathroom backward. As soon as he was back in the bedroom, the growling stopped, and I could hear Betty's tags hitting rhythmically against the feed pan.

Chip got up and walked over to the nightstand to turn on the light. I noticed that there wasn't a picture of Ellen and the children there. Nor was there one on the dresser.

"Don't," I said.

I heard Betty's tags hit the tile floor. I couldn't see Dashiell, but I could hear him snoring.

"You want to talk in the dark?"

"It might be easier."

"Anything to please you," he said, his voice thick with emotion. Or was he just hoarse from hanging out in a smoke-filled room for most of the night? My throat was sore, too, and I couldn't stand the smell of the stale cigar smoke coming from my hair and clothes.

"May I use your shower?" I asked.

"That's the urgent thing you had to say?"

"No—I had too much to drink, and I can't stand the smell of smoke on myself. I'd like to take a shower and wake myself up, and then I have something important to say to you. Okay?"

Chip nodded. Without saying a word, he walked over to his dresser, opened the second drawer, took out a clean shirt, and handed it to me. "You might feel fresher in this. I'm going to stretch out my back and close my eyes until you're finished, then I'll do the same. Afterward, we can do whatever you like."

I didn't like the look in his eyes.

Well, I did. But I had something completely different in mind.

"Talk," I told him.

"Talk," he repeated, trying to keep a poker face.

Everything was aching. I decided on a bath instead of a shower. The radio was in the other room, where it belonged. I could hear it playing.

I emptied the complimentary bubble bath into the tub. I didn't think Chip would mind. Sliding into the hot water, I thought about what I wanted to say to him and how I'd put it. The next thing I knew, I was waking up in chilly water, the bubbles all gone, my mouth tasting like a sewer, complete with alligators.

I washed my hair, rinsed off, brushed my teeth with Chip's toothbrush, and got dressed.

The radio was still on, and Chip was lying on his side, his head on the pillow, both dogs up on the bed, mine pressed up against his back. They were all sleeping.

Apparently Betty had changed her tune again. She'd not only allowed Dashiell up on the bed but her head was lying across Chip's legs so that her muzzle was against Dashiell's ear, whispering sweet nothings as he slept blissfully.

I looked at the clock radio. It was morning—six-twenty-two, to be exact. We'd been asleep for nearly two hours.

I woke Chip and walked over to the window seat, moved the drape back, and sat against the wall on one side. I listened to the water running, then heard the faucet squeak again as Chip turned the water off. A few minutes later, wearing a navy blue T-shirt and khaki pants now, his feet bare, he came over and sat on the other side, facing me.

"I'm not here for the reason you think I am," I said.

With Chip sitting so close, his green eyes looking into mine, I understood what all those people had been doing here every night, leaving the loneliness of their own room and going to someone else's, where under a veil of alcohol and excitement and in the suspension of reality of being away from home, they would fall into the arms of a stranger, and for a moment there was that silent promise that what would follow would be perfect and different and for a few hours would make the world go very, very quiet and seem very far away.

"I'm here because Sam hired me to prevent the very thing that's been happening since we got here."

"And what would that be?"

"Murder."

"Rachel," he said, taking hold of my arms and pulling me against his chest, "it's all right. You're just tired," he said as if I were one of his children. "There've been a couple of terrible accidents, but no one—"

I pushed myself away. "No, you're wrong. They weren't accidents. Someone's winnowing away the competition. You've heard all the fighting, all the—"

"Rachel, are you telling me you think Bucky King or Martyn Eliot is a murderer? And anyway, what on earth do you mean Sam hired you to—"

"I'm not a dog trainer anymore. Since my divorce. I just couldn't go back to it. I don't know why. Well, you know what they say. One door closes. Another door opens. I'm a private investigator now. Sam hired me to work undercover because she was afraid—"

"A what?"

"A private investigator. This is real, Chip. It's not a joke."

"Okay. If it's real, show me your license."

He was trying to keep it serious, but his eyes were dancing with what he saw as the humor of the situation, same old, same old. Didn't we live to goof on each other? Hadn't we always done that? Or maybe he thought it was different this time, that I was too drunk to know fantasy from reality, that because of the alcohol I was telling a whopper of a story.

"I—"

"Come on. If you're a private investigator, show me your license."

I just sat there.

"You know what a license is, don't you? One of those little laminated things with your picture on it you keep in your wallet and whip out on occasions such as this."

"I never got one."

"I see." The way he was grinning, you'd think he'd just won the lottery.

"No, you don't see. I work without a license. I didn't want to do all the paperwork, but that doesn't mean—"

"Then your business card. Surely, you have a business card, Rachel. Show me." He held his hand out.

I took a card out of my wallet and handed it to him.

"Rachel Alexander, research assistance?"

"It's just that. . . I mean, you don't want to put on a business card . . . I work mainly on referrals, and the thing is, people need answers, you see, and I do the research necessary to help them find out what it is they need to know. Understand?"

"And tonight?" He reached out and took my hand. "It's okay," he whispered. "It's okay."

He'd figured it out. Or so he thought. I had changed my mind about the meaningless roll in the hay and didn't know how to say it.

I took my hand back.

"I don't know who is doing this. I don't know when it's going to happen next. I suggested the poker game because it seems evident that men are the targets here. And when I couldn't keep it going any longer—" I turned toward the window, but the sun hurt my eyes. I looked back at Chip. "When you got up to leave, I thought that if anything happened to you, I'd never forgive myself."

"Rachel—"

I held up my hand like a Supreme. "Let me finish," I said.

"That's very sweet, really, that you're a PI and you're going to protect me." He couldn't hold it in any longer. He was laughing out loud now. "Maybe vodka's not your drink," he said. "Anyway, you've forgotten about Betty."

"No, I haven't." I was really annoyed now, and it must have been evident, because Chip had stopped laughing. "Dashiell will protect Betty."

"No, I mean I have Betty to protect me."

"See if you can follow this," I said. "I was a dog trainer. I'm no longer a dog trainer. I'm an unlicensed private investigator working undercover. I know it's pretty complicated, a lot to absorb at once, so how about if you don't worry your pretty little head about any of this. I'll do the thinking for both of us."

"Seriously, Rachel. Enough kidding around. Even if what you say is true," he said, and I could see that he was humoring me, "you don't need to protect me."

"I do," I told him. "Look, we only have a few hours. You take the bed. I'll curl up in the chair. Just make believe I'm not here, okay?"

I moved over to the chair to try to catch some sleep. Chip sat there in the window seat, nervous as a mouse in the terrier ring, not knowing what to make of this. I closed my eyes, trying not to think about the way he smelled, like taking a walk in the woods early in the morning, when the mist is just lifting and everything is fresh. Oh, hell, it was probably aftershave.

I heard him get up and hoped he'd get into bed. But he didn't. He had come over to where I was and he was leaning down over me, his hands on the arms of the chair. I opened my eyes and looked into his, moss green with flecks of brown in them. And for just a moment I thought of something I'd left in my room, carefully wrapped in tissue paper that had been sprinkled with

rose water. Less is more, I thought. And less of what I was thinking was exactly what I needed.

I tried to push him away. I thought I'd go back to where I'd
been, sit in the window seat, looking out at Central Park. It would
help me to keep my mind where it belonged. But Chip's arms
stayed put, and when I tried to duck under one of them, he
stopped me with a hand on my collar, like a mother dog picking
up an errant pup by the scruff of its neck.

"I listened to you. Now you listen to me."

"I don't think there's anything else to say. I know you think
I'm full of hot air, so—"

"It's not about that, Rachel. It's about me, about us."

I sat up straight, my back pressed against the back of the
chair. "There is no *us*, Chip. You're a married man."

Who was I fooling? Certainly not Chip.

He squatted in front of the chair, his hands on my knees.
"Remember I told you at Westminster I'd gotten divorced? I'm
still divorced."

"Well, so what? That's just a technicality, isn't it? You're
living at home again, what difference does it make if there's a
piece of paper or not?"

"No difference at all."

"So, then what is this all about?"

"Rachel, I've tried to talk to you so many times this week,
and you just keep blowing me off."

"You said what you have to say. That you've gone back to
your family, and I've wished you good luck, so what else—"

He shook his head. "I've been trying to tell you. That's not
the end of it. That was the beginning, what happened right after
I saw you last time, when I said I'd call you. I moved back in with
Ellen and the kids, that's true, but it didn't work out. The recon-
ciliation was a flop."

I sat there saying nothing, just looking at him long enough for human beings to crawl out of the sea, stand upright, and invent no-iron cotton.

"Why didn't you just say so?" I finally asked.

"I've been trying to, Rachel, since Sunday. You kept interrupting me or running away. Three months after the divorce, I moved back in. But it was all wrong. We both knew it. Ellen's thinking of moving back to California, to be near her family. That's why I took this job, so that I could give her the money to help her with the move. Sometimes—" he whispered, "whenever I saw you, Rachel, I—"

I reached out to pull him close. It seems I'd waited forever for this moment.

That's when I heard the knock. Well, it was more like banging. Only it wasn't on Chip's door. It was on mine, next door. It was Sam. I could hear her calling my name.

We jumped up and ran to the door, pulling it open at the same moment my door opened.

"What? What is it? Why you wake Boris?" He stood there scratching his hairy stomach, which was sticking out of his open shirt.

Woody was already in the hallway, standing next to Sam.

But his hair was wet. And he wasn't wearing what he'd worn at the poker game.

I walked into the hall and looked past Boris to see if Bucky were there, but it was only Boris. He was the only rat that hadn't deserted the stinking ship.

Sam looked at me, then at Chip, then back at me.

"What *is* it?" I asked her.

But she didn't answer me. What the hell was going on? I wondered. Had she made all this fuss just to tell me she'd finally found Mr. Wright?

But her cheeks weren't flushed. Even with makeup on, she looked as if she needed a transfusion.

"Someone else is dead." Her voice was barely above a whisper now. "They've just found the body."

"Who? Who's dead?"

Sam turned away. I saw her shoulders shaking.

Woody reached out and took my hand in both of his.

"It's Martyn," he said.

I pulled away and began to shake my head, as if saying no could make this nightmare go away.

"How?" Chip asked.

"Suicide."

"No *way*," I said. "You can't be serious."

"Unfortunately, I am. The porter found him on the sidewalk as he was coming in a little while ago."

"Why he do that?" Boris asked.

Sam faced us again, wiping her eyes with the heels of her hands, smearing her mascara onto her temples. "The police are on the way. Let's get downstairs. I'm sure they'll have questions, particularly for those of you who were at the poker game."

She turned and headed for the elevator, Woody on one side, Boris on the other in his stocking feet.

I started to pull Chip's door closed, but he stopped me, pointing to his bare feet. We stood for a moment in the hallway, looking into each other's eyes, neither of us saying a word. Then he went inside for his shoes, and we headed downstairs to wait for the police.

KEEP YOUR DAY JOB, I TOLD HIM

Who had opened her door when I was coming back with the ice? Had that been Cathy, hoping it was Martyn, even though she knew there was another baby on the way at home in England? Had he managed to explain that away too, the way he'd explained away Graeme and Sheila and his wife, sitting with Cathy during Rick's last talk and laying it on with a steam shovel?

Sam, Woody, and Boris were nowhere in sight. I heard a siren in the distance, but I couldn't be sure if it was coming our way. There were so many accidents in the city.

I grabbed Chip's hand as he reached for the elevator button.

"I need a favor. I need the key to Martyn's room, or better yet, a passkey. The passkey would be in the office. I have a feeling that the old man won't be at his post, but out front where all the excitement is. Just have a lie ready, in case the old coot should come back and catch you in the office, which he probably won't."

Chip was looking at me as if he'd never seen me before, as if I were some stranger who had grabbed his hand in the hallway of a hotel and was in the middle of telling him some fantastic tale.

"Don't get too fancy. He's really gullible. You can tell him you were looking for a phone, to call the police. Tell him anything. Just get me the key and meet me at Martyn's room. I have something I have to do first."

I started for the stairs and then remembered something else. "403," I said. "If you get there first, don't go in without me."

He took my face in both hands and kissed me hard and fast on the mouth, then headed down the stairs. I headed up.

Sky barked even before I knocked. I could hear Cathy telling him, "Leave it." A moment later she was standing in the doorway in her unbleached, organic nightshirt, her eyes red and puffy, a disappointed look on her face.

"It's only me," I said, wondering if I should break her heart the rest of the way before I asked my questions or after. "Can I come in?"

Five minutes later I was across the hall, and Chip was slipping the passkey into the lock on Martyn's door.

"Don't touch anything," I said. "Just stand here in the doorway with me."

"What are we looking for?"

"An open window."

"It's closed," he whispered.

"Why are you whispering?"

"It seemed appropriate."

"I didn't think this is where it happened. I just wanted to make sure before the police get here and seal off the room. And one more thing," I said, bending down and looking under the neatly made bed. "Okay, we can go."

"What were you looking for under the bed, the traditional prowler?"

"Keep your day job," I told him. "A tennis ball. A scented one."

"Sky's? You mean Cathy was with him?"

"Yes, but not this morning. Still, if the cops found Sky's ball in there, they'd put her through hell."

"Okay, so Cathy had a thing with Martyn, is that what you're saying? And then what? He—"

"Don't even say it. No matter what this looks like, you know Martyn didn't do this himself."

"But you don't think Cathy—"

"No, but the only one I *know* didn't do it is you."

"You don't know that. You fell asleep in the bathtub, remember? I could have slipped out."

He was right. He could have.

What did I know about this man, anyway? Had I ever seen him take out the garbage or scramble eggs? Did I know if he hung up his clothes or threw them over the dresser for the wife to hang up, the way Jack had? Or if he had to have his dinner on the table the second he walked in the door the way my brother-in-law did, tap, tap, tapping on his stomach to show Lillian how hungry he was? Or if he used the force majeure clause as an excuse to break the contract he'd made with Ellen?

But then I thought, no, I did know him. Okay, I didn't know if he helped with the dishes or if he handled money well. But I knew how seriously he took his marriage vows—hell, if he was breaking them, wouldn't he have tried to break them with me, years ago?

"Did you?" I asked. "Did you slip out and push Martyn to his death?"

"No."

"I didn't think so. Let's get out of here."

We headed for the stairs.

"It's a schlep, but we have to walk."

He started down. I grabbed his sleeve and pointed up.

"The roof. We can't take the elevator because the cops are going to question Jimmy, and he'd tell them we went up there."

"Why would Martyn have gone up there?"

"I wish I knew. I wish I knew a lot more than that."

We walked for a while in silence.

"Rachel, why were you looking for Sky's tennis ball in Martyn's room?"

"Just to double-check. I don't know if Sky was with her, but if he was, he wouldn't have gone without his ball."

"That's not what I meant. Couldn't they have been in her room? Martyn didn't have a dog to worry about."

"It seems the females go to the males, just like in dog breeding."

With dogs, the bitch does the traveling, often by plane. The stud dog stays home, where he feels calm, confident, and relaxed. At home, feeling his oats, the stud dog is less likely to disappoint, more likely to perform.

Partway down the hall on five was the door to the roof, locked up tight, just as it had been when I'd photographed it on Sunday. There was a sign, too. It said No Entry. I wondered if I was right, thinking that this was where Martyn had been when he fell.

Chip reached for the door.

"Wait. Let me do this. This is the last place in the world you want to leave your prints."

I took two dog bags out of my pocket and put them on as gloves. Then I used the passkey and pushed the door open with my shoulder. There was a narrower flight of stairs behind the door, this one not carpeted. The door up top was a fire door. You could open it from the inside, but not from the outside without a key. I pushed it open with the side of my arm, and we walked out onto the tar roof.

There beneath us was Central Park, and beyond, the skyline of Fifth Avenue. On the roof there were exhaust fans and vents, a water tank, and an equipment shed. We walked forward, as cautiously as if we each thought the other was the one who had pushed Martyn off a few hours earlier.

Once at the edge, we leaned forward to look down so that we could locate the spot from which Martyn had gone over. I could feel a sour taste in my throat, and my knees seemed to be made of sand as I looked down to the sidewalk.

"Are you okay?" He took my arm.

"Just glad I haven't had breakfast yet." I stepped back from the edge.

"There's a little ledge down here," Chip said, still looking over the parapet.

"Big enough to stand on?"

"Not big enough for me to stand on."

"Are you thinking Martyn did? That he climbed down onto it and jumped?"

I stepped forward again, trying not to imagine toppling over and landing on the sidewalk below, right beside Martyn. Hands on the wall, one I would have made about three feet higher, I crouched low before looking down at the ledge, so I wouldn't be seen if anyone below looked up.

"There's Martyn," I whispered. He was lying on his back, one arm flung up over his head, the other at his side. His legs were apart. The way one turned in, you could see it was broken, even from up here. He looked almost like a rag doll, the way he lay there, so small and far away, so flat and still.

"The ledge is covered with pigeon droppings, feathers, and lots of good old-fashioned New York dirt. If Martyn had climbed down onto it, that mess there would have been disturbed."

Chip crouched next to me. "It is, sort of. There's one spot that looks cleaner than the rest of it. And it's right above where Martyn landed."

"Must have been from one of the birds. It's too small to have been made by Martyn standing there. He didn't jump, Chip. He was pushed. Three people can't have died accidentally in one hotel in just a few days. It just couldn't happen."

I duck-walked backward and stood, looking around the roof. It was spring, no snow to show footprints of Martyn or his killer. It hadn't rained either. There was nothing on the stairs we had climbed to get here. There was one thing, something black lying next to one of the huge exhaust fans.

"Chip, look."

"Is that Martyn's, do you think?"

"I do. I think it's the one he used in the temperament test."

The umbrella was closed, lying on the side of the fan farthest from the door to the roof. The little band that held the ribs neatly together was fastened, so that it almost appeared to be a cane.

"What's *that* all about? Was he going to float down to the street, as if he were the Penguin?"

"No. This was a temperament test."

"What was?"

"This murder."

"What do you mean?"

"I don't have the answer yet," I told him, starting to feel like a broken record, "but whatever happened here began as a test of Martyn's character. It was something clever, something he'd have to respond to. You know, the cops always say how dumb criminals are, that if they were half as smart as they thought they were, the detectives would be out of work because they'd never catch any of them. But whoever did this was no dummy. Come on. Let's get out of here before the detectives arrive, because you better believe if I thought to check out the roof, they will too."

"There won't be any prints on the umbrella, will there?"

"Other than Martyn's? No. Whoever is doing this is too damn smart to leave a signature."

We took the stairs down to the lobby, thinking our own thoughts as we walked. The old man still wasn't behind the desk.

"Shall I put the passkey back?" Chip whispered.

"No. We're going to need it again later."

"We are?"

"Yeah, I don't know when we're going to be able to squeeze it in—you're talking this morning, and we have the panel this afternoon. But there's at least one more room we have to get into today."

He held the front door for me. The police had arrived and were milling around waiting for the medical examiner to show up. From the top of the stairs, we could see Martyn splayed out on the sidewalk.

"Do you see a pattern in any of this?"

I looked up at the roof. I remembered looking up at it from across the street, after taking Dashiell to the park. The building seemed to have grown taller since then, the roof seemed so far above the cold, hard sidewalk below it.

"Yes and no. Rick and Martyn were killed—"

"None of this is what it appears to be?"

"None of this and probably not much about us—I don't mean *us*," I said, "I mean the other speakers. Rick and Martyn were killed after they spoke, but Alan was killed prior to his lecture. On the other hand, Alan's shtick is so blatant, why would anyone have to wait to hear him speak to want to kill him? Everyone already knew what he did and hated him for it. Well, almost everyone."

"What do you mean?"

"He had company his last night on earth."

"Who?"

"I don't know. Sam tried to make me think it was she, but I don't believe her."

"Rachel, why did you think I was in danger last night? No one knows much of anything about me. I haven't done a book, like Alan. I haven't done TV, like Bucky. And I haven't spoken yet."

"But you have. After the tracking demo."

"But that was—"

"Precisely. Only for the speakers."

"What about Boris? He spoke. Shit, he's irritated the hell out of everyone, repeatedly. How come he's still among the living?"

"I don't know. Maybe because of Sasha. None of the men who were killed were here with a protection-trained dog."

"Still, Rachel, he's not with Sasha all the time. He wasn't with him last night. Everyone knew where he was, where we all were."

"Maybe he's the doer," I said.

But what had Boris done that would make me suspect him—pretend he was a "wegetarian", that he was the world's greatest animal lover and didn't eat them the way the rest of us do?

Of course he had a temper. But everyone does, when you think about it. Maybe his boiling point was on the low side, but whoever did the killings seemed to me to be pretty cool, not a hothead like Boris. You couldn't be so neat, so clever, if you were working in the heat of passion. Or could you?

"What are you saying, that he could have gotten up and left

after we did, then gone back to your room afterward and gone back to sleep? Or pretended to? But if he could have, then Woody could have. Or Bucky."

"I don't know what to think. I mean, yeah, it's possible it was Boris. I suppose anything's possible. But what would the motive be? If it's competition, shit, Martyn wasn't taking dog jobs away from Boris. He was in England half the year. The other half he spent teaching seminars. He didn't take private clients in this country at all. He didn't have a book—and if he did, it would have nothing to do with Boris's book. Boris, God bless him, is in a class by himself, and no matter what you think of his methods, he sells, year in, year out. The more things change, the more they seem to stay the same."

"What about the other two?"

"Bucky and Woody?"

"Right."

"Why? What's the motive?"

He shrugged. "I don't know."

"Me neither. That's the problem. If I knew *why*, I mean *really* knew why, not all this guessing, I'd know *who*."

"So now what?"

"Well, first the cops grill us under hot lights while we squeal and writhe, claiming we have a right to call our lawyers." I watched the dark blue circle form around Martyn, listening to the sound of an ambulance approaching.

"And then?"

"Then we get breakfast," I said, unable to take my eyes off the spectacle on the sidewalk and hoping like hell I'd figure out who was doing this before the next sad, gruesome scene.

"And after that?"

"You deliver your talk on aggression. And while you do, I see if I can get my hands on the phone records."

"How? The hotel won't just give them to you, will they?"

"No. But they have to give them to Sam. She's the one who has to pay the bill."

Sam and Woody were standing near the body in a sea of uniforms.

"She's not going to be happy if they want to stop the symposium," I whispered.

"She may not have a choice now."

"She's pretty persuasive. Look at the group she assembled here."

Sam and Woody were talking to Detective DeAndrea now. Woody seemed to be doing most of the talking, but I had the feeling he was speaking with Sam's agenda in mind.

"I'll be back in the auditorium before the end of your talk."

"And?"

"I don't know yet, but I think we need to stick together."

"Good idea," he said. "But we shouldn't walk out at the same time."

"Why not?"

He shrugged. "That's what they always say in the movies. I've been watching a lot of bad TV lately," he said, "late-night movies. Keep my mind off my troubles."

"Does it work?"

"No," he said. "Not one tiny little bit. So where were you when I was stealing the passkey?"

"Last night, when I went for the ice, I went down the wrong corridor. Too much vodka. Instead of going back to three, I stayed on four. I ended up trying to fit my key into Beryl's door."

"The old broad must have demolished you for waking her."

"But I didn't. She doesn't sleep with her hearing aid in. Never heard a thing. Then, when I was walking back down the corridor to come back to three, I heard a door open. At the time,

I thought maybe I was wrong, maybe Cecilia woke her when she heard me at the door. I went back to apologize, to tell her not to be alarmed, it was only me. But when I got back to that part of the hallway, all the doors were closed. This morning, it occurred to me it might have been Cathy, that she might have waited up for Martyn. I thought maybe if she'd seen him, or talked to him, we might learn something helpful."

"What did she say?"

"That she had waited up. She hadn't meant to, but she was crying and couldn't sleep."

"Over Martyn?"

"Yeah. Man, he laid some real big line on her about how fucked-up his wife is, that he might leave her later on, and Cathy apparently went for it in a big way. Anyway, then subsequently, someone let her know he and the Mrs. were expecting another kid, just to see her reaction."

"Who did that?"

I winced. "Me. I had to check out Martyn's story, try to find out what was really going on. That's my job."

"And?"

"And I felt I had confirmed my suspicion that they'd been together when I saw the steam coming out of Cathy's ears, so to speak."

"But you don't think she—"

"Gut feeling? No. Sky must have heard me. She said she opened the door and thought, What am I thinking? and closed it without ever looking out. Martyn must have gone down the other way. We probably missed each other by seconds."

"You believe her?"

"I do," I said. "Something has to tie all this together. True, Martyn lied to her and hurt her. For some, that could be a reason to kill. People kill for a lot less."

"For leather jackets, sneakers, sunglasses, a buck fifty, an imagined insult."

"True."

"So?"

"Okay, suppose Cathy did kill Martyn. What about the other two? Can you figure out something that makes sense where Cathy killed them all? You know, I was thinking along those lines at first, the black widow spider bit. But I can't get it to make sense."

"That's because you're convinced it's a man."

"Maybe so."

"Fewer assumptions that way," he said. "If it's business, killing off the competition, it's easier to believe, more straightforward."

"Occam's razor."

"Exactly."

"Except that that's science. This is human emotion, twisted all out of shape. So in this case, choosing the simplest explanation may not lead us to the killer. It's true that sometimes—often—the cops find someone dead, they go right to the doer, the husband, the boyfriend, the business partner, the whatever. And sometimes the trigger is something that to others would seem so small, the sting of an insult, something said in front of others that causes humiliation. Or worse, the insult resonates in the heart of one human being, because it turns out it's something they have always secretly believed to be true about themselves.

"But there are times when the motive is convoluted, complex, dense, the result of an event that happened long ago that floats back up to the surface after years of remaining buried, God knows why. Sometimes—"

"I get it, Rachel."

"Well, I don't. I don't know who, and I don't know why, and

it's eating me alive. It's hell not knowing, not being able to stop it."

He shook his head. "No, Rachel, it's work. Hell is something far more personal."

It was personal for me. But I didn't say so. Chip was looking elsewhere, thinking other thoughts. Besides, Detective Flowers was headed our way.

"They're going to talk to us separately," I said. "Leave out the part about the passkey, okay?"

"Count on it," he said. He slid his hand into his pocket and slipped the passkey into my hand. "I wasn't planning on mentioning violating the crime scene either. So unless they sweat it out of me, I'll see you at breakfast."

"Okay."

But I wasn't thinking about breakfast. I was thinking about what he'd said a minute ago, that I was convinced it was a man. I began wondering if the cops would be thinking the same way.

I turned my back to the approaching detective. "Say we were together all night," I whispered.

"We were," he said. But he wasn't looking at me. He was looking over my shoulder.

I could hear her heels clicking on the pavement. I turned around. She had great legs, for a cop.

"Ms. Alexander, Mr. Pressman, I didn't expect to be seeing either of you again so soon."

There was a bit of early-morning frost in her voice.

Too much, if you ask me.

And now it was too late to tell Chip to leave out the part about us both falling asleep. If he included that little detail, I couldn't be his alibi.

Nor, should it be necessary, would he be able to be mine.

WHAT'S WITH YOU PEOPLE? HE ASKED

I sat in the back of the auditorium, slouched down in my seat, my ankles resting on Dashiell's back, listening to Sam introducing Chip. Even from this far back, I could see that her hands were trembling, and I could hear the strain in her voice, but she was a trouper at heart, and the threat of bankruptcy aside, she knew that for all our sakes, the show must go on.

When she finished talking about Chip, and while the audience were putting their hands together to give him the warm welcome she'd suggested he so richly deserved, she left the stage and took a seat in the front row, off to the side. Right next to Woody Wright. I wanted to talk to her alone, so I sent Dashiell to get her.

Chip had gotten up, and so had Betty. When he walked up to the mike, she did, too. Only a couple of people had noticed. I could hear them laughing, and when Chip did, he looked down at her standing at his side and shrugged.

"Shepherds are more prone to allelomimetic behavior than

most other dog breeds," he said, "and this is as good a place as any to begin this morning." His posture was relaxed, and so was Betty's. When he looked around the room, making eye contact with one person in the audience and then another, Betty did too. Monkey see, monkey do. Which was the principle of allelomimetic behavior.

Dashiell was making his way down the aisle to where Sam was sitting, walking slowly, wagging his tail as he walked, the note I'd written her rolled up and stuck under his collar, sticking up over his head like a feather.

"This means that the dog views herself, in this case, as a member of a group, and acts the way the other group members behave, especially the highest-ranked member of the group. In Betty's case, that's me, and this morning we are going to talk about why that's appropriate, but also about how that can sometimes be the cause of the aggression we are trying to stop.

"It's mostly the attitude of alpha that is aped, which of course means that if you are alert, worried, angry, relaxed, frightened, or happy, your dog will tend to be, too. In Betty's case, well, she also tends to mimic postures and activities. Which is sometimes humorous. But it is the mimicking of attitudes and feelings that is the real issue for us today."

I watched Sam pull the note out of Dash's collar, read it, and then turn around to look for me. She whispered something to Woody, then got up and followed Dashiell back to where I was sitting.

"I need to check the phone records. Can you get them for me?"

"Rachel, what on earth is happening here?"

"What did the police say?"

"Not much. They're asking questions, not answering them. Did they talk to you?"

I nodded. "They did. But I'm still on the loose."

"We all are. But I'm starting to wonder if we all should be."

"Me, too. That's why I need the—"

"I'll be right back."

I looked around the auditorium for our dwindling group. I spotted everyone but Cathy, but I could pretty well guess where she was and what she was doing.

After Sam handed me the phone bills and went back to her seat in the front of the auditorium, I slipped out the back and headed for the elevator. After walking all the way up to the roof, I didn't want to see the stairs again for a while.

Jimmy tucked himself against the wall and pulled the gate closed.

"Three," I said.

"I know. I know." He was looking forward, not at me and Dashiell. "What's with you people?" he asked. "You're dropping like flies."

We landed on three, and Jimmy opened the door. The hall was empty as far as I could see, all the way to the bend.

"How'd that feller get up on the roof this morning? That's what I want to know. It's locked up tight."

"Was that what the police said, that he jumped off the roof?"

"Insurance," he said, sounding just like his dad. "Got to keep it locked."

"Is it possible someone left the door unlocked?" I asked him. "You know, last time they were up there, checking the exhaust fans or whatever."

"Door self-locks. Just like the rooms. Closes and locks without a key."

"Anyone missing a passkey?"

He stuck his skinny neck out of the cage, checking out the empty hallway. Then he stood straight as a lamppost in his little corner, chin in, hands on the wheel. "I wouldn't know about that, missus," he said.

Yeah, right.

"I thought maybe your dad might have mentioned something," I said, sticking my hand in my pocket, pulling out a twenty, folding it in half, then in half again. Money talks, they say. I wanted to see if it was so.

Jimmy cleared his throat. "Didn't," he said. "The mean old coot. I hardly talk to him, if I can avoid it."

"Well, thank the good Lord you're an adult. At least you don't have to live with him."

"But I do. It's my duty, he says, as his son. What kind of a man would leave his old da alone? he asks me, any damn time I even think about moving out. He can read my mind, that one. And he's mean. Always has been. He's not going to change now."

"Guess not," I said. "Well, thanks for the ride. And for trying to answer my question. I know you would have if you could have." I handed him the twenty and walked off the elevator. But then I stopped, because I didn't hear the gate closing.

"Maid said one was missing," he told my back.

I turned around.

"Is that a fact?"

"Mercedes. The redhead? One that found the body in the bathtub," he whispered. He stepped out of the elevator now, stood next to me in the hallway. "Asked me what to do. Was afraid she'd get fired."

"How'd she lose it?"

"Didn't lose it," he said. "Someone swiped it off her cart. Happens from time to time. A guest forgets to pick up the key at the front desk and doesn't want the bother of going all the way back downstairs again, so he picks up the maid's key. Wouldn't be so bad if he were decent enough to put it back. I told her it happens, told her just like I told you, but don't tell the manager, I said. He might not be so understanding. She said the door was propped open—you don't prop it, it locks. Always leaves it open when she's cleaning. Feels safer that way. Cart was right in front of the doorway. Someone would have had to move it to get in the room. Didn't see anyone near the cart. Doesn't know how it could have happened. I said, Don't you worry. I'll get you another one. Told Pop to go get hisself a coffee, I'd watch the front. She's supporting a little girl and her mum. Can't have her losing her job."

We heard the buzzer ring inside the cage.

"Thanks, Jimmy."

"Now, don't go telling nobody what I told you, get Mercedes fired."

"You can trust me," I told him, heading for my room to go snooping around in other people's business.

I got back downstairs in time to hear the end of Chip's talk. Sam was sitting in the back now.

"There you are," she said. "I looked around for you in the break, but I didn't see you."

"Headache," I said. "I went upstairs for a while."

She nodded. "Do you need an aspirin?"

"No, I'm better now. Any news?"

"Detective DeAndrea came by. He said they're going to handle Martyn's death as a homicide. I'm not sure what their thinking is. It's possible they're doing this because of the children. Martyn's wife can't collect on his insurance if his death goes on the books as a suicide."

"They know about his children?"

"They asked about his family," Sam said, "where they were, if he got along with them, if he'd had any phone calls in the last twenty-four hours, something that might have upset him, if he seemed depressed, all of that."

"And you said?"

"That he was a devoted husband and father, that he didn't seem in the least bit depressed. What did you find in the phone records?"

"I haven't had the chance to look at them yet," I lied.

She was looking up at the stage.

"He's so good at this. Listen to him, Rachel."

"And you will have to keep reminding your clients—once will not be enough to say it," Chip was saying, "that when they allow an aggressive dog up on the bed or couch, the message the dog receives, loud and clear, is, We are equals. It's far more appropriate for the aggressive dog to have to work for what he gets, to live in a no-free-lunch culture, because if he keeps getting the wrong message, the message that he rather than his owner is in charge, eventually his aggression will be impossible to contain."

Betty was lying down, her pretty paws hanging off the front of the stage. Every once in a while she'd close her eyes. But you could tell she wasn't asleep. Her breathing pattern never varied.

I closed my eyes too, listening to the sound of Chip's voice but not his words. One of us was imitating behavior, too, the behavior of a professional colleague, blending in, acting like part of the group while carrying on some sinister project at the same time.

I knew how the passkey was stolen without Mercedes seeing anyone near the cart. The thief was short enough not to show when he or she was on the far side of the little wagon that held all the cleaning supplies, the free bubble bath, and the key that fit every lock in the hotel. It was a piece of cake for me to figure out how. Now all I needed to know was who: Who had sent the dog to steal the passkey, who had unlocked the door to the roof, whose aggression had become impossible to contain.

"He seems at ease in front of an audience. I don't know why he doesn't do this more often."

"Well, after this experience," I said, looking up at Chip on the stage, "nothing personal, Sam, but I wouldn't count on him ever doing it again."

"He may not be the only one," she said. She was picking the red polish off her nails. Little chips of it, like flakes of dried blood, were all over her skirt.

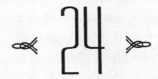

GOOD BOY, I SAID

I waited for Chip at the back of the auditorium, watching him taking people's hands as they spoke to him, looking at them as if each were the most important person on the face of the earth, and he had nothing more urgent to do than listen to their concerns.

When he finally got away, we left the empty auditorium and took the dogs across the street to the park.

"Something really strange is going on this week."

"Tell me about it," Chip said.

Dashiell had turned to look at me for direction. I nodded my head to the right, and he ran ahead off the path and into a copse of trees.

"I wish I could. That's the problem, I have all these pieces of information that don't fit together."

"Wouldn't that indicate that there are still pieces missing?"

I thought about that. "Okay, suppose we don't rule out anything that happened," I said. "What do we know? Three men have been killed, all after their ideas on dog training were expressed. Alan hadn't delivered his talk yet, but with Alan, it was coming out of his pores. Everyone knew how he worked, and they all hated it. In addition, he insulted everyone he could, given the constraints of the short time he had in which to do so."

"What about Rick and Martyn?"

"You know how dog people are—love my method, love me. If the opposite was true in Alan's case, why not for Rick and Martyn? They surely had their detractors too.

He nodded. "And Boris. You think Sasha protected him, or he'd be dead, too? And that I'm next?"

"There's one more element here that I discarded with Sam's encouragement."

"Ah, sex rears its ugly head."

"Precisely. Each of the three victims spent the night before they were killed having sex."

Chip looked puzzled, and then he began to laugh.

"And you think I might be next on the killer's list?"

I nodded.

"Did I miss something, Kaminsky? Did you molest me in my sleep? I hate when that happens."

"In your dreams, Pressman."

"Then why do you think I'm in danger?"

He'd stopped walking and had turned to face me, the humor now gone from his eyes.

"Because we're the only ones who know for sure what we did."

"To the best of my recollection, we didn't *do* anything."

"Okay, then we're the only ones who know for sure what we *didn't* do."

"And we can't exactly advertise it, can we?"

I shook my head. "Who would believe us?"

"Not the cops," he said. "I'm sure from the look I saw passing between DeAndrea and O'Shea."

"What do you mean?"

"At first they only seemed interested in the fact that you were out of the room at the same time Martyn was."

"But that was barely five minutes. Did you tell them that?"

"I did. And I told them that until Sam showed up to tell us about Martyn, you weren't out of my sight. So then they wanted to know what we were doing for all those hours."

"And you said?"

"That we were talking."

"We were."

"Exactly."

I took a deep breath. "Okay, no big deal, right?"

"It didn't stop there."

"It didn't?"

He shook his head. "They wanted to know what we were talking about."

"That's weird. When they questioned me, they mainly wanted to know what I did when I was out of the room and if I saw anyone else in the hallway. But they didn't ask me what we were talking about." I screwed up my face. "Did you tell them?"

"Of course. I told them we were discussing positive and negative reinforcement."

"Good boy," I said. "Did they buy it?"

"We're here, aren't we? Not in jail. But I doubt very strongly that they believe we were talking about dog training all night."

"Then they don't know dog people."

"Apparently not. They asked me about phone calls, too—did Martyn receive any during the poker game? Did he leave the game to make or receive a phone call?"

"And you said?"

"That there were no calls for anyone during the game, and Martyn left because he was still jet-lagged. At least, that was the reason he gave. If it wasn't the truth, well, how would I know that? They were making notes like crazy, as if I'd actually told them something important."

"They were making a note to check the hotel's phone records. They'd have all the incoming and outgoing calls. It's SOP. I have a set right here," I said, opening my jacket where the folded papers were sticking out of the inside breast pocket.

"Let's have a look," he said.

He whistled to the dogs to let them know we were stopping, and we sat on a big rock that could have been flatter and more comfortable but wasn't. I pulled out the phone bills for each of our rooms and opened them up.

"It's not what you think," he said. "I call to say good night to the kids, not to speak to Ellen."

"I didn't say a word."

"Well, I just thought—"

"You think too much." I put that page in the back and we looked at the calls from Martyn's room. There were two calls to England.

"I guess he called to say good night to his kids, too," Chip said. "Twenty-seven bucks for one call. Eleven ninety-five for the other. I hope that's cool with Sam."

"That's not our concern," I said. "It's Sam's. We're looking for missing pieces, for something that might tie these deaths together."

"Like if we found out that it was all the same woman, sleeping with each of them and then killing them afterward. Are the room-to-room calls listed as well as the outside calls?"

"Unfortunately not."

"What's that local call that Martyn made? Were you able to check that?"

"Read it to me," I said, pulling my cell phone out of my pocket. I punched in the number and waited for someone to pick up, smiling when they finally did. "Oh, sorry. Wrong number," I said into the phone. "It's the gift shop at the zoo," I told Chip. "He bought some puppets for his kids there. But he didn't buy them when he said he did. See, the call was made on Sunday, check-in day. He must have been calling to see if they were open. If he used his credit card or saved the receipt, I'd bet it was dated Sunday as well. Later, when I sat with him at breakfast and he showed me the puppets, he said he'd bought them for the children the afternoon before, which is the afternoon he spent with Cathy."

"Sounds like a man who's used to covering his tracks."

"It does indeed."

"Maybe the calls to England weren't to his kids, Rachel. They're young, aren't they?"

"Young enough to still get a kick out of hand puppets."

"Well, how long can you stay on the phone with a little kid? Maybe he's got a girlfriend back in England, too."

"Could be he said good night to the kids and then talked to his wife."

"Twenty-seven bucks' worth? Given his track record, I somehow doubt it. Unless that's how he expiates his guilt?"

"Let's find out right now. Let's boot up Sam's computer and see if that's his home number."

"Do you have access to her computer?"

"Not exactly."

"Then what?"

"I'm a detective, aren't I?"

"You're going to break into Sam's room?"

"Not exactly."

"Then what?"

"By a stroke of good fortune, a friend of mine, well, this thief I happen to know, stole a passkey for me."

"Was that the other room you were referring to earlier? You said not to return the key because there was at least one more room you had to get into."

I nodded.

"Rachel, you're working for Sam. Why do this behind her back? Why not just ask her for access?"

"She's already lied to me once. At least, I'm pretty sure she has. I'd rather be able to check this out myself without Sam breathing down my neck. There's a conflict of interests here. She needs to keep this thing going, because she's spent a fortune on it. I need to find out all I can, no matter where it leads. Or to whom. It doesn't matter who's paying me. The truth is all that counts. Because that's the only thing that's going to stop this."

I folded the phone records and put them back in that inside pocket. "Come on. If we go now, we still have time to do this while Sam's at lunch."

We put the dogs on leash and headed out of the park. Waiting for the light to change, we stood next to a boy with a white rat hanging halfway out of his shirt pocket, its nose vibrating a mile a minute—like there aren't enough rats in the city already, you have to go out and buy one.

Once inside, we rang for Jimmy, then waited for the elevator with a woman who had blue hair and who exhaled in disgust when either of the dogs looked at her. Dashiell, who thought she was trying to play one of his favorite games, began to sneeze.

"Four," she told Jimmy when the gate opened.

"Five, please," I said.

"She's not there," he said. "She's at lunch. All of them are."

"I know. We have to pick up something from her room."

He nodded and closed the gate.

We knocked first. You never know. Then I took the passkey out of my pocket and unlocked Sam's door. She had a suite. We walked into what looked like a living room. The door to the bedroom was off to the left. Her laptop and printer were sitting on the large desk that was against the wall to our right.

I sat at the desk and turned on the computer, waiting for it to boot up before I could search for her seminar records. Chip walked over to the window to check the view from a higher floor, whistled softly, and then came back to the desk, pulling a chair from next to it around to the front so that he could see the screen too.

"Maybe the history of who Sam booked where will explain some of this," I said, and we started calling up the seminar lists from the last two years.

"It looks as if, until this week, she never booked any of the men together," Chip said.

"Still, they all knew each other. Or at least, they knew of each other."

I pulled a small pad out of my pocket and began to make notes, dates and speakers, who was where when, and then I checked the list of names of attendees, just to see if something looked like a connection we hadn't thought of.

"Look at this," I said. "Audrey and Alan worked together late last year. After that, she attended two of his seminars."

"Really? Audrey and Alan?"

"Maybe Audrey was the one who gave Alan his big send-off."

"Which send-off do you mean?" he asked.

I looked away from the screen and into his eyes. "Maybe both, for all we know."

I kept scrolling through her records.

"I wonder if Cathy and Martyn ever met before."

"It looks like Sam almost always booked Martyn alone. He's probably a big enough draw."

"I think you're right. He does so much lecturing here, he's probably got"—I stopped in mid-sentence—"he probably had a really strong following. Sam was talking about people who follow their heroes from talk to talk, from state to state."

I scrolled down the lists of people in the audience for Martyn's talks.

"Cathy's name doesn't show. Looks like she'd never attended any of his talks. But when he finally met her, it was lust at first sight."

"How the hell did you—"

"I was sitting a row behind them. I couldn't have missed it. I saw Cupid flying around over Cathy's head, and then, whomp, the arrow hit her right in the chest."

"I wonder who else he's hit on?"

I began to scroll down the list again. "You said he sounded like a man who was used to covering his tracks, didn't you? We have no reason to think that the dalliance with Cathy was a first for him. Look, the number he called in England *isn't* his home number."

"Big surprise."

"It gets better. Check this out. Tina Darling worked with Martyn at the beginning of this last tour, three months ago."

"Isn't she the speaker who canceled out, the one I filled in for with today's talk?"

I nodded. "After she was on the program with Martyn in Minneapolis, she went to seven out of ten of his next talks. That means hearing the same lecture seven times—eight actually, if you count the time they worked together."

"Sounds like she was a really motivated student."

"Sounds like something else to me."

"So you think what? He dumped her after only seven seminars. And so she snuck into the hotel last night and—"

"I just thought it was interesting, that's all. She probably didn't show because they had a thing."

"A dalliance?" He was grinning.

"Yes. Wouldn't it be totally embarrassing to be on a program with someone who'd just dumped you?"

"I wouldn't know," he said.

"Yeah, yeah," I told him. "It must be hell being perfect."

"I wouldn't know that either." Betty came over for a head scratch, and Chip moved his chair back to make room for her. "So what else is on there?"

"How much she's paying you."

"More than you, I trust."

I flashed him the Kaminsky grin.

"What else?"

"I don't see anything in the files that would tie it all together. I mean, we could go back to the black widow spider thing. But wouldn't that mean that three different spiders, so to speak, killed their mates? I can't buy that. It's too far-fetched. I could see it happening once, but not three times."

"So we're back to the men."

"If the shoe fits."

"Men are no good," he said. "We're an easily corrupted gender. Take me, for example. I've only been helping you out for half a day, and I've already stolen, violated a crime scene, broken into someone else's room and surfed their computer files, and lied to the police."

"And your point is?"

"No point, Kaminsky. Just hoping for a big raise when my

review comes up." He stopped scratching Betty's head and leaned toward me. "How much time do we have before the panel?" He looked toward Sam's bedroom.

"Not long enough."

"I'm very quick."

"I don't want to hear that."

There must have been something in the air. Betty began teasing Dash, play-bowing, smiling, wiggling her cute behind. Mistaking flirtatiousness for serious intent, he went aft and climbed aboard. A split second later he was pinned against the side of the bed, his eyes looking anywhere but into Betty's.

It was a tough time for the menfolk. Neither of the bitches in Sam's room was in the mood for a quickie.

"It's getting late. We better finish up and get out of here."

"Leave it," he told Betty. Then he turned back to me. "Print the stuff. Print everything you think we might need. We can look at it in my room after the panel." He reached over and turned on the printer.

I began printing the seminar files, lists of who spoke where, lists of who was in the audience, files of all the speakers Sam had booked in the last two years, their phone numbers, addresses, fees, and special requirements.

Dashiell came over and dumped his big head onto my lap, stressed and depressed by his own foolishly high hopes and Betty's clear refusal.

"Let's get back," I said, shutting down everything and stuffing the papers I'd printed into the pocket with the phone records. "It's nearly show time."

Walking down the stairs, I watched Dashiell running on ahead with Betty. Like most dogs, given a minute, he could rewrite history. His tail was wagging, and he seemed to be smiling. When I turned to look at Chip, he wasn't, and neither was I.

"I was just thinking, if you are in danger," I said, "it's my fault. It was me who insisted on coming into your room, remember? You didn't exactly hit me on the head and drag me there. So no matter what happens, for the rest of this week, there's no way I'm going to let you out of my sight."

"Don't be ridiculous, Rachel. I know it's obvious we've been together. For one thing, you're wearing my shirt. But even if you weren't, Boris, Woody, Bucky, and Sam knew we were alone in my room. And no one would imagine that you would have been able to resist me."

I opened my mouth, but he put one finger over my lips.

"That actually worked to our advantage with the cops. Since they think we were multiplying like fruit flies last night, they don't think either of us pushed Martyn off the roof."

"But—"

He nodded. "Exactly my point. Why would someone want to kill us for spending the night together? We're both adults. Whose business would it be but ours?"

The dogs waited for us at each landing, bounding on ahead just before we caught up to them.

"Wait a minute," I said, taking Chip's arm. It was quiet below. The dogs had stopped too.

"What's up?"

"What if it's not business?"

"We're back to the black widow spider? I still don't see how that puts me in danger, Rachel. I haven't been with anyone but you."

"What if it's a man, someone who's *not* getting lucky, someone who's so envious he could kill?"

"You mean Boris?"

"Or Bucky?"

"But, Rachel, how could you find out something like that,

that one of them was trying to join the party, so to speak, and failing?"

"I don't know."

But that wasn't true. I did know. Because given half a chance, people talk.

But if that was how I was going to find out who had gone over the edge at this symposium, someone had better start talking soon, before another of the men ended up dead.

SHE WAS NODDING

Our abbreviated panel sat behind a long table covered with a white cloth on the stage of the auditorium. I was on the left side of the table, with Chip to my right; then there was Cathy, her eyes still red; Tracy, her face strangely hostile; Bucky, who always had to sit in the middle of things; Beryl, in her tweed jacket and plaid woolen hat; Woody, who kept looking at Sam in the front row; Boris, looking red-faced and ready to pop; and on the far end, Audrey, who appeared as small as if she were a child sitting on a grown-up's chair. Magic, of course, was on her lap. The other dogs were lying in front of the table on down-stays, a visible show of our consummate skills. In fact, Sasha was asleep and snoring, the best testimony on earth to his master's talent. It meant the dog understood he wasn't going anywhere without a word from Boris, so there was no compelling reason to stay awake.

I was as tired as he was, but unlike Sasha, I had work to do.

Having been to panels before and knowing as well as Bucky did that the best-known trainers would be asked most of the questions, I had the printouts from Sam's computer and the phone records, all tucked inside a copy of *Modern Maturity* I'd pilfered off the lap of an old geezer who was asleep on one of the chairs in the lobby. I held it on my lap so that I could study the material while the panel went on. I told Chip to poke me if I missed my name or on those occasions where we were all expected to give an opinion on the same topic. Or if I just needed to look up and smile.

I opened the magazine and began to study the lists in earnest, first the list of people in this audience, checking all the other participant lists for the last two years to see if any name popped up in a telling way. But while there were people in attendance here who had been to a Bucky talk or a Martyn weekend symposium, there was no name that appeared in the audience of all three deceased colleagues. This was not to say that perusing the lists wasn't worthy of my attention. Not at all.

Of note, it seemed to me, was that while Bucky was the most demanding of the speakers—spelling out the publicity he had to have, demanding first-class travel and lodging, requiring limos and escorts instead of taking cabs, even submitting his own introduction, which was three pages long, single-spaced—his draw, and consequently his fee, had gone not up but down over the last two years. Despite all the self-inflation, Bucky's popularity was slipping. And Bucky, I'd guess, was not a man to take that lightly.

I remembered that quite a few years back Bucky had had a nice gig as a steady guest on some daytime TV show, and Rick Shelbert had wheedled his way in there with some little tap dance about what he could do, causing Bucky to get fired and Rick—Dr. Rick, as they called him on the show—to get the job.

Had he had a bone to pick with Alan and Martyn as well? Where was he when I was sleeping in the bathtub?

But what was I thinking here? Sure, someone could have used a passkey and gotten into Alan's room, surprised him as he was getting out of the tub and knocked the radio, shelf and all, into the bath with him. But what about Rick? He'd died right in front of us. He'd choked on breakfast. And it was Chip and Martyn who had worked on him and failed to save him, not Bucky. Or Boris.

This was great. The more I learned, the less I knew.

I'd told Chip that things weren't what they seemed to be. So fine. What were they?

What if Rick hadn't choked? Was there something that could have made it seem he was choking? Some drug the killer could have slipped into his morning juice? And what a clever scheme that would be. Wouldn't choking be the obvious thing for us to think, watching a man start to cough, turn pale, and be unable to breathe in the middle of a meal?

Then there was Martyn. Was he competition for Bucky?

I looked up his seminars. He was pulling twice to three times the crowd Bucky pulled in. As Bucky's popularity went down, Martyn's had ascended. Sure, Bucky got the media to show up. But when it came to black-and-white figures, he wasn't doing as hot as he'd like everyone to believe.

I felt a jab in my side and looked up.

Audrey was speaking. "Yes, it was more difficult for a woman to get started in dog training years ago, but I don't think that's as true today."

"She wants you all to answer," Chip whispered, his hand covering his mike. "The good old macho days of yesteryear versus politically correct today."

"I may barf," I whispered.

There was a ripple of movement in the audience, then laughter. Everyone was looking at me. That's when I realized I hadn't covered my microphone.

"That's what I get for eating before a panel discussion," I told them. "Food's not a great idea when you're nervous." I smiled ingratiatingly at the sea of faces, still intensely focused on me. "Well, as long as I have your attention," I told them, "I don't pay attention to the sort of thing you're talking about."

The woman who'd asked the question was standing, taking notes at a furious pace. She was tiny, even smaller than Audrey, and dressed in pale violet, including the scarf that held her ponytail.

"I figure out what it is I want to do with my life and then go out and do the absolute best job I can. You can't ask more of anyone, male or female, can you?" I wondered if I should slow down so that she could record me verbatim, but I'm much too much of a New Yorker. I couldn't do it. "I think by doing that," I continued, "you can keep your choices open. Even in male-dominated professions, women have a good chance of succeeding, if they believe in themselves and don't listen to what other people say."

"But what about the men?"

"What about them?"

"They don't take women trainers seriously."

"So what? Take yourself seriously. No one else can prevent you from doing that. And the way someone else views you can't hold you back or make you fail. Only you can do that. Or not do that."

I heard Bucky exhale loudly. He had little patience for anyone else holding the floor.

"What Bucky is probably thinking is that you shouldn't pay so much attention to what other people are doing. Or thinking." I smiled down the table at Bucky. "That's one of the reasons why he's so successful. He uses his energy productively rather than worrying about what you or I are up to. There's a wonderful lesson there."

With Beryl's voice as a backdrop, I turned my attention back to the papers on my lap. And perhaps since it was Beryl speaking, I turned to the phone records from her room. She'd only made a couple of calls, both to the same number, probably telling her grandchild about Cecilia's antics. It was a 718 area code. I circled the number to remind me to check it out later.

Tracy was next to speak. I looked up as she began to answer.

"I disagree. Things are no better today." She looked even angrier now than she had when we all sat down to begin the panel. "This has always been a male-dominated profession, and as far as I can see, it still is. I'm reminded of the Ginger Rogers quote. You know, when she said she did everything that Fred did, but backwards and in high heels."

She waited for her laugh, but it didn't come. No one wanted to hear that even today women weren't getting an even break in the profession they practiced or, in most cases, longed to practice. I saw a few of the women looking back toward me, perhaps thinking that I would argue Tracy's point. But that wasn't the way the panel worked. Each of us, even Tracy, was entitled to her own opinion, and the fact that I disagreed not only with the content of it but with her negative attitude was beside the point.

A young man in the audience got up to ask a question. It was the brittle young man with the flat-coat that Beryl had worked with. He stood silently for a while, holding our attention without making good use of it.

"In my area," he said, spacing his words carefully, the way some children separate the food on their plates so that nothing touches anything else, "there are two women trainers. And as far as I can see, they're getting more business than I am. Which is why I came here," he added. "To improve my skills in the hope that it would improve my business. Nevertheless, I don't see evidence of what Ms. Nevins is saying. If I recall correctly, at least half the books and tapes in my home library are by women. Of course my favorite," he said, turning toward Beryl, "is Ms. Potter's series, from the TV show she did in Britain. It's just brilliant."

Tracy's dark look became even darker, her eyes hooded, her fingers tearing nervously at her cuticles. I turned to the phone bill from her room; nothing was logged there, but of course, room-to-room calls wouldn't be. So all I could do was wonder what Tracy Nevins was doing while nearly everyone else was playing musical beds. Had she seen what was going on? Had she tried to cozy up to Alan or Rick or Martyn and been rejected? Maybe it wasn't an unlucky man but a woman scorned.

I pulled out the seminar lists and looked for Tracy's name, first as a speaker. Sam had booked her only twice before, and she'd had a modest draw both times. She'd never done a video or a book. It was usually the people who did who pulled the biggest crowds. I wondered if she'd tried. There were several local trainers I knew of who, upon failing to get their method published, had self-published pamphlets. I wondered if there was a Gospel According to Tracy, and if the bitterness written across her face had to do with the words she'd just spoken and the envy she felt toward the successful men in the field. Again the same question: business or pleasure?

I began to flip through the names of attendees at the seminars given by the three speakers who had died this week. And there Tracy's name showed up more often. She'd attended three of Martyn's talks, all on the East Coast, four of Rick's, and two of Alan's, which, since she was a foodie, should have surprised me. But it didn't. I would never understand it, but for years I'd seen people embracing disparate methods as if they could take a little of this and a little of that and make something new and wonderful, something that made sense and would work, when if they had given the least little bit of thought, it should have been clear that it was an impossible combination. Still, there was Tracy's name, and for one talk, one of Rick's, she had traveled all the way to Phoenix. Fancy that.

"Being successful requires determination, good scholarship, and lots and lots of hard work, no matter your gender. There are no shortcuts, my dears, no magic answers. Even if your mum's in the business, you still have to make it on your own, don't you?"

Something was bothering me, one of those things you almost remember but not quite, but I had to let it go. Cathy was talking, and I wanted to hear what she had to say.

"Beryl's right," Cathy said. "Personally, I've found nothing but acceptance in this profession. I'm a bit surprised by what I'm hearing today. From the very first, I've met people who were generous, helpful, and willing to share information."

If Cathy had wanted our attention, she'd just earned it. Panelists and audience alike, we were all staring, wondering on which planet Cathy had started out as a dog trainer, because wherever it was, it sure as hell wasn't Earth.

"I think women have not only found a comfortable niche in dog training, we've had a beneficial effect on methodology. We're not as rough as the men. Well, as the men used to be," she said, showing off the contrast between her California tan and her pearly white smile.

As Cathy elaborated, once again her voice growing stronger as she concentrated on work, I looked past her, back at Tracy. She didn't seem to be paying attention to Cathy. Still, she was nodding, her eyes checking out the molding in one of the far corners of the room as her head bobbed up and down, up and down, as if she might be approving not of what the rest of us were hearing but of some private thought or plan, something, perhaps, of her own making.

Maybe I'd made a mistake with the poker game. Maybe in order to keep the men safe, I should have organized a quilting bee.

MY MOTHER WOULD HAVE BEEN PROUD

There's got to be a connection we're missing between the killer and the victims," I whispered to Chip after the panel, this time remembering to shut off my microphone. "There must be something that would tie all this together, that would explain it."

"But how do you get to it, from the victims' lives? We can't get to it from the killer's life. We don't know who the killer is."

I got up to go.

"Where to now?"

"I have to go upstairs for a minute. I want to put on something of my own. This was careless of me," I said, pulling on the front of the shirt he'd given me to put on after my bath. "I feel as if I'm waving a red flag in front of a bull."

We walked up to three, heading down the hall toward my room. But I stopped before I got there, staring at the door to 303.

"What's up?"

"I'm not sure."

"Speak up, Rachel, don't be shy. What do you need from me this time? A felony? Grand theft auto? B and E?"

"Oh, no way. I have a passkey. But that's not it. I'm just trying to recall something from a long time ago. But I need help. How much time is there before dinner?"

He looked at his watch. "An hour and a half."

"Come on," I said, heading back to the stairs. "We have to hurry."

"We do?" he asked.

"Stop being cute. You're with me, aren't you?"

"In sickness and in health. I just wish we were doing something less sick. Where are we going now?"

"My house."

It must have been something in my tone, or the way I yanked on his arm. He didn't say another word. When we hit the street, I went straight to the curb and put my arm out and, God bless New York City, a taxi pulled over to the curb to pick us up with both dogs.

"Tenth and Bleecker, please."

The driver's turban bobbed forward and back, and we were on our way.

We rode downtown in silence, the dogs jammed between us. When the cab stopped in front of Kim's Video, we got out and walked west, past the Sixth Precinct, jaywalking across the street to the gate that led to my cottage. There was a thin young man leaning on the gate, his nails painted a frosty blue, the blue arcing around platinum moons on each nail. It must have taken forever to do them so neatly. He moved away when Dashiell, followed by Betty, headed for where he was standing.

I unlocked the gate, and we walked down the brick passageway into the garden. After Westminster, I'd often imagined Chip coming here. I even made up what he might say, and what I might answer back. I'd thought about it a lot after he said he'd call, but this afternoon, there wasn't time for us to think about ourselves. Back at the hotel, someone could be in danger.

Chip must have been thinking the same thing. He didn't tell me how beautiful the garden was or how at home he felt in my living room. He didn't look into my eyes until my body heated up and I ached for him to touch me. He didn't touch me, either. Without speaking, he followed me upstairs to my office, and when I'd found the videos I was after and had put them inside the leather backpack that had been hanging on the back of the office door, he followed me back down the stairs. We whistled for the dogs, who were having a sniffathon in the garden, and headed back to the Ritz.

"What do you expect to find in those?" he asked, this time sitting pressed against me, the dogs smudging up the windows on either side of the taxi as the city pulled by.

"I'm not sure. Maybe the missing link we've been after."

"When and where are we going to look at those?"

"I think we have to go to dinner. It would be pretty blatant for us to skip it. I don't want to act strange in any way, or to call any more attention to ourselves than we already have."

"It's a little late for that, Kaminsky." He tugged on my shirt collar. Actually, *his* shirt collar.

"When we get to the hotel, I'll run upstairs and change."

"What about the tapes?"

"We'll find a friendly video store later tonight. I don't care if you have to buy a fucking VCR to accomplish this, but one way or another, we're going to watch these tonight. Are you with me?"

"Of course. And that's not a bad idea."

"What isn't?"

"Buying a VCR. I lost the one I had in the settlement."

The cab stopped a block from the Ritz, as instructed. Chip began to reach into his pocket for money, but I got to my wallet faster. "Allow me," I said. "It's on Sam anyway."

When I opened the door, Dashiell practically fell out, and Betty got out, too, by walking across Chip's lap and mine. Even good training has its limitations. Sometimes a dog has a better idea than you do about how to get something done.

"Go on ahead," he said. "I'll see you at dinner."

I took the elevator this time. Once in my room, I changed out of Chip's shirt, hanging it all by itself in my closet. Then I stashed the backpack on the floor and actually closed the closet door. My mother would have been proud.

I was the last to arrive at dinner. There we were, all sitting as we always had, except that there were three fewer people around the table. We apparently pattern-trained as easily as our dogs did, forming comforting habits almost immediately in new situations. My spot. My chair. My place in the world.

"Ah, there she is," Sam said.

It seemed to me her chair was a little closer to Woody's than it had been at yesterday's dinner.

When I'd looked at his phone records, I noticed he was calling home every day, usually before breakfast. When he'd taken my hand in the hallway, just before telling me that Martyn was dead, I'd felt the callus his wedding band had made on the ring finger of his left hand, a hard ridge just above where the ring would be, were he wearing it. There was no telltale tan line. Then again, it wasn't summer.

But Sam was a big girl. If Woody was married, she knew that. If she decided to be his perk for this symposium, she knew what that meant, too.

"We all took a lovely walk in the park, but we didn't know

where you were," she went on. "Some of the students came too. Bucky did an impromptu talk about promotion for their fledgling businesses. Woody told a group how to condition their dogs for agility competition. And Beryl took a small group birding."

"I was working on my notes," I told her. "For Saturday."

Sam nodded. The waiters began serving. I sipped my wine and looked around at the group, no longer seeing them only as professional colleagues. Now as I looked at each one, I wondered which of them had killed the three of us who were no longer here. And why?

Sure, I could tell Chip stories, some of them even plausible sounding. It was one of the men, killing off the competition. It was one of the men, green with envy over the lovemaking that others were enjoying. It was one of the women, unlucky at love, lucky in murder. But I couldn't buy any of them. Somehow, when you looked more closely, things didn't add up.

It's said that people kill over nothing. But it's never *really* over nothing. Certainly not to the killer. Quite the contrary—the slight, the promise not kept, the display of disrespect, these could blacken the sky. They could leave nothing but hopelessness in their wake. And a desperate need to get even.

If an offense could be undetectable to everyone but the killer, how would we see it? How would we find the corner to peel away the top layer and see what lay underneath?

"It's not so," I heard Tracy say, wondering what came before that I'd missed.

"But Cathy never had a problem," Bucky said, smiling at Tracy's crushed-looking face.

"Of course she didn't," Tracy said, a lot too loud, "look at her."

So of course we all did.

"Women who look like that never have trouble. In anything."

I turned to look at Cathy, who had a look of panic in her eyes now, having just lost the philanderer she thought she loved.

"That's not fair," Audrey said. "You have no idea how hard Cathy works. You're assuming that success fell in her lap because she's beautiful. Well, let me tell you. Life is never that simple. And right now, she's feeling—"

"Stop it," Cathy shouted. "Stop it right now. First of all, you're talking about me as if I weren't here. And second, I haven't asked for a reading, and I don't want one. Don't you people have any sensitivity at all?"

That shut us up. For a moment, but not long enough, there was only the sound of forks on salad plates. But this was not a dinner of mimes. This was not a group who could leave bad enough alone.

"You think being woman is difficult, Boris comes here from Russia with no money, no family, only incredible skill as dog trainer to start new life—"

"I don't believe this." Woody pushed his salad dish to the side. "How about we go our separate ways this evening? How about I go out and eat Chinese food—Bucky, what'll it be? Thai? French? Or maybe just good old Burger King. I'm sure there's one around Columbus Circle. This is bizarre, sitting here every night and having these petty fights. Where the hell does it get us?"

He pushed back his chair, picked up Rhonda's leash, and headed for the door, and suddenly I felt the kind of panic I used to feel when things were going badly with Jack. We'd have words, and he'd head for the door, and I'd become terrified I'd never see him again, even though a moment earlier that's exactly what I was wishing for.

"Wait," I said. "Chinese. Wow. I have a real yen for Peking duck, don't you?" I asked Chip, who was sitting, as usual, to my left.

"I do," he said. "That crisp skin, the spicy sauce, the cold, fresh taste of the cucumbers. Count me in." And now he was up, too.

"I know just how you feel. But it's the soup I love, the wontons, shrimp, pork, chicken, veggies, and that aromatic broth. I can't resist." Sam was standing, too.

Before anyone else had the chance to stand and testify, we were all laughing. And all sitting around the table again. The waiters cleared the salads and brought steaming pots of mussels and thick white bread to dip into the sauce, and as quickly as the storm came, it had blown over.

So how could I believe that for the reasons I'd imagined, any one of these people who were now laughing and telling each other hilarious stories had killed, not once, but three times?

27

YOU DON'T KNOW THE HALF OF IT, I TOLD HIM

Had we spent another hour telling war stories and drinking wine, we would have gotten to Broadway Electronics after they'd closed. As it was, there wouldn't be time to watch all four tapes. I'd have to scan them. And since I wasn't sure where the tiny part I thought I remembered was, I'd have to do it not only quickly but carefully.

I walked around the store looking at TVs and cordless phones while Chip began schmoozing up the clerk, pretending he wanted to buy a large-screen TV, one of the ones that sold for close to a thousand dollars. He was right, I thought, listening to him from an aisle away. His gender did corrupt easily. Perhaps, in the name of science, there'd be time to test that theory further later on in the evening. But first, there was something urgent I had to do.

I walked over and interrupted the big sale.

"I was thinking of getting a new VCR, right?" The thin,

pimply clerk with the prominent Adam's apple and unfortunate teeth looked annoyed. "I can try one or two of them out, right?"

"No prob." He stepped back behind the counter and came up with *Ace Ventura, Pet Detective*. Everyone's a wit.

"Way in the back," he told me, turning his attention back to Chip. He probably worked on commission.

I took the tape and went to the back of the store, laid the tape on top of one of the TVs, put the first of the four tapes I had in my backpack into one of the VCRs, and hit play on the remote.

The music came on first. Next, as an announcer spoke, there were dogs doing a long sit—a Great Dane, a chocolate lab, a boxer, two corgis, and what we call an English cocker, though where this tape was shot, it was just called a cocker spaniel.

And then there she was, her hair flaming red, or rather flaming orange, the color of the setting sun, her face twenty years younger, the jaw better defined, the cheeks higher, her skin without wrinkles, even though she'd been close to fifty when she'd done the TV series. Clearly she was at the top of her form, strong, confident, full of energy. Hands on her hips, she was directing her students.

I hit fast-forward, remembering that the part I was looking for was at the end of one of the sessions, not in the middle of it.

As I watched the screen, the training class looked like an old silent film, everyone moving much too fast and no one saying a word, even when their mouths were moving. My eyes began to burn, but I couldn't take my eyes off the screen; if I blinked, I might miss what I had come here to see.

The end of a session was coming up, and I hit play again.

"And so, my dears," she said, in that same strong voice, "when you practice this week, remember to praise with enthusiasm. Here now, give me that darling corgi, no, no, the little girl. Watch me, students," she said, leading the corgi to the heel position, signaling her to sit, and then bending down and hugging the little girl against her leg. "There's a *clever* girl," Beryl cooed, her voice warm and animated. The little dog gazed up at her, totally enthralled.

"See," she said, standing again, "nothing to it."

God, she was good. But this wasn't the spot.

I fast-forwarded, watching the jerky movements. Beryl was teaching the stay, demonstrating with the Dane and then watching her students try with their dogs, moving away so quickly that some of the dogs got confused and followed their owners instead of staying put.

I scanned the first tape and checked my watch. Time was running out. Chip might not be able to keep the clerk busy much longer, and at the rate this was going, I might not have time to find what I was after before the store closed. I put the second tape in and popped the third tape into the machine next to it, pressing play twice and looking back and forth between the two sets as Beryl sped through her training classes. I must have looked as if I were watching a tennis game played by midgets.

Then, on the third tape, the scene I was looking for began, something I had only vaguely remembered as I'd stood outside 303 back at the Ritz.

I rewound the tape so that I would hear the whole thing.

"So, dear people, now you have the down. But remember how to practice this, please. Those of you who had a little growling problem, teach the command at home first, where there are no other dogs about. The down puts your dog in a submissive posture, and for some of the males, this is quite embarrassing in class, in front of the other gents. It hurts your doggy's pride. But once he learns the down at home, and you give him that nice tummy rub I showed you, he'll do it very nicely in class and anywhere else you might need it. Any *questions*?"

She looked around, her orange hair escaping the combs she used to try to keep it in place, just as her gray hair did now.

"All right, then. Where's my little darling?" she asked, her gaze leaving the viewer and going off to her left, a loving smile on her face now.

I felt my stomach flip. This was the part I'd been waiting for. When the scene was over, I knew what I had to do, first thing in the morning. The music played again. As the credits rolled, the dogs romped in the background.

I ejected the tapes, packed them up, and brought *Ace Ventura* back to the clerk.

"I like the JVC one," I told him. "I have to check with my roommate."

He closed his eyes and nodded wearily. Surely he'd heard that before.

"I'll give you a call about that later in the week," Chip said. "I need a little time to think about it. Sure is a honey of a set, though."

"What did you find out?" he asked as soon as we'd left the store.

"The explanation for something that was too much of a co-incidence for me to buy."

He nodded.

"Something you don't care to elaborate on just yet?"

I nodded.

"Are we going back to the hotel?" he asked.

"I have to make two quick stops first."

We were a few doors from the drugstore where I'd dropped off the film I'd shot on Sunday. I opened the envelope right in the store, looking through the pictures with Chip, stopping on the one of the locked roof door with the No Entry sign, and again on a shot of the maid's cart parked outside one of the rooms, the passkey hanging on a hook to the left of the handle.

"What next?" Chip asked.

"Potato chips."

"A girl after my own heart."

We walked into one of the ubiquitous Korean delis that dot half the corners in Manhattan and stay open all night.

"How about some beer to go with them?"

"Oh, they're not to eat."

He frowned. "I'm not going to touch this with a ten-foot pole," he said, reaching for his money.

"Allow me. I can expense them."

"You're a hell of a date, Kaminsky."

I picked up a bag of Ridgies and put a five on the counter with them. "You don't know the half of it," I told him.

My cell phone rang, and I took it out of my pocket and flipped it open.

"Hello?"

"It's me, Sam. I've been looking all over for you. Detective Flowers called." I grabbed Chip's arm and pulled him closer, holding the phone away from my ear so that he could hear. "The ME has results on Rick. He didn't choke, Rachel. He died from anaphylactic shock, from an aspirin allergy. Flowers said she'd spoken to his wife, and she said Rick knew he was highly allergic to aspirin. It's not uncommon for asthmatics. She said he was very careful—he only took Tylenol, brand-name stuff, none of that generic stuff, because he figured, you never know for sure that way."

"There was Tylenol on his nightstand," I told her. "But I didn't find a bee sting kit. The only other meds were those asthma inhalers he used, two besides the one he had with him."

"Flowers said something about a bee sting kit. They took it, she said, when they checked his room. I don't get it. Was he worried about bees in Central Park? What does that have to do—"

"It's for any allergy that causes severe anaphylaxis. It's got injectable epinephrine in it," I said, keenly aware that one of the men who'd tried to rescue him was standing next to me, "which would have saved his life. But, of course, none of us knew about his allergy."

And as I said it, I realized that it wasn't true. Anyone of us could have known, with all the times aspirin had been passed around the table to alleviate hangovers after a night of heavy drinking. Anyone could have noticed Rick turning it down and taking two Tylenol instead. In fact, he might easily have explained why he was doing that.

And what about the person who had stood by so patiently while Rick spread out a towel to prevent soiling the hotel sheets? Couldn't she know, too? She might have even seen the anaphylaxis emergency treatment kit. She might have asked what it was he'd been so allergic to.

"What are the detectives going to do about this, did Flowers say?"

"They'll be here in the morning, early, and they want to talk to everyone. They want to rule out foul play."

"I'm not so sure they're going to be able to do that, Sam. You ought to prepare yourself for another possibility."

"You mean that someone did this on purpose?"

"Yes. But the big question is—"

"Who?" she asked.

I didn't say anything.

"And the others?"

"I don't think any of them were accidents, Sam."

Now she didn't say anything.

"I'm working on this. I don't have it yet, but I will. I wish it were neater. I wish it were easier. I wish I could have—"

Chip stepped back and shook his head.

"I'll see you in the morning, Sam. I'll talk to you then."

"It's not your fault." He put his warm hand on my face for a second. "These things always get solved *after* people have lost their lives. Think of all those interviews with the neighbors of serial killers, people who saw them every day, watched them grow up, and never had a clue. 'He was the nicest boy,' they say, 'quiet, polite, and good to his mother. We had no idea.' It's the same way people are with their aggressive dogs, saying that the biting started out of the blue, because they'd missed a year and a half of warning signs."

"Thanks for saying that."

I put the phone back into my pocket.

"Listen to me," I told him. "There's something I've got to do. I'm going to put you in a cab now." I ignored the amazed look on his face. "I need you to take the dogs and go to the cottage."

"Rachel, it's late. Everyone's gone to bed by now. The hotel is only three blocks from here. I'll have a German shepherd and a pit bull with me. What could possibly—?"

"Electrocution. Anaphylaxis. A lethal push from a high place. We were guessing before. Now we know. It's not safe at the hotel." I was holding his arms now, looking into his eyes. "Please do this. Do it for yourself. Do it for your kids. Do it for me, Chip. I don't care why, just do it."

"This is ridiculous. Where will you be?"

"I can't say just yet. But it's some place I thought I could get to tomorrow morning. I no longer think it can wait."

"I'm going with you."

"You can't," I told him. "It's too overwhelming if two people show up. She'll feel outnumbered. She'll never talk."

"She? She who?"

"The missing link we've been looking for." I reached into my pocket for my keys. "Please," I said, handing them to Chip. "I'll be home as soon as I can."

"But—"

I put my fingers over his mouth.

"I have to go."

I put my hand up for a cab. When one pulled up to the curb, I opened the door, and the dogs jumped in.

"I'll grab the next one," I said, practically shoving Chip inside. I tossed the bag of chips onto his lap. "Change of plans. You *can* have these after all. Beer's in the fridge. And wait up for me, okay? Otherwise I'll be locked out."

I told the driver where to go and slammed the door.

We could have shared a cab. I could have dropped him off in the Village and continued on alone. But I needed to think about what I was going to say. And I didn't want to give Chip a chance to reconsider letting me go on alone.

Once inside the second cab, I pulled out my cell phone again, punching in the number, then listening to the lonely sound that told me the phone was ringing on the other end. Unless she'd shut it off.

"Please be there," I whispered. "Please pick up."

"Hello?"

I was so startled when she answered that I didn't respond immediately.

"Hello? Is anyone there?"

I took a breath before answering.

"It's Rachel Alexander," I said. "I don't know if you remember me. We met at a dog show, a few years ago. I'm at the symposium that Sam Lewis organized, and—"

"What do you want? Why are you calling so late?"

"I'm sorry about that. But it's really important that I see you, as soon as possible. Tonight, if I can."

"Tonight? Why? What is it?"

"Something's wrong," I said. "I need your help."

There was silence on the line as the cab sped across the Brooklyn Bridge. I was almost there, and she hadn't agreed to see me yet.

"Something's wrong?" she repeated.

"Yes, very wrong."

"What does it have to do with me?" she asked.

"I'm not sure. That's what I need to find out."

The cab took the first right off the bridge and then veered left.

"Can't you tell me on the phone?"

"No, I can't. Look, I'm five minutes away. Will you see me, please?"

"Rachel, do you know what time it is?"

"I do."

"Well then, can't it wait until morning?"

"I'm sorry. It's already waited much too long."

There was another silence. I thought perhaps she'd put the phone down.

"Do you know where I am?" she asked at last.

"I do," I told her as the cab turned the corner onto Cranberry Street.

"Are you coming straightaway, then?"

"I'm nearly there."

Literally, I thought, as the cab stopped in front of her house. But I had the feeling it was figuratively so as well.

YOU CAN SEE HOW LUCKY I WAS

She stood in the doorway in a long, pink nightgown, her bare feet sticking out at the hem, looking more like a child than a grown woman. The same dark curls framed her face, but her clear blue eyes no longer looked as innocent as they did when she'd been a child.

"What's this all about?" she asked.

"May I come in?"

Her mouth opened, but nothing came out. Then she stepped back inside to allow me in.

She turned and walked into the living room, taking the place where she'd been before I came, her half-finished cup of tea waiting for her. I looked around the room and then back at her. It was too late in every way to start beating about the bush, something I had little patience for anyway. I took a breath and, standing in the middle of the room, began.

"How did Beryl come to take your place at the symposium?" I asked.

"Mummy's *here?*"

I nodded and pulled a chair closer to the couch, sitting across from where she sat, her legs curled under her, her cheeks pale, her eyes red, as if before I'd come she had been crying.

She stared at me for a few seconds before speaking. "She never said she was here." I could see her struggling with more than she was saying. "I thought she was calling from England."

She hadn't talked at all on the tape. It seemed she'd never wanted to appear on camera. After all, she'd only been five or six, a pretty thing, but too shy for all the hoopla that must have accompanied the filming of her mum's training classes for the BBC.

"Come here, Christine," Beryl had said, looking off to the side, at the child who wasn't coming. "Come and wave good-bye to everyone. Christina, darling, come to Mummy."

Beryl looked straight into the camera. "Wouldn't it be lovely if our little ones were as obedient as our dogs?"

She'd disappeared for a moment, the camera not following her. Instead it showed the dogs, all their heads turned to watch the teacher. And there she was again, carrying a serious-faced little girl of five or six with thick, dark, curly hair and startling blue eyes, quite a big child to be carried, but Beryl didn't seem to be having any difficulty at all. She seemed not to notice the weight as she kissed the little girl repeatedly, then whispered something into her ear.

After that, Tina and her mother were all smiles, waving at the camera until the screen went dark.

"You didn't say why Beryl is teaching instead of you, Tina."

"Well, I don't know what to say," she said, sitting straighter, trying to keep it all together now. "I was talking to Mummy and I told her I'd made this commitment but I simply couldn't keep it. I felt awful about it, because Sam's always been so good to me. I just told Mummy how difficult a time I was having calling Sam and disappointing her with the news. Well, then she said she'd take care of it. Naturally I thought she meant she'd call Sam and apologize for me. I even gave her the number. I had no idea she'd offered to come and speak in my place."

"And why was it that you couldn't speak at the symposium?" I asked.

"I don't see that that's any of your business, Rachel. Is that it?" She stood, ready to dismiss me.

"I was wondering why you changed your name, Tina?"

She sighed and sat down again. "Rachel, I don't see—"

"Please. It's important."

"Mummy throws a big shadow. You've met her now, haven't you?"

I nodded.

"Well, then."

I waited.

"When Daddy was gone, she moved us back to England. I was only three at the time, so mostly I lived there. But I knew I'd been born here and that my father was an American, and I was curious, do you know what I mean? When it came time for college, I decided to come back to the States. After I graduated, I went home again. But living with your mother after you've been on your own—" She shrugged. "Anyway, by then I knew I wanted to work with dogs, and there isn't business enough in Chipping Camden for *two* dog trainers. There really isn't enough work for one, but Mummy can make a living anyway because she's so famous. People come to her from miles and miles away.

"Mummy said if I stayed, I could help her. There was enough

work for both of us. But I didn't want to be thought of as Beryl Potter's little kid. I wanted to make it on my own. So I came back here. And I changed my name. Is that so difficult to understand?"

"Not at all. So Sam doesn't know that it was your mother calling to take—"

"My stepmother," she said. "My mother died when I was very little. I don't remember her. But Beryl always used to tell me that she must have been both beautiful and sweet, else I wouldn't be. She was a wonderful mother to me—please don't think otherwise, I mean, because of the name change. Actually, it's what she always called me."

"I know," I said.

"And Mummy never minded. She kept my secret for me. She thought it was the right way to do things, to soldier on, she'd say, manage on your own. It's what she did, after all, when Daddy died."

"When was that?" I asked.

"A couple of years after my mother died."

"His heart?"

She nodded.

"And your mother? She must have been very young."

"She was. She was only twenty. She committed suicide. So you can see how lucky I was that Beryl kept me, can't you?"

I nodded.

"Another woman, someone less strong, someone selfish, might have passed me on to any of my parents' relatives to raise. After all, I wasn't hers. But she didn't feel that way. She felt I was. You can't imagine how good she is, how fiercely loyal. Even coming here, taking my place. It was simply brilliant of her to do that. But does that mean—"

"No, she never told Sam about the relationship. It all seemed a happy coincidence, the deus ex machina saving the day."

She clapped her hands together.

"Oh, good for Mummy, she didn't tell."

"Yes, she's full of surprises," I said, thinking about Cecilia and looking around the neat little room for what seemed like the first time, looking and seeing now what wasn't there.

Frank was right. People will tell you the most astonishing things if you give them half a chance. It was late—it was nearly one by now. But we'd only just begun. And what I was going to ask next was going to get those tears flowing again. I was starting to be sure about several things, none more than that.

"Tina, I'm sorry to cause you more pain," I said, "but I have to ask you a few more questions. I have to ask you to tell me about Martyn."

Her eyes opened wide, and she shook her head, as if by doing so she could make what had happened to hurt her no longer true.

I nodded, then got up and moved to the couch, touching her hand after I sat down next to her. "Tell me about it."

"He's why I couldn't go." Her voice sounded small, almost inaudible. One tear rolled down her cheek.

"You met some months ago, when you spoke together."

She nodded, looking into her lap.

"We fell in love," she said, wiping her eyes with the heels of her hands. "No, that's not true. *I* fell in love. Martyn only fell in lust."

"He didn't say he was married?"

"Oh, he did. But he told me it was a bad marriage and that his wife was a very weak person, neurotic, he said, and that she was in therapy and he was hoping that when she got stronger he would—"

She paused, looking behind her, out the window to a small garden. There was a light on outside, shining on the little bench and the ivy that surrounded it, a pristine place to sit when the weather was warm enough.

"It sounds pretty lame, doesn't it?"

I nodded. "He can be pretty persuasive, can't he? And he's a very charming man."

She nodded.

Then she looked suspiciously at me. "Is that why you're here? Are you and Martyn—?"

"No, Tina."

"I'm so ashamed, Rachel. Not only did I follow him from seminar to seminar, but now it's all over, and I'm still acting like a jealous—"

"Don't do this to yourself, Tina. You're sincere, so you made the assumption that he was too."

"He *seemed* to be," she said.

I picked up the napkin from next to her teacup and handed it to her. She blew her nose and held it crumpled in one hand.

"He encouraged me to come to his talks. He even paid for one of my tickets. 'Come to Denver,' he said. '*Be* with me.' Then 'Come to Minneapolis.' But then—"

"Did you tell him about the baby?"

"How did you know that?"

"Just a guess."

"I did tell him."

"And what did he say?"

Tina began to sob. I slid closer and put my arm around her, rubbing her back. I felt her tears running into my neck, felt how thin she was beneath her nightgown.

"What did he say, Tina?"

" 'What are you trying to pull?' he said. 'I've had a vasectomy. It can't be mine.' "

"Good Lord."

"He'd said he loved me, then he was so cold. I couldn't face going to the symposium, knowing he'd be there. And I couldn't tell Sam I'd been such a fool." She pulled away and looked at me. "Did Sam send you? Is that why you're here?"

"Tina," I said, ignoring her question, "did Beryl know about this?"

She nodded. Then I looked to see if the door to the garden had blown open, because suddenly I felt very cold.

"What did you tell her?"

"That I'd take care of it. But I was so grateful, with all of this, that she was going to take care of calling Sam for me, that I didn't have to do that as well."

"Tina, I know it's late," I said, "but can you make us some tea? There's something I need to tell you, and I need a minute to think."

She stood up and bent to pick up her cup. "I still don't know why you came, Rachel, but I'm awfully glad you did."

I stood and hugged her, my heart feeling as cold and hard as stone, knowing what I had to say next and what it would do to this vulnerable woman.

I watched her walk away, not an ounce of fat on her. Then I looked around the room.

Beryl didn't have a grandchild. There was no tricycle in the garden, no Dr. Seuss on the coffee table.

Nor was there a grandchild on the way. There was no Dr. Spock, no *What to Expect When You're Expecting*, no bag of knitting, and no saltine crumbs next to where her teacup had sat.

Tina had taken care of it, as she'd promised Beryl. But not in the way that Beryl had imagined, had dreamed.

And clearly Beryl had taken care of her end of the deal. But not in the way Tina had imagined. Nor anyone, possibly not even Beryl.

But why the other two?

In order to get that answer, I suspected I was going to need a little help from my friends.

WE TOOK SEPARATE CABS

I rang the bell next to the wrought-iron gate and waited for Chip to come and open it.

"This is Tina Darling," I said when the gate swung open. "Beryl's daughter. She's staying here tonight."

He took a look at Tina, stepped closer, put an arm around her shoulders, and walked her to the cottage. I locked the gate and followed behind them, Dashiell and Betty circling around me, sneezing with joy that I'd returned.

Tina was so exhausted, she could hardly keep her eyes open. I took her upstairs to my room, turned down the covers, and when she sat, I bent and slipped off her shoes. Without saying a word, she lay back on the pillow, drew up her knees, and closed her eyes.

"Do you want me to leave Dashiell with you?" I asked.

She nodded without opening her eyes.

He'd followed us up, his nails ticking on the oak stairs. He stood at the side of the bed, watching her, his forehead wrinkled with concern, dowsing for where she hurt. But this wasn't a stomachache or a pulled muscle. The hurt Tina felt was everywhere, leaving room for nothing else.

I patted the bed next to her, and Dashiell hopped up, snuggling against her. As I pulled the cover over both of them, I saw her arm reach out to embrace him.

Downstairs, I poured two glasses of wine and joined Chip on the couch. "Chip, when Sam called to ask you to speak, did she tell you you'd be covering a spot left by another speaker who had seemed to abandon ship?"

"She did. She said Tina had agreed to teach, but that at the last minute, she was unable to reach her for a confirmation."

"I was able to buy that one. She'd been after you for a long time. And the topic is one any number of people could have handled."

"But none as brilliantly as I did."

"Correct." I took a sip of wine. "But for that speaker's other slot, we have a situation that tests credibility. Tina's forte is breed temperament. She contracts to deliver this important talk, the opening talk of the program, then fails to respond to all of Sam's attempts to reach her. So far, it's not too bad a stretch. But then, the day before the symposium, the only other person who could do as brilliant a job on the talk, someone who had refused repeatedly to come to the States to lecture, calls Sam and volunteers to speak on the very topic that is her specialty and that happens to be going begging."

"How do you know it was at the last minute?"

"Because the evening before, Sam had asked me if I'd cover it, because she hadn't been able to reach Tina, and she had to be sure everything was covered for the students."

"You would have been spectacular."

"This is true. But I never thought I'd be giving that talk. I assumed Tina would show, that she'd been away or something, which would explain her not getting back to Sam. I figured she'd be back just in the nick of time. Sam even saved a room for her, 303, the room on the other side of mine, just in case."

"But she didn't show. And now you know why."

"She'd had an abortion," I said even more softly than I was already speaking, wanting to be absolutely sure my voice didn't carry up the stairs to Tina.

Chip didn't say anything right away, but he reached for Betty, who was lying on the other end of the couch.

"Martyn?"

I nodded, watching him get it.

"But aren't we back where we were before? Why the others? Why Alan and Rick, too?"

"That's what I've yet to find out."

"How do you plan to do that?"

"I thought I might ask Beryl," I told him.

"You've got to be kidding."

"Not at all. Sometimes if you ask in the right way, you get whatever it is you're after."

"I'll keep that in mind."

"Good boy."

As he reached out for me, the same look in his eyes that Dashiell gets when I order in pizza, we heard the bedroom door open, and a moment later the bathroom door closed.

"I never knew it could be like this." He sat back, shaking his head.

"I find it often is. I've been thinking of hiring a personal assistant to do for me all those things I no longer get the chance to do—converse, eat out, go to the movies, have sex."

"It sounds like marriage," he said.

Strings of light were coming in through the slats of the shutters. Chip reached out and took my hand. Sitting there quietly, we heard a lone bird begin to sing. While we waited for Tina to come downstairs, I told him what I planned to do, and asked if he would help.

I fed the dogs while Chip showered and dressed. Then he took them out for a walk while Tina and I got ready. Afterward, he made breakfast, while I made some urgent phone calls.

We took separate cabs. Chip and Betty took Tina with them. Dashiell and I rode with each other, he watching the city slip by on one side of the backseat, me leaning against the window on the other side, thinking about how sometimes even the best of intentions go hideously awry and wondering what would become of Tina when all this was over.

ONE DOOR CLOSES

When we got out of the cab, Dashiell looked at me and then looked over toward the park, sending a message without saying a word. But I headed for the hotel instead. It was six-forty-five, time for us to get to work.

Sometimes killers play games with the cops, I thought, using the service entrance around the corner. They write notes, or leave maddening, conflicting clues on purpose.

Some killers want to show how smart they are, and so they brag.

Some are dumb as pigeon shit. No matter what they do, even tying their shoelaces, they fuck it up royally.

But this killer was one smart cookie. She'd done everything she could not to get caught, staging the crime scenes so that they appeared to be other than they were, accidents or suicide instead of calculated murders.

Had she killed the other two to muddy the waters, so that

the death she needed wouldn't stand out and eventually point to her?

Or worse, her daughter?

One door closes, I'd told Chip, talking about the inability I'd felt to go back to the profession I so loved after my divorce. Had I felt I didn't deserve even that?

Another door opens. I'd become a detective.

A door also closed the night I'd gone for ice. Cathy's door.

She'd opened it, hoping to see Martyn. Was she thinking she could rewrite history? Whatever she'd been thinking, she'd come to her senses and closed it without peering out to see who was there, to see that it wasn't Martyn. It was only me.

But then another door opened.

Martyn was tired. He unlocked his door and opened it. He wanted to go to bed. Why didn't he?

Was it because Beryl's door had opened?

But how the hell did she get him up to the roof?

I handed the package I'd brought from home to one of the waiters. When everything was ready, I headed for the elevator. Getting out on four, I told Dashiell to drop and wait. Then I knocked softly on her door.

"Have you had your breakfast yet?" I asked, holding the tray in front of me.

"Oh, brilliant," she said. "You've brought tea and scones. Come in, Rachel. Come right in."

She'd already been out for a walk. I could see where the dew had taken the shine off her sturdy nun's shoes.

"Here, let me put that on the dresser," she said. Then she pulled her chair close to the window seat. "Which would you prefer?"

"Either is fine."

"Save the chair for me," she said. "It'll remind me to keep my back straight. Shall I serve, dear?"

Without waiting for an answer, she walked back to the tray and lifted the lid off the teapot. "How did you get them to use loose tea?" she asked. "I've been trying unsuccessfully all week."

"I brought my own from home," I whispered to her back.

"Clever thing," she said.

Cecilia was scratching at the doorjamb, then turning around to try to catch Beryl's eye. But Beryl didn't notice. She was pouring tea.

I walked into the bathroom.

"My mother always told me," she said, loud enough for me to hear her over the sound of the running water, "keep your back straight, Beryl. Head high. The rest will take care of itself. Now, isn't that the silliest thing you ever heard?"

I came out and took my seat. Beryl was smiling when she turned around, my cup in one hand, a plate with a raspberry scone in the other. I took them and placed them carefully next to me on the window seat. Beryl went back for the napkins, cream, and sugar. And again for her own cup and scone.

"Isn't this cozy?" She poured some of the heavy cream into her thick, dark tea, stirred, and took a sip. "Just like home."

"Sam was so thrilled when you decided at last to come and speak here, to be part of her symposium."

"Yes, she was. She seemed de*light*ed to hear from me."

"What made you change your mind?"

"Oh, I saw a wonderful article in the *Gazette*, Rachel. It sounded like something one couldn't afford to miss."

"And it has been quite something, hasn't it?"

"Well, much more exciting than anyone dreamed," she said, leaning toward me over her cup. "Poor things, those men who died."

She was looking down at her lap now, and I could clearly see that there was no hearing aid in either ear, yet she'd heard me when I'd whispered. I gave it one more try.

I broke off a piece of my scone and took a bite. "I feel so sorry for their families," I said, rudely talking with my mouth full.

"Oh, yes, the wives. I feel such *em*pathy for the wives, alone now, having to cope by themselves. Grieving, but carrying on." She seemed not to be seeing me, but looking off into the past.

"Detective Flowers called Sam," I said.

"Oh?"

"They don't think the deaths were accidental."

"You don't say."

"I do. I've never thought so myself, Beryl."

"Is that *so*, dear?" Holding her cup at chest level, she peered at me with unblinking eyes.

"I was thinking that maybe Alan's door hadn't closed all the way when his lady friend left. Then, of course, someone else would have been able to open it without a key, wouldn't they?"

"Well, I suppose that's—"

She turned because Dashiell had opened the door to her room, the door I'd stopped from closing all the way by using my foot to push Dashiell's ball into the corner of the door frame as soon as Beryl had taken the tray of goodies and headed for the dresser, the way the ball Beau had hopefully tossed to the departing Audrey had gotten wedged in Alan's door and had kept it from clicking shut.

"Possible," she said, finishing her thought.

I saw caution creep into her eyes.

"Oh, look, dear," she said, a smile as false as a four-pound note spreading across her lips but leaving her eyes unchanged. "It's happened here. The door didn't shut all the way. How careless of me. But something good's come out of it, hasn't it? Now Cecilia has your beautiful boy to play with."

"Did something good come out of Alan's door being left ajar when his lady friend exited? She was in such a rush, wasn't she?"

We sat there then holding our teacups and looking at each other, sending messages without saying a word. We could hear the dogs wrestling on the other side of the room, but neither of us turned to watch them.

"Audrey? Oh, yes, dear. She was anxious to get back to her room unseen. She never even looked in my direction."

"Why, Beryl?"

She ignored me, taking a sip of her tea.

"Wonderful," she said. "I don't understand why you Americans use those silly little bags."

"It had to do with Tina, didn't it?"

"I see. So that's where you and Chip were last night. Then you understand, of course."

And just then, I did.

"She never told you *who*. That's it, isn't it? Of course," I said. "Who would know better than your own daughter what a fuss you would have made. And she was right, wasn't she?"

"It's not what you think," she said, holding her cup in front of her, balancing the plate with the scone on her lap.

"Then tell me what it was."

"I'd gotten up early, you see. Well, early isn't the word for it. It was four in the bloody morning. Jet lag, I suppose. I tossed and turned for half an hour, then tried a warm bath. But I couldn't get back to sleep. We had to get up early anyway, I told myself, for the tracking. So I decided I'd take the little one out for a walk. I thought it would calm my nerves, make me feel better, fresh air and all that. That's when I saw her, sneaking out of Alan's room.

"I'd only meant to get cross with him, you see. I know it was foolish of me to think my anger would stop him from hurting other vulnerable young girls."

"The way he'd hurt Tina."

Beryl winced.

"At the time," she said, talking slowly, thinking she shouldn't have to explain all this, "I *thought* it was he. Else I never would have walked in on him when he was in his bath, would I?"

"Of course not."

"I'd only gone in there to vent, Rachel. You're absolutely right. Tina never told me *who*. 'You know how you are, Mummy,' she said to me. 'You'll only make a scene. It's none of your business,' she said. 'I'll take care of it myself. I'll do whatever has to be done.' "

She pulled a large handkerchief from her jacket pocket and blew her nose.

"I came because I thought she'd need my help, working when she was pregnant. I thought we might take a little place together so that—" She blew her nose a second time. "Well, never mind that, dear. There won't *be* a baby for me to care for now, will there?"

I shook my head.

"I knew it had been one of these men. That's what kept Tina from honoring her commitment to Sam and to the students. And I knew it was a married man. One who didn't think twice about breaking his vows. Well, there I was checking my pocket for the keys, holding the little one under my arm so that she wouldn't start all the other dogs barking and wake the lot of them, and I saw Audrey backing out of Alan's room, disheveled looking. I thought, aha, I have my man. But you must believe me, I only meant to scare him, Rachel, to let him know his hurtful behavior was not going unnoticed.

"It was completely irrational, to think that by walking in on him in the tub and yelling at him I could change his ways, as if he were a dog I were correcting. Once a cocksman, always a cocksman, wouldn't you say? Of course, I wasn't rational. You see, I'd called Tina on Sunday night, to tell her my surprise, but before I'd had the chance to say I was here, I heard she sounded just terrible, that she'd been crying. Well, I knew she'd been abandoned. And that she was pregnant. But as it turns out, the tears were because she'd had an abortion, and it made her feel so awfully blue. So of course I was in a state myself. Not only was Tina so *mis*erable, but I'd lost my—"

Cecilia came over to sit near Beryl, and Dashiell came and stood by my side, his forehead wrinkled, his one-track mind on Beryl now.

" 'It's none of your business,' she said. Imagine thinking that." Beryl took a sip of tea. "At any rate, dear, I saw this chance to tell this man what a snake I thought he was, and when I showed up in his bathroom, he had the nerve to deny any affair with my daughter. In fact, he said I sounded like a dotty old fool and told me to get the hell out of his bathroom. He stood up. What a sight. He was buck naked, raging at me. But he'd just soaped himself, and as he lifted his leg to get out of the tub, only the good Lord knows what he would have done to me then, probably grab me by the collar, call me a nosy old biddy, and toss me out of his hotel room, well, instead, he slipped. And as he was going down backward, his arms flailing at his sides as if he were trying to fly, he grabbed the towel rack with the radio on it."

She bent her head and covered her face with her hands.

"Of course it was all my fault. If I hadn't been there, he wouldn't have been in such a rush. He would have paid more attention to what he was doing when he got up out of that slippery tub. But I most certainly didn't go in there with the idea of doing harm. I only thought I might do some good."

"And how did you find out it wasn't Alan?"

"When I called Tina and told her about the accident. There wasn't the reaction there would have been were he the one. Oh, dear, I thought to myself, you *are* an old fool. But you know what, Rachel? I was glad it had happened. I felt rather satisfied, not at the time of course, at the time it was just gruesome. But afterward. Afterward I felt good about it. Don't you see?"

I tried to keep looking neutral, but Beryl was a dog trainer. She knew body language and saw that I was appalled.

"It *was* an accident, Rachel. But not a mistake. He'd broken his marriage vows."

"And you were worried about Audrey, how she'd feel afterward, when he had no further interest in her? You were worried she'd suffer, the way Tina was suffering?"

"No, dear. I wasn't thinking about *her* at all. I was thinking about Alan's poor wife. Suppose he had a change of heart and left her after this *fling* with pretty little Audrey? That's what I was thinking."

"I see," I told her. But of course, I didn't. Not yet, anyway. "And what about Rick Shelbert?" I asked. "Did he break his marriage vows as well?"

"Why, of course, dear. I certainly wasn't going around the hotel randomly killing people for nothing."

I felt the hair on my arms standing up. Dashiell knew something was wrong too. He looked at me, then back at Beryl. I could feel his tension rising with my own.

"How did you, uh, focus on Rick next?"

"I'm not much of a sleeper, even without the jet lag. I suppose it's my age. I usually stay up quite late, and then I'm up bright and early anyway—with the birds, my mother used to say. So it wasn't too difficult to know when one of the gentlemen had company. Anyone could have done it, dear."

She broke off a piece of scone and popped it into her mouth. Then she took a second piece and gave it to Cecilia. "Naughty thing," she said, "begging like that."

"Tell me about Rick's accident."

"Oh, that wasn't an accident, Rachel. When I heard the commotion in *his* room—oh, my dear, the noise could have awakened the dead—I thought, *now* I have my man."

I closed my eyes, squeezing them shut, feeling a tear run down my cheek.

"The sugar bowl."

"Clever *girl*," she said.

"You crumbled them up."

"Powdered them, actually. I put them in a handkerchief and hit them with the heel of my shoe, the same as I do with Cecilia's *vit*amins. She so hates to take a pill. This way I can mix it in her food, can't I, love?" She looked dotingly at the little dog, breaking off another piece of scone for her. Then she poured some of her tea into the saucer and set it down on the floor for Cecilia to lap.

"Convenient, all of us taking the same seats at every meal," I said. "We apparently pattern-train as readily as our dogs."

"The aspirin wouldn't have hurt anyone else," Beryl said. She seemed annoyed that I might think her so careless. "Had I missed, no matter. I would have simply tried again."

"But then you found you'd made another mistake."

"Oh, no, dear. Not a mistake."

"Of course. And who was he with?" I asked, curiosity getting the better of me.

"Heaven knows, dear. That's not the point, is it?"

"I guess not."

"But I must confess," she said, leaning closer, "I did stay long enough to hear some talking. Afterward. Pillow talk, I think it's called. And, well, both voices sounded very deep." She sat back and fiddled with her shirt, tucking it neatly into her skirt. "It's quite possible Rick's lover was a man. But what earthly difference would that make?

"I must admit that after that, I really badgered Tina. Parents can do that, you know. We know all the buttons to push to get our children raging mad."

"Did she blurt out Martyn's name at last?"

"No, dear. But when I'd finally gotten her really angry, by naming trainers and nattering away at her, Was it he? Was it he? she said, No, Mummy, it's not any of those. He's foreign. So naturally I thought it was Boris."

"Did he have a sweetie, too?" I asked.

"Exactly my question, Rachel. So guess what I did," she said, taking on a conspiratorial tone, as if the two of us were in on this together.

I got up and walked to the door, opened it, and looked out into the hall, nodding to Mercedes, who patted her uniform pocket to show me where the twenty I'd given her had been squirreled away. Then I called to Dashiell. "Keys," I told him, pointing down the hall to where the supply cart had been parked. A moment later, Dash was back with the passkey. He sat and tossed it in the air for me to catch.

"Brilliant," she said, the muscles in her cheeks jumping. She looked at Dashiell and then at me, sizing us up anew.

"But what did you do about Sasha?" I asked her.

"Don't be a goose, dear. Do you think I can't handle a Rottweiler? Are you forgetting who I am?"

"Not in the least, Mrs. Potter, but we're discussing a protection-trained Rottweiler here, not a crooked sit."

"I bloody well know that."

"What was it you shoved through a crack in the door?" I asked, remembering the dog dead asleep on stage the following morning, "a couple of Valium in a bite of cheese? Halcyon? Then you waited a few minutes before opening the door and having yourself a *good* look."

"Yes, dear, a good look." She was glaring now, and I knew she was planning something, too. I had trained enough dogs to recognize escape behavior, no matter if the creature was human, not canine.

"At who?" I asked.

"Whom," she said. "At Boris, that's who." She sat back again, smiling now.

"And?"

"He was all alone, lying on his back, snoring. He looked like a beached whale. I thought to myself, Tina *couldn't* have meant Boris."

She picked up her cup of cold tea and took a sip.

"Of course, I hadn't thought of Martyn as *foreign*. But after this, I knew that that's who it was. Martyn Eliot, of all the ironies."

"How did you get him to go up to the roof, Beryl?"

"What did you say, dear?" she asked, fiddling with a wisp of hair that had come loose from its combs. "Oh, yes, the roof. Of course, you'd wonder about that. Well, you're such a terribly clever person, you tell me."

"As you wish. It had to be a test of character, in keeping with your theme."

She smiled, but her eyes were cold.

"First, you heard me at your door. Cecilia must have been all excited, because Dashiell was with me. Next—"

"I've had quite enough of this, dear. The tea is cold, and I'm afraid I'm getting bored with your company."

She stood, took her purse from the bureau, and stooped to scoop up her dog. Then she headed for the door.

I watched her reach for the knob, turn it, and pull the door partway open before sending Dashiell. Crossing the room, he didn't seem to touch the ground. When he came up on his hind legs and slammed the door shut with a satisfying thud, the room shook.

"Sit down, Mrs. Potter. We're not finished with our discussion."

Beryl reached for the doorknob again.

"Watch her," I said.

Dashiell wedged himself between Beryl and the door, using his hip to back her out of his way. Then he stood facing her, as quiet and unmovable as cement.

"Out," she commanded, her voice booming.

Dashiell never blinked.

"Haven't you trained him?" she asked me, desperation in her voice. Then without waiting for me to tell her what she had already learned for herself—that while Dashiell might sit for her, or even roll over if she asked him to, he had been proofed against taking commands from anyone but his handler when doing protection work—she made another mistake. She reached for Dashiell's collar.

Dashiell's muzzle wrinkled up like an accordion, retracting his lips. There were sound effects, too, a low rumble that made everything tremble, as if we were outside and the subway were passing underneath the sidewalk.

Beryl withdrew her hand.

"Sit down, Mrs. Potter. You aren't going anywhere. Even if Dashiell weren't here, I am. You don't have the advantage of surprise this time."

She backed up to the bed and sat, Dashiell watching her every move.

"It had to do with Cecilia," I said. "Because that would be the one request he couldn't turn down, and you knew it."

Even sitting on the bed, her back was as straight as a ramrod.

"I woke up at four again. It was Cecilia. She was at the door, and I heard the tags on her collar tinkling. She was just standing there, begging me to open up, her little tail wagging back and forth. Then she came back to bed. But a moment later, she was at the door again. That time I did get up, because I heard the key in the lock next door to me. It was our Martyn, home from your poker game."

"You locked Cecilia in the bathroom," I continued, having recently felt the scratches on the inside of the door to make sure my theory was correct. "And then you went to knock on his door."

"He looked so tired, so out of sorts. It was a demanding lifestyle he kept, trying to make *so* many women happy. It would wear a man down, I'd think. It wouldn't leave much for the woman waiting at home."

"No, it wouldn't."

"I was quite hysterical, you know. I grabbed at his shirt and began to pull him out into the hall. 'It's Cecilia,' I told him; 'she awakened me crying, had to go and do her business, poor thing, but Samantha had warned us about the dangers of New York City,' I told him, doing my best frail and frightened old lady in a bathrobe for him. 'I'm afraid I've done a naughty thing,' I said. 'I took her up on the roof. I thought she could take care of things there, and we'd be safe.'

"He was frowning, almost too tired to follow the little story I was telling him. 'Well, somehow,' I said, rushing on with it, 'she'd gotten herself into some sort of pipe and was too frightened to come to me. Oh, could you help, Martyn?' I asked him.

" 'Perhaps we should call the desk,' he said. I could see he was annoyed. He was dying to get to sleep. 'There's no time,' I told him, 'it's a matter of life and death.' Well, *that* was certainly true," Beryl said. "I begged him to fetch his umbrella, I said perhaps we could use the handle to hook her collar and pull her out. We headed for the stairs. I assured him that the elevator man would be fast asleep in the basement, and there wasn't a moment to waste with Cecilia's life in the balance, now was there?"

"So he passed his character test?"

"So he did, my dear. So he did. However, in general, I thought his character to be the lowest. Wouldn't you agree?"

"And once you were up there?"

"I tossed the umbrella down and looked over the ledge. Good Lord, I said, see what she's gone and done. He came running, the dear man, *so* concerned."

Again, there was that faraway look in Beryl's eyes.

"He was a wee thing, wasn't he? Couldn't have weighed much more than nine stone, nowhere near as heavy as Charles."

"Charles?"

"Carl's bullmastiff, dear. Remember?"

"Your Carl was a veterinarian, too, wasn't he?"

"He was indeed."

"An American?"

"Yes, dear."

"And you loved him with all your being?"

"You have no idea."

She lifted Cecilia and held her against her bosom, squeezing the little terrier so tightly that she began to squirm.

"I used to kill him off every day," she said. "In my imagination, of course."

"After he left you?"

"No, dear, before. I loved him so desperately, I used to think, what if anything ever happened to him? I wouldn't be able to go on. So every day, I'd kill him off and then imagine how I'd cope, how I'd care for Christina and make a life for us. It assuaged my anxiety. But at the time, I had no idea—"

She looked at me for the first time in what seemed like ages, and I could see the years of pain in her eyes now, all exposed.

"It was his heart," I whispered.

"Yes, dear, his heart."

"He fell in love with someone else."

"Yes, dear, that's what he did."

"And abandoned you and his child."

Beryl nodded. "At first no one knew his whereabouts. And in my shock and grief, all I could think about was that someone would take Tina from me."

"You wanted to keep her."

"Wanted to keep her? She was all I had left. She was my life. So as soon as we could, we moved to England, not to London, where I'd lived when I met Carl, but the Cotswolds, where I hoped none of his family would be able to find me."

"And did you ever find out what happened to Carl, where he went and with whom, and what became of him?"

"Oh, yes, dear. Actually, I did. He'd disappeared with a wealthy client. That was clear from the first."

"He left a note?"

Beryl smiled the saddest smile I'd ever seen. "A note? Why, no, he didn't think to do that, Rachel. No, there was no note. But *she* went missing too. That part wasn't hard to figure out."

"And what became of them?"

"I don't know about her," she said, "but shortly after they came back from France, poor Martyn—"

"You mean Carl."

"Yes, shortly after they came back from France, poor Carl had a terrible accident."

"Fatal?"

"As it happens, it was. A lucky thing, too. With him gone, I was able to sell his practice. That gave me the money I needed to raise my daughter and get on with my life."

The longer it cooks, my grandmother Sonya used to say, the thicker the stew. No matter if you were a dog or a person, you only got to be more like yourself as time passed.

I looked out the window. People were on their way to work. Traffic had picked up, too.

"I'll get ready now," Beryl said.

I reached into my pocket and shut off the tape recorder. Then I walked over to the phone and called downstairs. Beryl waited until I hung up. She whispered something in her little dog's ear; then, back straight, head held high, she handed her to me and began to pack her things.

"If you hug me,
then I'll hug you!"

"Well . . .
It's easy peasy.
Don't you know?
It's one plus one.
A hug takes two."

PERFECT HUG

Do you suppose,
    there might be a **hug** right under my nose?

        What's the secret?
        "Tell!"

I've roved the wide seas, over and under, and still I wonder . . .

One that will suit me down to the ground?
One that will fit me all the way round?

Where will I find one that's just my size?

Gymnastic,
enthusiastic hugs!
But . . .

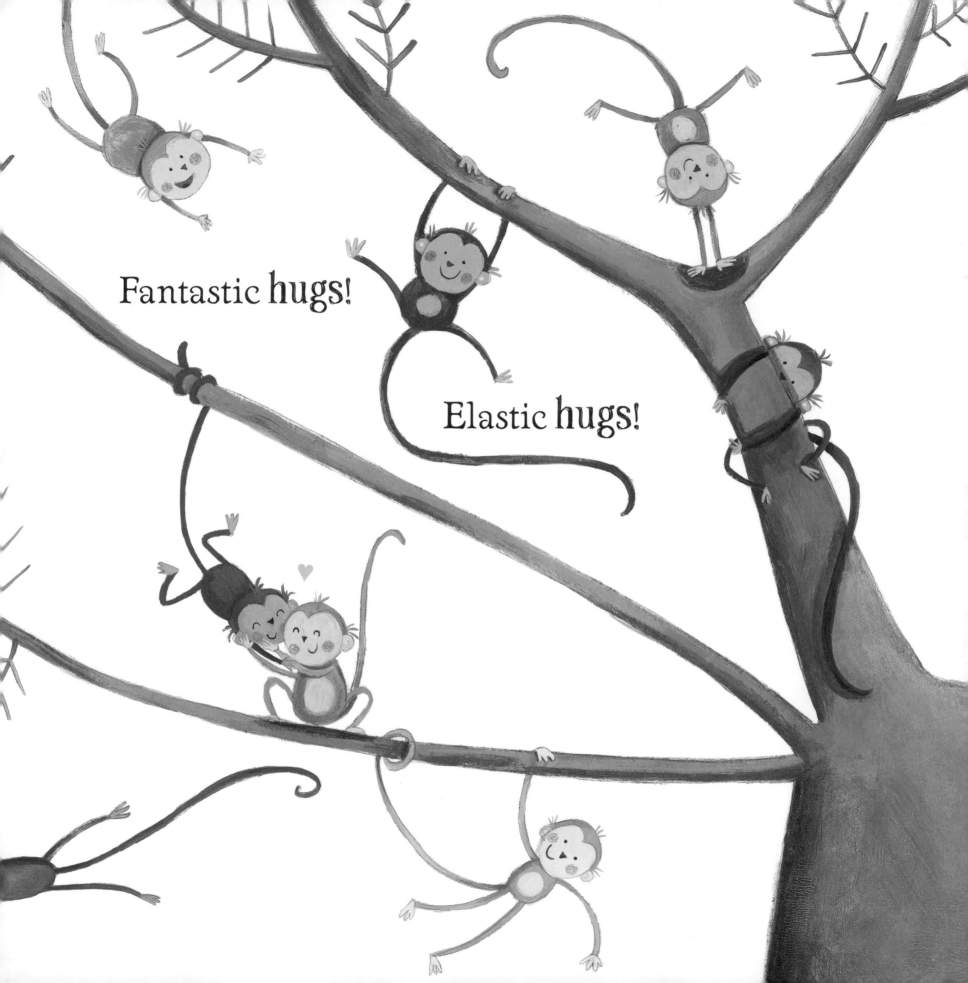

Fantastic hugs!

Elastic hugs!

BIG

and small.

I've tried them all,

short and TALL,

far out, on stars in a galaxy far, far away?
How DO they **hug** the Milky Way way?

Could there be **hugs** light-years from here?
Hugs we know nothing about,

I'd **hug** her with rubber gloves on my fingers.

None of these **hugs** is quite the height for,
not too tight for, oh-so-right for me.
But . . .

And what about a jellyfish, with all those stingers?

And some not any!

Then there's the question of arms.
What's too many?

Some have lots.

A **hug** from a grizzly
is **big** but scary.

Grin and bear it,
but do be wary.

A boa constrictor's **hug's**

a bit STRICTER

than any sort of **hug**

ought to be (at least for me)!

How big is a **hug**?

A bug may mean well,
but how can I feel his tiny squeeze
around my knees?

But none is exactly the right **hug** for me!

I'm out to find the perfect kind.

PERFECT HUG

There are **hugs** for wrigglers,

and **hugs** for gigglers.

Hugs that are tickly,

and **hugs** that are prickly....

The Perfect Hug

Joanna Walsh

Illustrated by Judi Abbot

A Paula Wiseman Book
Simon & Schuster Books for Young Readers
New York London Toronto Sydney New Delhi

To Isaac and Freya,
wishing them many hugs
– *J. W.*

A chi mi stringe da sempre
nell'abbra cio perfetto,
papà Pino emma Rita!
– *J. A.*

SIMON & SCHUSTER BOOKS FOR YOUNG READERS
An imprint of Simon & Schuster Children's Publishing Division
1230 Avenue of the Americas, New York, New York 10020
Text copyright © 2011 by Joanna Walsh
Illustrations copyright © 2011 by Giuditta Gaviraghi
First published in Great Britain in 2011 by Simon & Schuster UK Ltd.
Published by arrangement with Simon & Schuster UK Ltd.
First US edition, 2012
All rights reserved, including the right of reproduction in whole or in part in any form.
SIMON & SCHUSTER BOOKS FOR YOUNG READERS is a trademark of Simon & Schuster, Inc.
For information about special discounts for bulk purchases, please contact Simon & Schuster Special Sales
at 1-866-506-1949 or business@simonandschuster.com.
The Simon & Schuster Speakers Bureau can bring authors to your live event. For more information or to book an event,
contact the Simon & Schuster Speakers Bureau at 1-866-248-3049 or visit our website at www.simonspeakers.com.
Manufactured in China · 0512 SUK
2 4 6 8 10 9 7 5 3 1
CIP data for this book is available from the Library of Congress.
ISBN 978-1-4424-6606-7

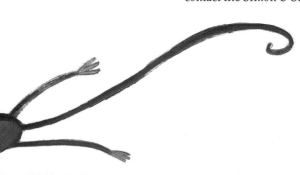